AUNT BESSIE DECIDES

AN ISLE OF MAN COZY MYSTERY

DIANA XARISSA

❀ Created with Vellum

For Adam, Penny and William (Bill),
who kindly lent me their names for this book.
In the real world they are all very talented
individuals and nothing like their
namesakes here.

AUTHOR'S NOTE

This is the fourth book in the Aunt Bessie Cozy Mystery series that grew out of my Isle of Man Romance, *Island Inheritance.* As Bessie was the source of the inheritance in that novel, I've had to bring her back to life for this series by setting the cozy mystery books about fifteen years before the romance. This series, therefore, began in early 1998 and moves forward about one month per book.

There are characters who appear in both series. Obviously, they are somewhat younger in the Aunt Bessie series than they are in the romance series. The romances are all stand-alone titles, however, and you don't need to read them to enjoy Aunt Bessie, either.

I've used British and Manx terminologies and spellings throughout the book (although one or two American words or spellings might have slipped past me). A couple of pages of translations and explanations, mostly for readers outside of the United Kingdom, appear at the end of the book. I've also identified the quotations used in the text in the back of the book.

The setting for the series is the Isle of Man, which is a small island located between England and Ireland in the Irish Sea. It is a Crown Dependency, and is a country in its own right, with its own currency, stamps, language and government.

CHAPTER 1

"I hope we have enough to eat," Hugh said anxiously from the driver's seat of his car.

Bessie laughed from the passenger seat. "I'm sure we have plenty," she assured the young policeman. "Doona, Grace, and I all brought hampers full of food. We have enough for a small army."

"Or one Hugh Watterson," Grace laughed from the backseat.

"Hey, I'm a growing boy," the man protested.

"Hugh, you're twenty-six. You're done growing," Grace told him affectionately.

Hugh shrugged. "Well, I'm still hungry," he grumbled.

Bessie laughed. She'd known Hugh since he was a baby, and in spite of his now being six feet tall with broad shoulders, he still looked almost exactly like the teenager whose appetite he possessed.

"I know John is bringing food as well," Doona added from her seat next to Grace. "I'm sure he'll bring extra. We've all brought extra."

"Yeah, but he's bringing his kids," Hugh argued. "They probably eat loads themselves."

"Henry told me there will be food vendors at the show as well," Bessie said soothingly. "I wouldn't let you starve, would I?"

Hugh gave her an affectionate look. "Nah, you always take good care of me," he acknowledged.

Bessie sat back in her seat and smiled to herself. She was always trying to take care of her friends, and that was what today was all about.

Elizabeth Cubbon had lived in the small village of Laxey for more years than anyone else in the car had been alive. It was just barely possible that you could add all of their ages together and still not get to hers, but that was not the sort of thing Bessie was likely to even consider. In her mind, she was just a bit past middle-aged and she was quite happy to stay there for the next sixty or seventy years.

Known as Aunt Bessie to nearly everyone, she made friends easily, but counted very few people as close friends. A recent series of shocking events had strengthened her relationships with a few very special people. Those same recent events had generated a great deal of stress for Bessie and her friends. Accordingly, she had decided they all needed a pleasant diversion. After some consideration, she'd invited them to an evening picnic and open-air theatre performance of a Shakespearean play.

Bessie had suggested that Hugh, her favourite neighbourhood constable, invite his girlfriend, Grace, along for the fun, and he'd been happy to include her. Doona, Bessie's forty-something best friend was currently single, and she'd been happy to agree to an evening out. Hugh offered to drive. Bessie had never learned and Doona was pleased to agree, as that allowed her to add a bottle of wine to her hamper.

The last member of their little group, CID Inspector John Rockwell, was going to meet them all at their destination. Officially, Hugh and Doona worked for Inspector Rockwell, but that didn't get in the way of their friendship. Bessie had insisted that the inspector include his wife and children in the night out, and she was looking forward to meeting them.

The car made its way across the island, heading from Laxey towards Peel. Bessie nodded as they passed Tynwald Hill.

"Not long now until Tynwald Day," she remarked.

"My cousin's school choir is performing," Grace told her. "I've promised to come and watch and cheer, but not too loudly."

Bessie laughed. "How old is he?"

"He's nine. He's torn between loving the attention and being embarrassed that he has a family," Grace replied.

"We should make a day of it," Doona suggested. "There's loads to do and it's always fun to stay for the fireworks at the end of the night."

"I'd love to do that," Bessie told her friend.

"I'm going to have to wait and see if I'm working," Hugh told the others. "Not everyone will be at St. John's. A few shady types might stay behind in Laxey and cause some trouble."

"Sometimes I hate your job," Grace said.

"I'm sorry," Hugh told her, "but I wouldn't trade it for anything."

"I know," Grace laughed. "That's why it's a good thing you're so cute."

Bessie laughed as Hugh turned fuchsia. Even the tips of his ears brightened noticeably from the unexpected compliment.

"Anyway," Grace continued, "the Screamin' Manxmen are supposed to perform and I've been dying to see them again. They're fabulous."

Doona laughed. "Maybe Bessie and I will skip that particular performance," she told the others. "I think there's a ceilidh as well. That might be more our style."

"Speak for yourself," Bessie laughed. "I've never been any good at dancing and I've heard good things about the Screamin' Manxmen."

"Really?" Doona asked.

"Well, some of my young guests are quite enthusiastic about them," Bessie told her. "And I am really hopeless at dancing. I can never remember the patterns for more than a minute or two. Anyway, we can work it all out next month."

A few moments later, they arrived in the town of Peel.

"I haven't been to Peel Castle in years," Hugh said as they made their way through the streets of the town. "Where can I park?"

"There's a car park near the castle," Bessie told him. "It's only a short walk away from the entrance."

"I haven't been here since a school trip about ten years ago," Grace admitted. "And in those days I was more interested in trying to chat up the boys in my class than I was in history."

"Hey," Hugh protested with a laugh.

"It's a wonderful old pile of ruins," Bessie told the young woman. "I could spend hours walking you through the different sections and telling you all about the place, but tonight isn't a good night for that. Everything is set up for the show tonight."

"Which play did you say we're seeing?" Doona asked.

Bessie sighed deeply. The car slid into a parking space and Bessie turned around in her seat to look at her friend. "*Much Ado About the Shrew*," she said with yet another sigh.

Everyone climbed out of the car and, after gathering the hampers from the car's boot, they began the short walk to the castle.

"I'm sorry," Doona said to Bessie. "But what did you say the play was called?"

Bessie shook her head. "When they arranged things with Manx National Heritage, the theatre troupe said they would be doing classic Shakespeare. When I bought the tickets, Henry said he thought they were doing *Hamlet*, which would have been fine. Apparently the troupe just let MNH know last week that they've, quote, 'had a change in direction,' end of quote."

"What does that mean?" Hugh asked.

"From what I've been told, it means that they are doing some sort of modern reinterpretation of classic Shakespearean comedy and tragedy. Apparently, they've combined *Much Ado About Nothing* with *The Taming of the Shrew*, although I understand that they've also added in odd sections from other plays, including something from *Romeo and Juliet* and a nod to *Macbeth*." Bessie sighed again. "If we hadn't already made plans to come, I certainly wouldn't have bought tickets for this."

"I don't know," Hugh chuckled. "It sounds like it could be fun. I'm not a huge fan of Shakespeare, anyway. They spent way too much time forcing us to study him in school. Maybe a total jumble of his plays will make them interesting."

"And if it isn't any good," Doona added with a wicked grin, "I've got three bottles of wine in my hamper."

Bessie laughed. "The only reason I didn't cancel is because I know we'll have fun no matter what."

"We certainly will," Doona told her.

They made their way up the stone steps at the front of the castle and down a short corridor. It was dark and cool inside the old stone building after the bright warmth of a sunny day in the middle of June.

"Hello, Bessie." The sixty-something grey-haired man in the ticket booth gave them all a smile. "Henry told me you'd be coming through. He's got a section set up for you and your friends."

"Ah, thanks, Bob," Bessie replied. As an amateur historian, Bessie was well known to most of the staff of Manx National Heritage.

"Do you have your tickets?" he asked. "If you don't, it's no bother, really, but I'm supposed to ask."

"I do have my tickets," Bessie assured him, handing them over. "And I have four for another friend who's coming separately with his family. Can I leave them with you?"

"Is that Inspector Rockwell?" Bob asked. "He's already here. He said he was meeting you and I let him and his kids in. I assumed you had tickets for them."

Bessie chuckled. "I hope you're being stricter with the rest of the public," she remarked, "or it could get awfully crowded in there."

Bob shook his head. "I doubt it," he said in a whisper. "We were doing okay until they announced the play they were doing," he confided to Bessie. "We had a ton of cancellations after the change and I don't think we could give the rest of the tickets away now."

"Oh dear," Bessie said. "This is their first performance, right? They're meant to be doing shows for a fortnight, I thought."

"They are," Bob shook his head. "They're booked for tonight and tomorrow night, and then a matinee on Sunday for families, and the same next weekend. They're also meant to be doing school shows on Tuesday and Wednesday, but most of the schools have cancelled as well. Taking the kids to see Shakespeare is one thing, but this, well, no one knows what to expect."

"Good thing I brought wine," Doona muttered, making everyone laugh.

"Ooooh, there's a programme," Bob announced, handing a small stack of papers to Bessie. "There should be plenty there for everyone in your party," he told her. "Feel free to keep any extra; I can't imagine we'll need them."

Bessie just barely stopped herself from sighing again. "I suppose we should get in there," she said to her friends.

"The show doesn't start for over an hour. They're meant to go on at seven," Bob told her. "But the food vendors are ready to go now. I would think there's about a dozen folks inside, eating and getting ready to enjoy the show."

"Only a dozen?" Bessie did sigh now. "I hope it picks up before show time."

Bob shrugged. "I'm not sure *Much Ado About the Shrew* is going to pack them in," he told her.

Bessie and her friends made their way past Bob's ticket booth and into the castle grounds.

"It's gorgeous," Grace breathed as she looked around at the crumbling stone structures that surrounded them.

"Magnus Barefoot, an eleventh-century Viking king built a fort here, although the site was originally used as a place of worship," Bessie told the girl. She gestured towards a large ruined building. "The Cathedral of St. German was built in the thirteenth century and if we weren't here for a theatre show, we could explore its crypt."

"Ooooo, spooky," Grace shivered, clutching Hugh's arm.

He laughed. "I'd put my arm around you," he told her, "but I'm carrying too much food."

Doona chuckled. "I told you we brought too much," she said.

"Let's find Inspector Rockwell and work out where we're meant to be sitting," Bessie suggested.

Bob was right; there were only a small number of people wandering around the site, and no one had any trouble spotting the inspector.

He was tall, at least as far as Bessie was concerned. She was only a few inches over five feet tall herself and Rockwell was over six feet. He was in his early forties and athletically built with neatly trimmed brown hair and stunning green eyes.

Bessie waved to him and he quickly crossed the grass towards them. He dragged two children along with him and Bessie couldn't help but smile when she noticed that they both had their father's gorgeous eyes.

"Bessie," Rockwell said when he reached her small group, "it's good to see you." He gave Bessie a quick hug and then stepped back to greet Doona, Grace and Hugh as well.

"But where's Sue?" Bessie asked, looking around for the inspector's wife, whom she had yet to meet.

"Ah," Rockwell laughed. "Would you believe she's on a hen night? One of her old friends back in Manchester finally decided to marry the guy she's been living with for the last ten years and Sue and a few other friends decided that, after all this time, she deserved a hen night. I'm not on call this weekend, so I told her I'd keep the kids and she could go and have fun."

"I'm sorry I'm not going to get to meet her," Bessie told her friend. "I was really looking forward to it."

"Next time," Rockwell assured her. "And in the meantime, I suppose I must introduce these two monsters to you," he added. "This is Thomas," he said, nodding towards the taller of the two children. The boy grinned awkwardly.

"Nice to meet ya," he said, looking down at the ground.

"And this is Amy," Rockwell continued. The young girl nodded politely.

"Dad's told us so much about all of you," she said in a soft voice. "I feel as if I know you already."

"Well, your father hasn't told me near enough about you," Bessie said. "Tell me everything interesting about you."

Amy flushed and looked at her father, who laughed. "Why don't we get settled with some food while Amy thinks about what she wants to tell you?" he suggested.

"That sounds like a plan," Bessie agreed.

"Didn't Bob say that Henry had a spot for us?" Doona asked.

"He did," Bessie agreed. "I'm just not sure where it is."

"It's over there," Thomas said as he waved a hand vaguely towards the stage. "Mr. Costain showed it to us while we were waiting for you guys."

"Wonderful," Doona said. "Lead the way, Thomas."

The little group fell in behind Thomas as he led them across the bumpy terrain. Bessie studied the inspector's children as they walked. She knew Thomas was fourteen, and he looked exactly how Bessie imagined the inspector would have looked at that age. They had the same brown hair and the same build, although Thomas was still several inches shorter than his father. The child moved with the awkward gait of a young man whose body was growing faster than he could adapt to it.

Amy, at twelve, also seemed to be in the awkward stage somewhere between childhood and adulthood. She wore her brown hair long, and it was pulled back in a fairly haphazard ponytail. Her fringe was too long and she kept pushing it out if her eyes as she clomped across the grass. While she bore a strong resemblance to her brother, she looked less like the inspector than Thomas did. Bessie wondered how much young Amy looked like the missing Sue.

"Oh, this can't be right," Bessie said as the little group reached a small roped-off section right in front of the temporary stage.

"Henry said we're to make ourselves at home in the VIP section," Rockwell told her.

"Oh no," Bessie said, shaking her head. "I didn't buy VIP tickets. Henry shouldn't give us special treatment just because we're friends."

"Ah, we're more than friends." The voice came from behind Bessie and she quickly turned around to greet the speaker.

"Fastyr mie, Henry," Bessie greeted the man in Manx. She and Henry had already known each other for many years before they'd both taken the same beginner's class in the Manx language, and the class, which Doona also attended, had strengthened their friendship.

"Oh, fastyr mie," Henry replied with wink. He was in his fifties and had worked for Manx National Heritage since he'd left school. "Now, this VIP section is for you and you friends," Henry told Bessie, unhooking one of the ropes from the short poles that had been pushed into the ground and motioning for Bessie and the others to enter.

"Now, Henry," Bessie said firmly. "I didn't pay for special treatment. We'll just set up our picnic on the grass out here like everyone else."

Henry flushed and took a step closer to Bessie. "Ah, Bessie, I know you don't like anyone to make a fuss over you, but, well…." He glanced around and lowered his voice, even though there was no one around to overhear him.

"The thing is," he confided, "everyone else has cancelled, like. The VIP section was meant to be full. It was booked by some group of bankers from Douglas who were going to bring their families. We set it up to accommodate forty people, like. But when we rang this afternoon to let them know about the change in the programme, they cancelled. Now we have this big space, right in front of the stage, and no one to use it. We can't take the whole section down; the actors have already seen it. And I don't want to put just anyone in here. Besides which, there aren't that many folks here anyway. I'd be ever so grateful if you and your friends would sit in here. If you can spread out and try to look like a whole crowd, that'd be great too."

Doona laughed. "I reckon I look like at least two people these days," she told Henry. "I'll do my part."

Bessie frowned at her pretty friend. Doona was taller than Bessie and somewhat heavier. A couple of eventful months meant that Doona had added a few extra pounds to her somewhat generous build, but her highlighted hair and bright green eyes remained unchanged. Bessie knew the eye colour was courtesy of coloured contact lenses, but she had been relieved lately to see some of Doona's zest for life shining out of them again.

"Exercise classes start Monday," Rockwell said to Doona. "I'll make a fool of myself in beginning aerobics if you will."

Doona smiled. "I told you I'm willing to come to one class and try it," she answered. "No promises after that."

Rockwell had recently taken over the running of the small police station in Laxey and one of his new innovations was adding an exercise facility to the site. He'd brought his own exercise bike, treadmill and weights from home, and the department had paid to have a matted floor laid in the small storage room that the Chief Constable had given permission for them to convert. Now Rockwell had persuaded one of the local gyms to offer exercise classes at the station three mornings a week.

"I'm not going to be trying it," Hugh said firmly. "I'll stick to lifting weights a couple of times a week."

"I know I'm not invited," Bessie said, "but I'd be sticking to walking anyway." Bessie walked on the beach outside her cottage home every day, enjoying the fresh sea air and the exercise. She was sure her morning walks were one of the secrets of her long life and continued good health.

The group made their way into the VIP area and Hugh finally put down the hampers he'd been carrying since they'd left the car. "Where do you want to set up, then?" he asked, surveying the area.

"That's where the troupe is going to be getting changed between scenes and whatever," Henry told them, pointing to a small tent that was set up immediately to the right of the VIP section.

"Let's spread out as far away from them as we can, then," Bessie suggested. "Watching them dash in and out throughout the show might be distracting."

"Or it might be entertaining," Doona suggested with a laugh.

"There's another small group booked into the VIP section," Henry told them now as Doona and Grace each grabbed picnic blankets and began to lay them out on the grass. "Make sure you leave enough room for them. I think there's about five in their group."

Doona nodded. "We aren't even using half the space," she told Henry. "They'll have plenty of room to spread out."

Within minutes, Grace and Doona had four blankets laid down together to make a large rectangle for the group to sit on. Hugh had set out plates, napkins and cutlery while Rockwell opened his own hamper and started unpacking the goodies inside.

Bessie unpacked cold ham, loaves of crusty bread, and a selection of cheeses. She had pork pies and Scotch eggs as well as enough sandwiches to give everyone in the group at least two. She pulled out a few plastic containers filled with various salads and added them to the collection.

"My goodness," Bessie exclaimed as the hampers were emptied and the food spread out across one blanket. "We have enough for an army." Half an hour later, she was reconsidering that remark, as nearly all of the food had disappeared.

"I'm stuffed," Doona announced, lying back on the blanket.

"That's just as well," Bessie told her. "There isn't a lot of food left."

Doona laughed. "I noticed that. We may have to buy something from the vendors to keep us going through the show."

"I'm planning on it," Hugh announced.

Everyone laughed.

"Why am I not surprised?" Grace asked. "I think I'd explode if I ate as much as you do."

Bessie smiled at the young woman. "I don't think anyone can eat as much as Hugh," she told her. "Although I do think young Thomas tried."

Thomas blushed. "I was really hungry," he told Bessie. "I didn't eat much lunch."

Rockwell laughed. "Teenaged boys are always hungry," he remarked. "They have a lot of growing to do."

"Well, there's meant to be an interval. I think we should all get something from the vendors then. They've turned up expecting to cater to a crowd and they certainly don't have one," Bessie said.

"I think…." Doona cut her comment short when a sudden flurry of activity at the entrance to the small tent next to them caught everyone's attention.

"This is the dressing room?" The voice was loud and strident. "We've sunk to a new low now, haven't we?"

"Hush, Penny, someone will hear you." The second voice was much quieter, but still carried clearly over the short distance to where Bessie and her friends were sitting.

They watched with interest as the two speakers, both of whom had their backs to them, struggled with the tent flaps. They were both dressed in jeans and T-shirts, and from the back Bessie was uncertain as to either person's gender. Both were carrying large boxes that were filled to overflowing with what must have been costumes. Finally, one of them managed to find an opening and the pair slipped into the tent.

"Well, that was interesting," Doona said. "I would have thought they would have been in costume ready to go by now, though. The show is meant to start in twenty minutes or so, isn't it?"

Rockwell shrugged. "And I would have thought there would be a lot more of them, as well," he said.

Bessie opened her mouth to reply, but she was interrupted by activity in another direction. Henry was ushering a small group towards the VIP section.

"Oh, my heavens," Doona gasped when she noticed the group. "It can't be."

"What can't be?" Bessie asked.

"That man, it can't be, can it?" Doona said, staring at the group with Henry.

"I think it might be," Grace giggled from her spot on the blanket next to Hugh. "I really think it might be."

Bessie looked at Inspector Rockwell, who shrugged and shook his head.

"It's Scott Carson, isn't it?" young Amy whispered in an awed tone.

"It is, isn't it?" Doona hissed back.

"I can't believe it," Grace giggled. "It really is."

"Who's Scott Carson?" Bessie asked, looking from one flushed face to the next in confusion.

"Shhhhh, he'll hear you," Doona said.

"I can't believe you don't know who he is," Amy said, giggling again.

The group had now reached the ropes and Henry stopped to unhook the rope that marked the entrance.

"Here you are, then," he said. "That half of the space is all yours."

"That's simply not acceptable." The woman who spoke glanced

around the small area and then shook her head. "We must have the entire space to ourselves. Mr. Carson needs to be protected from, well, ordinary people."

The man himself laughed. "Knock it off, Candy," he said, smiling at Henry and then nodding towards Bessie's group. "This is absolutely fine. I'm sure these lovely folks are just here to enjoy the show, same as us."

"Oh, but Scott...." the woman began.

He held up a hand. "Really, Candy, enough. This is fine." He turned to Henry and beamed at him. "Thank you so much," he said, offering a hand. Henry took it cautiously. When Henry pulled his hand back, he looked at it and then shook his head.

"Oh, no," he said, holding up the note that Scott had slipped to him. "I don't need tipping for just doing my job."

Scott tried to wave the money away, but Henry insisted on giving it back to him. "Thank you kindly, anyway," he said, giving the man an awkward bow as he hastily left the VIP section.

Scott nodded at Bessie's little group. "Good evening," he said loudly in what Bessie took to be an American accent. "I'm Scott Carson and I'm beyond excited to be here."

Doona got to her feet and made a beeline for the handsome man. "Hello, there," she said excitedly when she reached him. "I'm Doona Moore."

"Very nice to meet you, Doona," the man said, offering a hand. Doona took it and then turned pink as her hand touched his.

Bessie had risen to her feet more slowly and now she joined the others who were also now standing and making their way towards the new arrivals.

Whoever the man was, Bessie had to admit to herself that he was gorgeous. His sandy brown hair fell in a very carefully haphazard fashion to frame a nearly perfect face. A small scar across his chin gave him a slightly dangerous look and his dark eyes provided an attractive contrast to his light hair. He looked to be somewhere around forty and he seemed to tower over Doona, whose hand he was still holding.

"I'm John Rockwell, CID Inspector with the Isle of Man Constabulary," Rockwell told Scott, holding out his hand.

Scott chuckled and then, seemingly reluctantly, released Doona's hand to shake Rockwell's. "Nice to meet you," Scott said.

"These are my children, Thomas and Amy," Rockwell introduced the children who shook hands politely. Amy giggled again and then hid behind her father and brother.

"I'm Grace Christian," Grace said, her face flushed with excitement.

"And it's a pleasure to meet you as well," Scott said, taking her hand. Bessie watched as the man's eyes moved up and down Grace's slender figure. Grace turned a brighter shade of pink under his inspection. She was fair-skinned, with blonde hair and blue eyes, and Bessie could see even the back of her neck turning pink.

"And I'm Hugh Watterson," Hugh interjected, quickly shoving his hand out. "I'm with Grace."

"Lucky you," Scott remarked casually, releasing Grace's hand to shake Hugh's.

"And I'm Elizabeth Cubbon," Bessie told him. "Everyone calls me Bessie, so you may as well, but I'm afraid I haven't the slightest idea who you are."

Scott laughed. "How refreshingly honest of you," he said with a laugh. "I'm not really anyone special."

"Bessie doesn't watch television," Doona told the man, slipping an arm around Bessie's shoulders. "I'm sure she'd be a huge fan if she did."

"Am I to take it you're a fan, then?" Scott asked, giving Doona a beautiful smile.

"Oh, definitely," Doona enthused. "Bessie, Mr. Carson is the newest star of *Market Square*, Britain's favourite daily soap. I watch it every night or I record it, if I can't watch."

Bessie nodded. "Sorry," she said to the man. "As Doona says, I don't watch television."

Scott shrugged. "Not everyone can be a fan," he said.

"But everyone should," Scott's companion chimed in now.

"Ah, Candy," Scott said. "Everyone, may I present my manager, Candy Sparkles?"

Everyone turned to look at the woman who had now thrown an arm around Scott. She was older than her client. Bessie guessed her to be somewhere around fifty, but it was hard to be certain. Candy was so deeply tanned as to resemble old leather and her face had a strange, sort of permanently surprised look to it that suggested that she'd had some sort of surgery on it. Her long blonde hair looked brittle and dry, and huge dark sunglasses shaded her eyes. Her curves were extremely generous, something else that Bessie suspected had had outside assistance.

"It's great to meet ya'll," Candy drawled in a southern American accent. "I hope you don't think I'm too rude," she continued in a low and husky voice that sounded as if it had been honed on whiskey and four packs of cigarettes a day. "I'm just always trying to protect Scott. You all seem like nice enough folks, but you wouldn't believe what people can be like. He's been nearly trampled to death by rabid fans. That's why we have the bodyguards, you know." Candy motioned to the two men who were standing behind her. They were nearly carbon copies of one another, dressed all in black with dark glasses and determinedly expressionless faces.

"And because you love having big strong men around," Scott said in a teasing tone.

Candy laughed wickedly. "You've got me on that one," she said, slapping Scott's back. "I do love having them around."

"The show's meant to start in fifteen minutes or so," Scott said, after a glance at his watch. "I guess we'd better get settled in."

Candy nodded. "Carl, go and get our stuff," she instructed one of the bodyguards. He nodded once and then turned and headed back out towards the small crowd that was dotted around on the grass behind them.

The second man turned and stood facing the crowd, his arms linked behind his back. Bessie was childishly tempted to wave a hand in front of his face to see if he reacted. Clearly Candy had a similar thought as she studied the mountainous man, but Candy didn't have any qualms about acting on hers. Candy walked around behind the guard and Bessie almost gasped when she saw the other woman reach out and pinch his bottom. The man didn't visibly react to the touch, and Candy just laughed when Scott told her to behave.

A few moments later, Carl was back with his arms full, and Bessie and her friends retreated to their half of the area and watched. Two folding chairs were set up and then rearranged repeatedly until Candy was satisfied. A picnic hamper was opened and a bottle of wine extracted. Candy filled two glasses and handed one to Scott.

"I guess we're ready for show time," Candy said with a laugh as she took a healthy sip of her drink.

"Cheers," Scott said, smiling over at Doona, who flushed and then raised her own glass in a toast with the handsome actor.

The pair settled into their seats and the two guards took up position right behind them, both planting themselves firmly in place with their eyes fixed on something in the distance above Scott's and Candy's heads.

There was another flurry of activity at the small tent. Bessie watched as a couple of people went into the tent. A moment later, a woman walked out. She glanced casually over at the VIP section and Bessie was surprised when she saw the colour drain from the woman's face. The woman spun around and went back into the tent. A moment later, everyone in the VIP section could hear raised voices coming from the tent. The sound was muffled, and Bessie couldn't make out any words, but clearly there was an argument taking place in the makeshift dressing room.

A few moments later the tent flap opened again. This time a tall man, dressed as a king or perhaps a nobleman, strode out. He seemed to deliberately avoid looking towards the audience as he took the few short steps to the side of the stage. There he had a quick conversation with Bob, who was standing at the light and sound control panels. Bob nodded and then the man headed back into the tent, without looking around.

"Um, hello," Bob's voice came out over the tannoy. "I just wanted to let you all know that the show will be starting in about ten minutes. If you haven't already done so, please take a minute to read the introduction in your programme so that you, um, know what to expect."

"I forgot to pass around the programmes," Bessie exclaimed. She quickly dug into her handbag and pulled out the stack of papers that Bob had given her. There were more than enough to go around and she was happy to pass a couple to Scott and Candy as well. Once everyone had a copy, Bessie settled in to take Bob's advice and read the play's introduction.

Shakespeare's boring.

Shakespeare's hard to understand.

Shakespeare's not relevant anymore.

How often do we hear, or even say that?

And yet, theatre groups around the world still insist on performing Shakespeare's work as it was written. Oh, sometimes someone might try to give it a more modern twist, but basically, if you "do" Shakespeare, you're expected to follow his script.

But why?

Shakespeare was writing for everyone. He wanted to attract a large audience and he used humour and wordplay to entertain his crowds. What we wanted to do is take that idea and run with it.

What we've done is take some of Shakespeare's very best writing, the funny and the interesting sections, and combined them into a new show that offers something for everyone. We mixed up comedy with tragedy, drama with history and Shakespearean language with modern slang. We've created a modern masterpiece that we feel is exactly what William Shakespeare would have written last week, if he were still around.

We invite you to sit back, open your minds, and enjoy:

Much Ado About the Shrew.

"Oh dear," Bessie said to herself.

CHAPTER 2

A few moments later a hush fell over the small crowd as a group of people left a large tent that was set up behind the stage. They slowly approached the stage, which was simply a large wooden platform that had been built on a flat area of grass. A small section of the stage had a second, higher platform built on to it and then, rising above that, a small balcony with its own narrow flight of stairs. Because it was open-air theatre, there was no curtain between the stage and audience. Now, the group of actors climbed onto the main platform and the show began.

"To be or not to be," a voice rang out from somewhere amid the clustered men and women on stage.

"Oh, Romeo, Romeo, wherefore art thou, Romeo?" someone else called.

"Out, damned spot! Out, I say!" a third voice chimed in.

A woman dressed in long hooded robes stepped forward. "Great lines deserve great actors," she intoned. A moment later the flap to the small tent next to the VIP area was flung open and several men and women flowed out from it towards the stage.

For the next hour or more, Bessie watched and wondered at the action that was taking place on the stage. Every so often she'd feel as if she'd started to understand a bit of the plot, only to find herself plunged back into confusion as something seemingly random interrupted the narrative. After the first half hour, she more or less gave up on understanding things and topped up her wine glass instead. Doona grabbed the bottle from her hand as soon as she'd done so and filled her own glass. The pair exchanged confused looks and silently toasted the fact that they were smart enough to bring wine.

As the first act drew to a close, most of the actors began to make their way off the back of the stage and gather near the sea wall. A few people had been in and out of the small tent throughout the show, disappearing as one character and re-emerging in a new costume to take the show in a different direction. Now, a couple of the actors headed into the small tent and began a conversation that grew loud quite quickly. Again, the exact words were unclear but the unhappy nature of the discussion was obvious to everyone in the VIP section.

"To sleep, perchance to dream." A tall man spoke loudly on the stage. From the annoyed look on his face, Bessie could guess that he, too, could hear the argument in the dressing room tent.

"But dreams are merely worlds we have yet to explore," the woman, the only other actor still on the stage, said in reply. "And we have many worlds yet to explore."

The two linked arms and headed off the stage, towards the small tent. The audience watched silently, many with stunned expressions on their faces. After a very brief pause, Bob came out from where he was sitting and made an announcement over the tannoy.

"There will now be a twenty-minute interval. I invite everyone to visit our many food vendors who would be happy to provide you with a snack for the second half of the show."

Bessie looked around at her friends. When she caught Doona's eye they both burst out laughing.

"What the heck was that?" Doona asked, trying to keep her voice down so that it didn't carry beyond her friends.

"I haven't the slightest idea," Bessie answered, shaking her head.

"It wasn't like the Shakespeare we've been learning at school," Amy announced.

"I didn't understand any of it," Thomas complained.

"Neither did I," Bessie told him. "It was all rather, um, complex."

"That's one word for it," Rockwell laughed. "I can think of a few others, but I wouldn't use them in front of my kids."

Hugh shook his head. "I was worried that I'm thick or something," he confessed. "I couldn't follow it at all."

"It was pretty awful," Grace told her boyfriend. "But in a funny way, I suppose."

Bessie nodded. "Unfortunately, I think it was only funny when it wasn't meant to be."

"So, what did we think of that?" Scott Carson had stepped over to join Bessie's little group.

"It was certainly different," Bessie said diplomatically. "What did you think?"

"I thought it was terrible," Scott said loudly. "It was just a huge jumbled-up mess that made no sense. It didn't even tell a story."

"Well, don't hold back," a voice from behind Scott said. "Tell us what you really thought."

Scott turned around and Bessie saw a sly grin cross his face. "Darling Penny, how wonderful to see you," he said silkily. "You look absolutely gorgeous, as always."

"As do you," the woman, who was still in her full elaborate Elizabethan-style costume, answered. "But then, you've the money to make sure of that now, don't you?"

"Oh, Penny, let's don't be bitter and horrible," Scott replied. "I took the time to come and see the show, to offer my support. That should count for something."

"Oh, aren't you kind?" the tall man who had been last to leave the stage now stood behind Penny just outside the little tent. "I can't tell you how much we appreciate your willingness to spend time with the little people in spite of your huge fame and fortune. If it's all the same to you, I'll skip kissing your ring and grovelling at your feet while I'm in costume."

"William, still so dramatic, and still so bitter," Scott said with a sigh. "I was hoping my coming today would do something to end the unnecessary unpleasantness between us."

"I hardly think that's going to happen," the man answered, turning his back on Scott, but not walking away.

"Oh, I must introduce everyone," Scott said, clapping his hands together. "Seriously, you all must meet my old friends."

Bessie got to her feet slowly, stretching tired muscles that were unaccustomed to sitting on the ground. While she was working out the kinks, the rest of her group rose as well. Now Scott began his introductions.

"Okay, let's see what I can remember," he said with a self-deprecating shrug. Bessie's friends had fallen into an untidy line and now Scott walked along behind it, announcing each person in turn with a grand gesture with his hands. Doona was last in the row and after he presented her with a flourish, he walked over to the two actors from the show.

"Everyone, these are my friends, William Baldwin and Penny Jakubowski, extraordinary actors being let down by a slightly underfinished script."

Bessie watched as William's face tightened. He looked to be about ten years older than Scott, maybe somewhere near fifty, with hair that was dark but was definitely grey at the roots. He was tall and thin and Bessie supposed that many women would consider him very good-looking, especially in the handsome nobleman's costume he was wearing.

Penny was probably forty, although she appeared to be fighting her age with even more makeup than the stage demanded. Her short hair was a coppery colour that definitely came out of a bottle, but her green eyes were possibly authentic. Bessie knew nothing about cosmetic surgery, but there was something decidedly odd about the woman's eyes that made Bessie wonder if she'd had something done to them. Penny was still wearing her costume from the last scene, a long flowing gown that was cut very low in the front and emphasised Penny's very generous cleavage. The dress was just a little bit too tight, though, as if Penny had gained a few pounds since the costume was made.

"Adam wrote the script," Penny said now in reply. "And we love it."

"Adam wrote the script?" Scott repeated. "Well, that explains a lot."

"And what is that supposed to mean?" An angry voice came from behind William and Penny.

"Ah, Adam, right on cue," Scott beamed. "Who else is hiding in that little tent of yours?"

The man who now stepped around William and Penny looked furious. He was probably thirty-five and somewhat shorter than William, but still tall to Bessie. He too was in costume, but his was a simple robe. His bald head seemed to shimmer in the setting sunlight and his dark eyes seemed to flash angrily at Scott. "I asked you a question," he said sharply to Scott.

"I just didn't follow the story," Scott answered airily. "I'm sure it's all my fault. I never was very bright."

Adam's eyes narrowed as he looked at Scott. "Just bright enough to get the job that was supposed to be mine," he said fiercely.

"Hey, now," William interrupted. "That was supposed to be my job," he said. "If anyone should have been plucked out of the group and made a star, it should have been me."

"Now, now," Scott said in a soothing voice. "You all know how grateful I am that I've had the opportunity I've had. And I'm grateful to you guys for keeping me working before I got my big break. That's why I'm here tonight. I wanted to see my old friends. I left in such a hurry, I feel like I never said good-bye properly."

"Ha," Adam snorted. "You couldn't wait to get away, and as far as I'm concerned, good riddance to you." He turned his back to everyone and stomped to the changing room tent. Shoving aside the tent flap, he disappeared inside.

"Penny?" Scott said in an appealing voice. "Please tell me you're not mad at me." He put his hand on her arm.

Penny gazed up at him for a minute and then sighed. "I can't stay mad at you," she admitted, giving Scott a hug. "But really, now you need to get me a part on your lovely show."

Scott laughed, but it sounded awkward. "I so wish that I could," he told Penny. "If it were up to me, I'd get parts for all of you, even Adam. But I'm just a teeny tiny fish in a massive pond. I'm lucky they haven't killed off my character yet, and I just keep hoping my luck holds."

"As long as you keep winning titles like 'Sexiest Newcomer to Soap Land,' they couldn't possibly get rid of you," Penny told him.

Scott beamed. "You saw that?" He glanced over at William and made a serious face. "I mean, it's just a way to sell magazines. It doesn't mean anything, really. Anyway, the writers can do what they like if they feel it fits the storyline. Look what happened to Maggie."

Penny nodded seriously. "I suppose you're right about that."

Bessie looked questioningly at Doona, who was still standing next to her. "Maggie Lawson was one of *Market Square's* biggest stars," Doona whispered. "The rumour is that she started having an affair with one of the writers. His wife is also a writer on the show, and when she found out, she wrote Maggie right out of the show; she killed her off in a huge car crash."

Bessie shook her head, glad to have yet another reason for not having a television.

"Anyway," Scott told Penny in a confiding tone, "it isn't anywhere near as glamourous or exciting as you'd think. Mostly it's all about sitting around all day to shoot for three minutes and then sit around for another couple of hours."

"And for that you get paid handsomely," William interjected.

Scott flushed. "I must admit, the pay is generous," he said with a shrug. "But by the time I give my agent her share, well, I'm not exactly filthy rich."

"Your agent?" William laughed. "Only you would drag around a washed-up old porn star everywhere you go and try to convince people that she's your 'agent.'" William made exaggerated air quotes around the last word.

Scott laughed as Candy got up from her chair. "Really, Billy boy," she drawled. "I think you should remember how we met. Hmmm, where was it now? Oh yeah, on the set of *Candy Takes the Cake,* wasn't it? I was the star and you, you were 'tall man in trench coat' in the opening scene."

Candy shook her head. "If you'd have listened to me, you could be where Scott is now, but you never gave me credit for what I know. I might not have been a star for long, but I learned a lot on my way up and on my way back down. And I'm using everything I've learned to shape Scott's career. He was smart enough to listen to me and now we're both reaping the rewards."

"The only skill you picked up in your time in the movies was how to...."

Candy's brittle laugh cut off William's words. "Sour grapes, my old friend," she said.

"Enough, you two," Penny said, glancing from William to Scott and back. She smiled at Scott and then took another step closer to him. Putting her hands on his arm, she gazed up at him. "Do you think there's any chance you could get me an audition?" she asked Scott in a breathlessly flirty voice. "I'd do anything to get an audition."

Scott looked down at her. "I'll see what I can do," he replied. "For you and for William as well."

"Don't worry your pretty little head about me," William said harshly. "I'll look after myself, and Penny as well."

William took Penny's arm and gave it a pull. After a last beseeching look at Scott, she let William lead her back into the tent.

"Well, that was fun," Candy laughed. "It's always so nice to see old friends."

Scott shook his head and sighed.

"Scotty? It really is you!" The excited squeal came from the tent opening, and then a small figure hurtled out of the tent and into Scott's arms.

"Ah, Sienna, there you are," Scott said, hugging the girl tightly. "Let me look at you."

The girl stepped back and spun slowly, giving Scott, and everyone else, a good look at her.

She couldn't have been much more than twenty-five, with long blonde hair and bright blue eyes that Bessie immediately suspected were artificially enhanced. She was no taller than Bessie's five feet, three inches. Unlike Bessie, however, she was endowed with generous curves that she was currently showing off in a tiny cropped T-shirt and a mini-skirt that only barely covered enough to be decent. As she twirled, Inspector Rockwell covered his son's eyes in case the skirt inched up any higher.

"Hey, Thomas and Amy, let's go grab something to eat from the vendors," Hugh suggested suddenly, grabbing the kids' hands. "We'll leave your dad here and I'll get you something he wouldn't approve of."

Rockwell laughed and quickly pulled out his wallet and handed Hugh some money. "Make sure you eat it all before you get back here," he teased the kids. "Otherwise, I might object."

Grace laughed. "I won't let them get too much junk food," she promised, as she linked her arm into Hugh's and they led the children out of the VIP section.

"You won't catch me leaving just when things are getting interesting," Doona hissed to Bessie.

Bessie shook her head. She wasn't interested in getting anything else to eat and she was fascinated by the scene that was unfolding in front of her. It was certainly a good deal more interesting than the play had been so far.

"So, how do I look?" Sienna giggled up at Scott.

"Amazing," Scott replied, pulling her into another hug. "I was afraid you didn't want to see me."

"Ha," she replied, snuggling up to the man. "More like Adam didn't want me to see you."

Scott shook his head and loosened his grip on the girl. "You're still with Adam?" he asked. "That's disappointing."

The girl giggled. "What else could I do, with you gone off to London?" she asked.

"But when I was in the troupe, you wouldn't even give me the time of day," he reminded her.

"Because I didn't know you were going to be a big star, did I?"

Sienna demanded. "If I'd known, I'd have given you a lot more than the time of day."

Scott shrugged and then changed the subject. "It's great to see everyone," he said. "But what's up with the play? *Much Ado About the Shrew*? What the devil is that?"

Sienna giggled again. "Adam wrote it, so I have to tell you I think it's brilliant," she said. "But, really, after you left we didn't have a choice. No one could agree on anything and William couldn't find anyone to replace you. He'd booked the shows here ages ago, so we had to come and perform something."

"What's wrong with *Hamlet*?" Scott asked. "Or, well, just about anything else?"

Sienna shook her pretty blonde head. "We just don't have enough people to do *Hamlet* anymore. It's hard to find people to join a troupe that hasn't any bookings, you know? We had to find a show with fewer big parts. Penny wanted to do *Romeo and Juliet,* if you can believe that."

"What's wrong with that?" Scott asked.

"She wanted to play Juliet," Sienna sighed. "I almost got myself fired when I suggested she was too old to play a teenager anymore." She sighed again, even more deeply. "Everything's changed without you in the company," she told Scott.

"I don't know. You're still with Adam, and Penny and William are still together. It all seems the same to me."

Sienna shook her head. "Everyone fights all the time. I'm pretty sure Adam and Penny are getting together behind my back, and William has been dropping hints that we should get together every time I'm alone with him."

"My dear girl, you can do much better than William," Scott told her. "Actually, you can do much better than Adam as well."

Sienna laughed. "Is that a proposition? Because I'd leave here right now with you if it was."

Scott ran his hand down her back and squeezed her bottom. "I couldn't possibly take you away from the company," he said in a sad voice. "Things would fall apart without you."

Sienna laughed harshly. "It's too late for that," she retorted. "We haven't had a decent performance since you left. William has auditioned and cast half a dozen different shows and then cancelled them, usually after just the read-through. When it became clear we had to get something ready for the shows here, Adam threw this mess together and we literally rehearsed it on the ferry. I think this fortnight will be our last time together as a theatre troupe."

"It can't be that bad," Scott said. "Will's Comedy/Tragedy Players were one of the best travelling Shakespearean performance troupes ever. I only ever played small parts. William and Adam were the geniuses behind its success. We toured the entire US, remember? Maybe taking the company across the ocean was a mistake," Scott conceded. "We should have known things would be different in the UK, and we didn't plan as well as we should have. But that's all in the past. You guys can have a brilliant future together. You just have to work as a team."

"The problem is, you deserted the team," Sienna told him. "We all used to feel like a family and then, one day, Candy starts acting like an agent. Suddenly there's a casting director in the audience and, like magic, you've landed the opportunity of a lifetime and the rest of us are left with nothing."

"You've still got each other," Scott said.

"Yeah, except now we're all trying to figure out how to get our own big break. We've all seen what's possible and we all want to follow in your footsteps, not hang around changing costumes in tiny tents on small islands in the middle of nowhere."

Scott shook his head. "I didn't mean to break up the group," he said sadly. "But I couldn't very well turn down my big break, could I?"

"Why couldn't you have taken us with you?" Sienna asked, tears welling up in her eyes.

"Before we left the US, you barely even knew my name," Scott replied. "I was just another member of the troupe and Adam was one of the stars. Now you're prepared to dump him and run off with me, because I'm a little bit famous?"

"Yeah," Sienna shrugged. "Is that a problem?"

Scott and Candy both laughed.

"My dear girl," Candy said, taking Sienna's arm. "You and I need to talk. I think I could be a big help to you. In fact, I'm sure I can make you a star."

Sienna's eyes lit up. "Really?"

Candy shrugged. "You're pretty and you're ruthlessly ambitious. I like that. I suppose you have to finish tonight's show, but we're leaving in the morning for London. That won't be a problem, will it?"

Sienna made a face. "Everyone will fuss if I leave in the middle of the run here," she said. "I guess I just won't tell them. They'll figure it out by lunchtime tomorrow."

Scott shook his head. "Don't you feel any loyalty to the troupe?" he asked. "I gave William a week's notice before I went."

"Except once you told him you were going, he threw you out on the spot," Sienna laughed. "I think I'd rather just sneak away. They'll be fine without me. Anyone can do my part."

"What about Adam?" Scott asked.

"He and William can fight over Penny," Sienna replied. "Or he can go after some pretty little thing in the chorus who can't actually act. He'll be fine."

"These people's real lives are more interesting than what happens on *Market Square*," Doona whispered to Bessie.

"I think it's all terribly sad and I'm glad the inspector's children aren't here to witness it," Bessie replied. "I've half a mind to sit that girl down and have a serious talk with her."

"I rather think you'd be wasting your breath," Doona told her friend. "She's far too self-absorbed to pay any attention to you."

"Sienna? Where the devil are you?" the voice boomed out from the small tent, causing Sienna to giggle nervously.

"I guess I'd better get back to it," she said with a sigh.

"Catch me after the show and we'll figure out exactly where and when to meet tomorrow," Candy told her. "I'll sort out your plane ticket and you can repay me from your first proper pay cheque."

"Oh, thank you." Sienna gave the older woman a huge hug and

then threw her arms around Scott. "Thank you as well," she said, batting her eyelashes at him.

"You can thank me properly later," he said with a lascivious chuckle.

"Oh, I will," Sienna promised with a wink.

"Oh, please," Doona muttered to Bessie.

Rockwell stepped over to stand behind the two. "They should have written some of this drama into the play," he whispered. "Although the characters certainly aren't very likable."

"Scott's not bad," Doona protested. Bessie looked at her for a long minute before Doona blushed.

"Okay, Scott's gorgeous and I think I could forgive him anything," she giggled.

Rockwell shook his head. "I think I should go and find my kids," he said grumpily.

"Maybe we should just sit back down and finish the wine," Doona suggested to Bessie.

"I do hope you two lovely ladies aren't whispering about me," Scott said. Sienna had disappeared into the tent, and he now turned his attention back to the others in the VIP section.

"Of course not," Doona said, blushing. "We were just talking about finishing our bottle of wine."

"That's a lovely idea," Scott said with an engaging smile. "I think I'll join you. But no worries, I'll bring my own bottle."

Bessie and Doona exchanged looks, with Bessie trying to telegraph her dislike for the man to her friend. Whatever they both thought, though, they were both too polite to tell the man he wasn't welcome.

Bessie headed back to her spot on the blankets and picked up her bag. She pulled out the light jacket she had packed. It was getting late and it was definitely getting cooler. She was about to sit down, but she was interrupted.

"Oh no, I saw how hard it was for you to get up," Scott said with an ingratiating look. "Take my chair, please."

Bessie protested for a moment, but Doona quickly joined in the argument, and together they persuaded Bessie to join Candy on the other side of the small enclosure. Doona brought Bessie's wine glass over to her and then filled it to the brim.

"Do you want me to move the chair over to our side?" she asked Bessie, as Bessie took a sip.

"Oh, don't do that," Candy said. "I'd love a chance to talk to Bessie about the island."

Bessie gave Doona a dubious look, but responded politely. "I'll stay here with Ms. Sparkles, then," she told her friend.

Doona raised an eyebrow, but took the handful of steps she needed to get back to her own corner of their blankets. Scott smiled up at her from where he'd already stretched himself out, a full bottle of wine within easy reach.

"Come join me, then," he coaxed Doona. "Tell me all about your beautiful self."

Doona sat down on the ground, grabbed her glass and emptied its contents. Scott was quick to refill it before the pair began their chat.

"So, have you lived on the island your entire life, then?" Candy asked Bessie.

"No," Bessie answered politely. "I was born here, and then my family moved to the US. We lived there through my teen years and then moved back here when I was seventeen."

"Really? That's fascinating," the other woman replied.

"Do you really think so?" Bessie asked. "Or are you just being polite?"

Candy laughed so hard that she had a coughing fit. Finally she drank a healthy swallow of wine and regained control. "Sorry, I smoked for so many years that I'm always just a tickle away from a coughing spell," she told Bessie. "And if I'm honest, I guess I'm not really that interested in your life." Candy shrugged. "It's all ancient history anyway. The present is so much more interesting than the past."

Bessie shook her head at her. "As an historian, I think I might have to disagree with you."

Candy laughed again. "My goodness, we've absolutely nothing in common, have we? Whatever will we talk about?"

Bessie glanced over at Doona and Scott. Doona was staring at the man as he talked, and she seemed to be hanging on his every word. "You did say you're leaving in the morning, right?" Bessie asked.

Candy let out yet another stream of laughter. "Don't like Scott playing up to your friend? Can't say as I blame you for that. He's too good-looking and he knows it. Women throw themselves at him and he is quick to catch as many of them as he can."

Bessie frowned. "Doona has had a rough time lately," she told Candy. "I'd rather he didn't play games with her emotions."

"Scott, you behave," Candy called over to the man who had just placed his hand over Doona's.

Scott flushed and then pulled his hand back. "We're just talking," he said crossly.

"Just make sure it stays that way," Candy said. "Doona's way too good for the likes of you."

"No doubt," Scott replied. "I'll behave."

"Better?" Candy asked Bessie.

"Yes, thanks," Bessie answered.

"Should I tell you about my life as a porn star?" Candy asked.

"Do you feel the need to talk about it?" Bessie asked.

Candy chuckled. "You're perfect," she told Bessie. "Here I am, trying to shock you, and you're way cooler than I am. No, I don't especially need to talk about it. I had a terrible childhood and I started taking care of myself when I was sixteen. Making movies was a way to make money, nothing more. Once I'd made as much as I could, I got out of it and started doing other things. And now I'm finally making decent money managing an actor who's never even been naked on camera. It's a weird old world."

"It is at that," Bessie agreed, feeling rather as if she were in the middle of a very strange dream. Certainly the cast of characters was completely unlike any people she'd ever met before.

A moment later Hugh and Grace returned.

"It's getting on towards sunset," Hugh said as they sank down on the blankets near Doona and Scott. "I thought it was meant to be a short interval, but it's been nearly an hour now."

"A lot of people have left," Grace added.

Bessie looked around and shook her head. The small crowd of maybe a hundred people who had been present for the first half of the show seemed to have shrunk by at least half.

"I think your friends are going to have trouble selling tickets for the rest of the fortnight," Doona told Scott.

"It's a shame," Scott replied. "There's a lot of talent in that little group, but Adam is no writer. I can't imagine what they were thinking, trying to put together an original show."

Rockwell and his children now appeared outside the ropes. Thomas jumped over and Amy was quick to follow while their father took the time to unhook one of the ropes from its post and walk through.

"Did we miss anything?" Rockwell asked the group, as he looked over the VIP area.

"We were just wondering why they haven't started back up again," Doona answered, standing up and taking a step towards her boss.

"That's a great question," Rockwell said. "The sun is going down and it's going to get dark soon. I'm not sure it would hurt the performance if it's too dark to see it, but it won't be safe for the actors moving around the stage if they can't see where they're walking."

"Let me go and see what's going on," Scott said, rising to his feet. He crossed to the little tent and shouted into it. "Hey, William? It's show time, you need to get on with things."

A long silence followed Scott's words, and then the tent flap was pulled back. Penny's face appeared in the opening.

"We're just about ready," she said. She quickly disappeared, pulling the flap shut again behind her.

Bessie spotted Henry pacing anxiously near the stage. She got up and crossed to him. "Henry, what's going on?" she asked.

Henry jumped. "Oh, I didn't see you there," he muttered. "Sorry, Bessie, but this is just craziness. The show should have finished by now, or nearly, and they haven't even started the second act. We've got some floodlights in place, just in case they ran over, or whatever, but it looks as if we're going to need them for the whole second act. I worry about everyone trying to get out of here once the show is over, though. The castle grounds will be pitch black and there's so much to trip over."

"At least there aren't that many people here," Bessie reminded him.

"True," Henry said, his face brightening slightly. "I suppose we can take them all out in small groups with our torches."

"Anyway, I think they're almost ready," she said.

"I certainly hope so," Henry replied. "Some of us have to work again in the morning."

Bessie crossed back to her little group. They were just getting settled in for the second act.

"Oh, no, Bessie, you keep the chair," Scott said, as Bessie started to sit back on the ground. "Here, I'll move it over for you near your friends."

Bessie tried to protest, but first Scott and then everyone else overruled her objections. Scott set the chair up in the middle of the blankets and then headed over to his own side of the section. He flopped down on the ground on the far side of Candy, almost in the doorway to the small tent. His two bodyguards took up their positions behind him.

Bessie settled in to the borrowed chair with Doona on one side of her and Hugh on the other.

"Are you sure you can all see around me?" she asked.

"I don't want to see anyway," Thomas told her, lounging across the blanket behind her seat.

"Sit up and watch," Rockwell told his son. "The second half might be better."

Bessie bit back the laugh that bubbled up inside of her after that remark. From what she'd seen and heard during the interval, the second half was going to be just as tragic as the first.

A few moments later the group of robed actors and actresses were back, making their way towards the stage. Bessie sat back and sipped her wine, letting their words wash over her without giving them much attention. Various quotations from a myriad of Shakespeare's plays were mixed in a seemingly random fashion with lines from old movies and books. Bessie began to amuse herself by trying to guess whether lines were from Shakespeare, borrowed from some other play, or simply the product of Adam's seemingly unusual imagination.

Doona made one or two muttered comments, but Bessie was far too polite to engage in a conversation during the show, especially as they were essentially sitting in the front row. About halfway through the act, the floodlights were switched on. Now, actors leaving the stage to head for the small tent were essentially blinded as they left the bright lights of the stage for the total darkness that surrounded it. Henry was busy passing out torches to them to help them find their way back to the small tent, but the torches didn't provide nearly enough light for them to change by. It became increasingly amusing to everyone in the VIP section as they watched and listened to the various people tripping and stumbling on their way into the dressing room tent and within it as well.

More than once the action on stage had to pause as everyone waited for an actor to emerge from the unlit tent. William stomped out once with his shirt on back to front and no one on stage was brave enough to mention it until Penny managed to slide up to him and whisper in his ear. More than one of the actors stumbled in the tent entrance next to Scott, and Bessie was sure she heard Penny stop to have a chat with him at one point.

"They should have just done *A Comedy of Errors*," Doona hissed as Sienna made her way onto the stage in a pair of shoes that didn't match, the tiara on her head askew, wearing crooked lipstick.

Bessie was torn between feeling sorry for the troupe and feeling angry with them. She'd paid good money for a professional theatrical performance and she certainly wasn't getting it.

As the show wound down to its unbelievably confused and contrived ending, Bessie sighed with relief. She couldn't wait to get home and go to bed. By tomorrow, she was sure, everything that had happened would feel much funnier.

The show finally ended around half ten. At first the audience was slow to applaud, perhaps not entirely sure that the play was actually finished. Once the actors began to take their bows, Bessie and her friends clapped as loudly as they could, trying to make it sound as if they were a crowd. Bessie wasn't certain, but she had a feeling that many of the remaining audience members had slipped out during the interminable second act.

Now Bessie and her friends began to try to gather up their things in the darkness. Bessie could hear hurried discussions between Henry and Bob, and then one of the large floodlights that had illuminated the stage was turned towards the audience to enable people to find their belongings.

Bessie looked over at Candy and Scott. Candy looked to have fallen fast asleep in her chair, and Scott was still stretched out on the ground beside her. The two security guards, still wearing their dark glasses, hadn't moved from their posts.

Bessie rose from the chair and looked at it, wondering exactly how it folded up. She was too tired to experiment with it and risk pinching her fingers.

She crossed over to Candy and put a hand on her arm. "Candy? The show's over," she said to the other woman.

Candy shrieked and jumped in her seat. "What, huh, what?" she said.

"The show's over," Bessie repeated impatiently. "Thank you for letting me use the chair, but you can have it back now."

Candy blinked several times. The lighting cast odd shadows around the VIP section. Candy rubbed her eyes as she shook her head. "I was fast asleep," she told Bessie. "I'm sure I drank too much wine."

"I think Mr. Carson did as well," Bessie replied, nodding towards Scott, who hadn't moved.

"Okay, Scott, I've burnt my bridges; let's rock and roll." Sienna's singsong voice echoed through the space as she emerged from the tent, back in her mini-skirt and tiny T-shirt.

"Scott's had too much to drink," Candy sighed. "Again."

Sienna shrugged. "I guess the big guys can lift him, right?"

Inspector Rockwell had been standing next to Bessie during the conversation; now he held up a hand. "I don't think I want anyone lifting Mr. Carson," he said in his senior policeman's voice.

He took the few steps needed to reach Scott's side and bent down beside him. Rockwell shook Scott's shoulder. "Mr. Carson? Scott?"

There was no response, and Bessie's heart sank. The inspector pulled a small but powerful torch from his pocket and focussed it on Scott. The torchlight glinted off the jewelled hilt of the small knife that was sticking out of Scott's back.

Sienna's screams echoed around the castle grounds.

CHAPTER 3

ockwell was already in police inspector mode, but he was a father first. He turned to Doona. "Get the kids out of here," he told her. "I don't want them being a part of this."

Grace and Doona grabbed Thomas and Amy, who both protested only briefly, and pulled them away from the VIP section. Hugh exchanged glances with his boss.

"I could run them home," Hugh suggested. "But I don't want to leave you to cope with all of this on your own."

Rockwell frowned. "Tell them all to hang on for a few minutes. Once Inspector Warren gets here, we may all be able to leave."

Hugh nodded and walked over to have a few words with Grace, who was unnaturally pale.

The inspector turned back to Sienna, who was still screaming. For a moment Bessie thought he might slap the girl, but instead he grabbed her shoulders and twisted her away from the body. After a long moment, the screams suddenly stopped.

Henry and Bob came rushing up, presumably drawn by Sienna's shouting.

"What's going on?" Bob asked.

Henry took one look at Bessie's face and then looked at Scott's body. "Not again," he moaned.

Rockwell shook his head. "I'm afraid so, Henry. Can you ring 999, please? Tell them I'm here and I'm securing the scene, but we need backup. As soon as you've done that, you need to get to the gate and stop people from leaving."

Henry nodded and pulled out his mobile. He started to walk away and Bessie watched him press the nine button three times. She sighed.

"We need more lighting," Rockwell said, his voice revealing his frustration.

"I can try turning around more of the floodlights," Bob offered. "There are some on the other side of the stage."

"That would be great," Rockwell told him. Candy hadn't moved from her chair, but now she stood up, grabbing her wine glass as she rose.

"I'm going to need a lot more wine," she said huskily.

Sienna spun back around. "You're still going to make me a star, right? I mean, you said you'd take me with you. You aren't leaving this island without me."

Rockwell held up a hand. "No one is going anywhere right now," he said firmly. "I'd like you both to just sit down at the far end of the section and just relax. I'm sure Inspector Warren will have questions for you when he arrives. In the meantime, I'd like you to keep quiet. And I'm afraid I'm going to have to take that," he added, holding out his hand for Candy's drink.

"No way," Candy argued. "My best client, heck, my only client just turned up dead. I need a drink or ten."

"Stop," Rockwell barked as she raised the glass to her lips. "We don't know what happened to Mr. Carson, but there's a chance that he was drugged or poisoned. The only thing I saw him consume was that wine."

Candy laughed. "Oh, come on," she said. "I'm no police detective, but even I can see the knife in his back."

"It's a prop knife," Sienna said quietly. "It couldn't have killed him."

"You recognise the knife?" Rockwell asked her.

"Yeah," Sienna shrugged. "We used it in *Macbeth;* it's a prop. The blade retracts when you push on it."

"So Scott's not dead?" Candy demanded.

Rockwell knelt down beside the man and shone his torch on Scott's face. "He's definitely dead," he replied. "I really don't think you should drink that wine."

Candy turned pale in the odd bright lighting and her wine glass slipped from her fingers. Rockwell just managed to catch it before it hit the ground.

"Can't have you messing up my crime scene," he muttered.

Hugh stepped forward now. "If you ladies wouldn't mind, I think you'd be better off down here, out of the way." He escorted the pair to the furthest corner of the VIP section where they both sank to the ground.

Rockwell looked at the two bodyguards, who were still standing, motionless and expressionless, in their spots. "What exactly were you two meant to be doing here?" he asked.

"Nobody said anything about Mr. Carson getting murdered," one of them sputtered. "We were just meant to hold back the women, and then just the ugly old ones, that's all."

The inspector shook his head. "Go and sit with Ms. Sparkles, please. Someone will take your statements shortly."

As Rockwell turned back around, he seemed to suddenly notice Bessie. She'd slipped back into the borrowed chair and was busy trying to look inconspicuous.

"Ah, Bessie, what can I do with you?" the inspector asked with a sigh.

"Don't you worry about me," Bessie told him sternly. "Get the kids somewhere safe with Doona and Grace. I'll just stay out of everyone's way until you and Hugh are ready to go back to Laxey." For a moment she thought Rockwell was going to argue, but just then Bob managed to hook up another light and suddenly the outside of the small tent and the area around it were flooded with light.

"It's about time," a voice shouted from inside the tent. "Maybe now I can find my pants."

Bessie guessed that the light had illuminated the tent's interior as well. The voice was William's and she hoped he was using pants in the American way, meaning trousers, and not that he was roaming around in the tent without underwear.

A moment later sirens could be heard racing towards the castle. Inspector Rockwell sent Bob to meet the arrivals and escort them to the crime scene. Bob had a powerful torch with MNH stamped across it. Two uniformed constables were quickly led across the site to Rockwell.

"For now we're just securing the scene," the inspector told the two young men after brief introductions. "I'm assuming Inspector Warren is on his way, along with the coroner."

"Not likely," the shorter of the men said. "Inspector Warren had his appendix out this afternoon."

Rockwell frowned. "I didn't hear about that," he said. "Who's running the CID while he's off?"

The two men looked at each other and then back at Rockwell. They both seemed to shrug at the same time.

"Inspector Warren is pretty much the whole Peel CID," the taller constable told Rockwell. I suppose the Chief Constable will have to find someone to take charge."

Rockwell nodded. "We should...."

The scream cut through his words.

"Scott? Scott?"

Penny, now dressed all in black, came running from the small tent, straight towards the body. Inspector Rockwell motioned to the two constables, and they quickly intercepted her just before she reached it.

Rockwell looked down at the glass that he was still holding and frowned. He quickly and carefully set it down inside Candy's open picnic hamper. From where Bessie was sitting, the hamper looked empty, so apparently it had held nothing but the pair of glasses and two bottles of wine.

Penny was sobbing in the arms of a very unhappy looking constable.

"Ms. Jakubowski, please." Rockwell gave Penny an awkward pat on the back. "You need to calm down."

"What's going on out there?" William's strident voice cut through Penny's wailing.

"Oh, William, Scott's dead," Penny shouted.

"Nonsense," William shouted back. The tent flap opened and he strode out in long grey trousers and a matching short-sleeved shirt. "What are you shrieking about, my love?" William addressed Penny, ignoring everyone else.

"It's Scott," Penny sobbed. "He's, he's, he's, oh, I can't say it." She dissolved into more tears, while William slowly took in the scene.

"Heart attack? Must have been," William said to Rockwell.

"We'll know more when someone from the coroner's office arrives," Rockwell replied. "In the meantime, perhaps you and Ms. Jakubowksi would like to wait in the dressing room tent? Is there anyone else still in there?"

William blinked. "Wait? No, thank you. I'd like to get back to the hotel and get some sleep. Come along, Penny, let's go."

"I'm sorry," Inspector Rockwell said in his sternest tone. "But I need you to wait here until someone had had a chance to take a statement from you."

"That's preposterous," William blustered. "I mean it's tragic, old Scott passing away so suddenly, but it's nothing to do with us. We need to get our rest. We have a lot of rehearsing to get through tomorrow afternoon."

"I'm not going to disagree with that," Rockwell said dryly. "But you aren't going anywhere yet. Please wait in the tent."

The inspector turned away from William and Penny, while the uniformed constable that Penny was still clinging to began to try to usher them back into the tent. The constable pulled back the tent flap and then took a sudden step backwards as Adam appeared in the opening.

"What on earth is going on out here?" he demanded, looking from Penny's tear-stained face to Scott's body.

"Well, well, well," he said as he took a step towards Scott. "Has someone finally done what we all wanted to do?" Adam stared at the body for a moment and then began to laugh heartily.

Inspector Rockwell exchanged looks with Bessie and then took a step towards the man. "Mr., um, that is, I don't think I caught your last name, but you need to calm down and stop laughing."

Adam grinned at him. "It's Misnik, but please, call me Adam. I suppose I'm a suspect. How very exciting. When does the crime scene team get here? Are you going to take my fingerprints? Of course, that's our prop knife, so my fingerprints may well be on it. But then, if it's our prop knife, it couldn't have killed Scott, now could it? What a puzzle. Where is Sherlock Holmes when you need him?" Adam sighed dramatically.

"Shut up, Adam," Sienna called from her corner of the VIP area. "Just shut up before you talk yourself into getting arrested."

"Oh, Sienna, I forgot all about you. You were on your way to bigger and better things, weren't you?" Adam laughed again. "I guess that big dramatic goodbye scene you just played through was a little premature, huh? Scott can't make you a star now, can he?"

"Mr. Misnik, please," Rockwell stepped in. "I'd like you to go back in the tent with Mr. Baldwin and Ms. Jakubowski for now. Constable Hopkins will sit with you until we can get things organised here."

As Adam and the other players moved back into the tent with one of the constables, more sirens could be heard. A moment later Henry appeared with six more uniformed men. Before Rockwell could issue any instructions to the officers, his phone buzzed insistently. He took a few steps away from the group and answered it.

Bessie watched the others during Rockwell's call. Doona, Grace and the children appeared to be having a lively conversation about something. Grace was standing with her back to Scott's body and every time one of the children started to look towards it, Grace slid sideways to block their view. Bessie smiled to herself. If she could learn to live with the uncertainty of the job, she seemed perfect for Hugh.

Sienna and Candy were sitting on the ground in the dimly lit edge of the section. They were studiously ignoring each other and the two bodyguards who were kneeling on the grass next to them. Hugh stood between the two groups, watching Sienna and Candy closely, but occasionally glancing at Grace as well.

Rockwell pocketed his phone and glanced around at the scene in front of him. He sighed deeply and then cleared his throat. "There's a forensics team on its way," he announced. "In the meantime, with Inspector Warren out of commission, I'm in charge of the investigation. Let me get a few things sorted and then I'll start taking statements from everyone."

Several people began to speak at once, causing Rockwell to shake his head. "I know you're all tired and want to go home, but I'm sure you all understand how vital it is that we find out what happened to Scott. I know you'll all be very patient as we proceed."

Bessie heard a few mutters, but no one wanted to argue with the inspector. He walked over to Hugh and had a short conversation. Hugh nodded and walked over to Grace. Rockwell then turned his attention to Bessie.

"I'm sending Doona, Grace and my kids home with one of the uniformed constables. The kids can crash at Doona's until I get there. I'm afraid that's the best I can do under the circumstances. Unfortunately, there isn't room in the car for you as well. I hope you won't mind staying for a little while. I really need as many officers here as I can get."

"I don't mind at all," Bessie assured the man. She tried to keep her voice calm, aiming to sound almost bored at the prospect. It wouldn't do for the inspector to realise just how much she wanted to stay and watch things unfold. While Scott's death was sad, she was intrigued by the prospect of having a front-row seat for a real-life murder investigation.

Rockwell gave her a look she couldn't read, and then nodded and walked away. Bessie listened as he gave instructions to various officers. The handful of audience members that hadn't left before the body was found had to be questioned, and Rockwell set Hugh with the task of taking preliminary statements from them.

"It's highly unlikely that any of them saw anything that might help

43

with the investigation," Rockwell told Hugh. "I would think they were all rather too far away to see what was happening in our section, but they need to be questioned and we need contact information for them, just in case."

"Yes, sir," Hugh said smartly. Bessie could tell that Hugh was excited at being involved in another murder investigation. Rockwell had been working with some of the officers in Laxey, training them in investigative techniques. Now Hugh had a chance to put some of that training to good use.

"Get their impressions of the show as well," the inspector added. "I'm curious what they thought and why they stayed for the second act."

Hugh smothered a laugh. "Yeah, I've been wondering why anyone stayed," he muttered as he turned away.

"Henry?" Rockwell called to the man who was standing at the edge of the VIP section. "I'm assuming you left a constable guarding the gate?"

"Yes, sir, a young man called Constable Blake told me to come back up here in case you needed me."

"Excellent, is there an office or another similar space where Hugh can talk to the good folks who are waiting so patiently?" Rockwell asked.

Henry nodded. "I can let him use the ticket booth," he told Rockwell. "It isn't a very big space, but it has lights."

"Lights would be a bonus," Rockwell replied. "How many people are left from the general audience?"

"I think there are about a dozen people or so that hadn't actually left before I got to the gate," Henry answered. "I don't think more than one or two small groups left after the show finished and before I got there. One of your officers has everyone that was left on the grass over there." Henry pointed towards the sea wall, but with the lights focussed on the VIP section, Bessie couldn't see anything in the darkness.

"Great," Rockwell replied. "Please get the ticket booth opened up for Hugh and then tell the officer to start showing people in, one at a time."

"Yes, sir," Henry said smartly. He headed off, keys in hand, with Hugh following closely behind him.

"Oh, and Henry?" Rockwell called. "Come back here after you've set that up, please. I'm sure I'll need something else."

Bessie could just make out Henry's nod as he turned on his torch when he and Hugh reached the edge of the illuminated area.

A moving torch in the darkness let Bessie know that someone else had arrived. Several serious looking men and women emerged from the darkness behind Bob and greeted Rockwell. They had to be crime scene technicians, Bessie decided. They were all dressed in ordinary clothes, but several carried bags and cases.

Rockwell stepped to the edge of the VIP section to talk to them. Only a few odd words drifted to Bessie. She tried to work out a way to move closer to them without drawing attention to herself, but before she'd managed it, the conversation finished.

One of the men pulled out a phone and began barking orders. Within minutes, several large lights were being put into place around the crime scene. Bessie slid her chair backwards, trying to stay out of everyone's way. Rockwell and one of the men stepped over to the body, crouching down next to it. A man with a camera was taking photographs from every possible angle. After a minute he stopped and nodded at Rockwell.

The man with the inspector reached out a gloved hand and pulled up slowly on the knife handle. A sharp looking blade glinted in the bright light. Whatever Sienna thought, it was no prop knife.

"It's the knife Penny gave William," Sienna gasped.

Rockwell's head snapped up and he looked over at Sienna, who was now standing up and peering intently at Scott. "It's definitely not a prop," he muttered to the other man.

"No sir, it's not," the man agreed.

Rockwell got to his feet and stepped away from the body. He caught Bessie's eye and shrugged. A moment later, Henry was back.

"Hugh's all set up in the ticket booth and the officers are bringing him people to question one at a time," he reported to Rockwell.

"Good, what about the rest of the actors, the ones that were coming and going from the bigger tent behind the stage?" Rockwell asked.

"They're part of a local troupe," Henry told him. "The Peel Area Players, apparently."

The inspector looked around. "Gary?" he called. One of the uniformed men snapped to attention and rushed over to Rockwell's side.

"Yes, sir?" he asked smartly.

"I want you to talk to the actors from the local troupe who were working as extras in the show tonight," Rockwell told him. "Find out if any of them knew any of the actors who came in to do the show or if they knew Mr. Carson. Get their impressions of the show, whatever information you can get."

"Yes, sir," he answered.

"Henry, can you set up a few lights in the big tent at the back so that Constable Kewin can talk to the local troupe members?" Rockwell asked.

"I'd be happy to," Henry assured him.

"Great," Rockwell replied. "Now I just need a similar quiet space to do some questioning of my own."

Henry frowned. "There's a little storage room in between the loos," he said hesitantly. "It isn't very big, but I suppose we could find a table and a few chairs for you to use. It does have lights."

"That'll have to do," Rockwell replied. "I don't want to move off-site until the crime scene folks have had time for some initial impressions, at least. I'm just taking preliminary statements tonight, anyway."

"I'll get Constable Kewin set up and then go and see how much of a mess the storage room is," Henry told him. "Give me a couple of minutes."

Rockwell nodded and then looked back at the body. There were several men and women working around it. The photographer continued to snap pictures every few seconds, and another person seemed to be sketching the scene. Bessie was fascinated by the quiet hive of activity.

"Oh, I say, Inspector?" Adam had emerged from the tent again, with an angry looking constable on his heels. "Sorry to interrupt all the excitement out here," Adam said airily. "But I'm bored to death in there. Oh, pardon the pun."

Rockwell raised his eyebrows. "I'm sorry my crime scene isn't more exciting for you," he told the man.

"Yes, well, I suppose it can't be helped, but really, how much longer do we have to wait?" Adam's voice took on a whiny tone that angered Bessie. It seemed to have a similar effect on Rockwell.

"You have to wait until I say you can go," he answered in a deceptively calm voice. Bessie could hear the suppressed anger simmering under it. "If you would prefer, I can have you escorted down to the station and you can wait there for me. I'm sure it will be a good deal more exciting. There are nearly always a few drunk and disorderly folks hanging around in the cells."

Adam flushed. "Oh, good heavens, no," he gasped dramatically. "I was just checking to see if you had any idea how much longer it would be, that's all. I didn't mean to upset you. I'm just so very tired, you see."

"I'm sorry that Scott didn't have the good sense to get murdered at a more convenient time for you," Rockwell told him. "For now, though, I need you to be patient. We're just sorting out a space that I can use for interviews and then I'll be talking to each of you in turn."

"Fabulous," Adam replied. "I guess I'll just wait in the tent, then."

"If you don't mind," Rockwell said.

"Or even if I do," Adam remarked as he turned and disappeared back into the tent.

Rockwell cleared his throat, but Henry was back before he began to speak.

"Okay, Inspector," he said. "Constable Kewin is all set and I've done the best I can with the space for you as well."

Rockwell nodded. "I'm sure it will be fine," he said. "I'll follow you. Miss Cubbon, would you come with us, please?"

Bessie was so surprised to be addressed so formally that for a moment she simply sat and stared at the inspector. "Oh, yes, of course," she said finally, shaking her head at her own stupidity.

Henry began to lead them away, his torch bouncing about in the darkness that engulfed them as soon as they were outside the VIP area. Rockwell called for one of the uniformed officers to join them. He switched on his torch and the uniformed officer put his on as well, but even three torches didn't seem to do much to help cut through the darkness.

"I'm really sorry about this," Henry told Rockwell as he opened the door to the storage room. "It isn't really designed to be used for more than storage."

Rockwell and Bessie stepped inside the small space. Bessie looked around at the old stone walls. A few bare bulbs provided the only illumination in the room. The back wall of the space was covered in shelves, and the shelves were crammed full of boxes that had papers spilling out from them. Bessie could see old brochures and maps of the castle grounds as well as advertising materials for other MNH sites. There were several chairs stacked on top of one another shoved into one corner, and a collection of spades, shovels and other gardening tools were piled up in another.

A slightly lopsided table had been set up in the middle of the room, with a chair on either side of it. Rockwell sank down into one of the chairs and then motioned for Bessie to take the other.

"Thank you, Henry," he said. He addressed the uniformed constable who had accompanied them. "Wilson, I'd like you to wait outside while I speak with Miss Cubbon. After that, I'll need you to bring me the various people I want to speak with, one at a time."

"Yes, sir," the man replied smartly. Henry held the door open for him and the pair walked out. Wilson pulled it shut behind him and the inspector let out a huge sigh as the sound of the door clicking into place echoed through the cavernous space.

"Sorry, Bessie, I want to get this over with as quickly as possible, but I just need to ring Doona and check on the kids," the inspector said. Bessie nodded and then got up and walked towards the back wall of the room to give him some privacy. The call was fairly short.

"Okay, Doona's got them both snuggled up on the floor watching old movies and eating popcorn with Grace. I suspect they'll all end up sleeping on Doona's floor in one big pile. Doona reckons my kids were less upset by the murder than Grace was."

"I'm sure you'd rather be with them than here," Bessie said in reply.

Rockwell shrugged. "It's my job," he said. "I'm sure Sue isn't going to be very happy when she finds out what happened, though."

"Oh, but it's hardly your fault."

Rockwell shook his head. "Let's just move on, shall we? I'll need a formal statement from you, of course, but I think that can wait until some time tomorrow. I know you didn't kill Scott Carson, and as far as I can work out, the list of suspects is a pretty short one."

"It has to be one of the actors who was using the dressing room tent, doesn't it? In the dark, with all the tripping and stumbling they were doing getting in and out of the tent, one of them must have taken a moment to stab Scott, mustn't they?" Bessie asked.

"I think Candy Sparkles could have just about managed it," Rockwell told her. "She was leaning up and down, picking up her wine bottle, throughout the show. From the angle she was sitting at, it wouldn't have been impossible for her to reach Scott."

"Are you sure the stab wound killed him?" Bessie asked.

"At this point, I'm not sure of anything," Rockwell admitted. "And I'm too tired to think it all through. For tonight, I just want to get preliminary statements from everyone and then we can go from there."

"That sounds like a good idea."

"But what shall I do with you, while I'm questioning everyone?" Rockwell asked.

Bessie yawned and then shrugged. "I'm exhausted," she told him. "I was thinking, while you were on the phone, that maybe I could just curl up in the corner over there in a chair and take a nap?"

Rockwell raised an eyebrow. "Are you sure you'll be able to sleep?" he asked.

"I can certainly try," Bessie said, her eyes twinkling. Rockwell had to know that there was no way she was going to miss out on hearing what everyone had to say.

"Well, I suppose that will have to do," the inspector said.

"There are some large display boards along that wall," Bessie pointed out. "Perhaps we can put them up and screen me off from you and the others. That way I definitely won't be in the way."

Rockwell nodded. "I suppose that would make sense," he agreed. "I will have to tell everyone that you're there, but if you're sleeping behind the boards, no one should mind."

It only took a few seconds for them to arrange the room to Rockwell's satisfaction. Bessie settled into the most comfortable chair they could find, tucked up behind the boards.

"All set?" he asked Bessie.

"All set," she confirmed.

"Let's get the show on the road," Rockwell muttered as he headed towards the door. Bessie wondered whom he would send for first.

CHAPTER 4

*B*essie wasn't surprised when Constable Wilson escorted Sienna into the room. Behind the panels, she settled into her seat, sliding down so that she looked as if she were ready to fall asleep. She'd shifted her chair to just the right angle to give her a perfect view, between panels, of the table and chairs in the centre of the room.

"Ah, I'm afraid I didn't get your surname," Rockwell said as Sienna settled into the chair opposite him. Wilson pulled a third chair up to the table, and then sat down beside the inspector.

"It's Madison," Sienna told Rockwell, running her fingers through her hair. "Sienna Madison."

"Okay, thank you." He made a note. "Before we begin," he told the girl, "Constable Wilson will be taking notes, as will I. I'll also be recording our conversation, if that's okay with you."

"Whatever," Sienna shrugged.

The inspector smiled tightly. "Miss Cubbon has had a long day and is resting behind those display panels. If you'd feel more comfortable talking to me privately, I can find somewhere else for her to rest while she's waiting for a ride back to Laxey."

Sienna waved her hand. "It doesn't matter," she said. "I can't imagine what you want to talk to me about, anyway."

Rockwell raised an eyebrow. "A friend of yours was murdered tonight," he said. "Surely that gives us a great deal to discuss."

Sienna shrugged. "I didn't really know Scott well," she replied.

"Let's start at the beginning," the inspector suggested. "Tell me about the theatre troupe."

"What about it?"

Rockwell sighed. "Let's start with what the group is called."

"Will's Comedy 'slash' Tragedy Players," Sienna answered waving a hand through the air to draw the slash.

"And how long have you been together?"

Sienna wrinkled her nose. "Ah, um, maybe five years?" she said, making her answer a question.

"Did you join the troupe after it was formed, or have you been a member from the beginning?"

"Yes," Sienna said.

Bessie rolled her eyes. Getting information from the girl was like pulling teeth. She had new respect for Inspector Rockwell as he kept his cool.

"You've been a member since the group was formed?" Rockwell tried to clarify her answer.

"No, well, sort of." Sienna waved a hand. "What does that have to do with Scott, though?"

"Ms. Madison, you don't need to worry about that," Rockwell said tightly. "If you could just answer my questions, we'll both get done a lot faster."

Sienna sighed deeply. "I joined the troupe about five years ago," she said. "They'd already been together for a month or so, but they hadn't performed anywhere yet. They needed another leading actress and I auditioned and got the job."

"Thank you," Rockwell said, taking more notes. "And was Mr. Carson already a member when you joined?"

Sienna nodded and then shook her head. "Maybe," she said finally. "I really didn't pay that much attention to the minor players."

Rockwell made another note and then gave Sienna an engaging look. "Ms. Madison, I need you to help me out here. I don't know anything about how travelling theatre companies work. Can you educate me, please?"

Sienna smiled back and Bessie suspected that the girl had just realised how attractive the inspector was.

"Well, I'm not sure how other companies work," Sienna said, softly, "but I can tell you about ours. We're a Shakespearean group. All we've ever done is Shakespeare. I think that's William's choice. He told me once he was named after him, which is sort of weird, but anyway, I don't know if I believe him."

"No one else in the company ever suggested performing other shows?" Rockwell asked.

Sienna shrugged. "It's William's troupe," she said. "He put it together and he's the director, so he gets to pick the plays. It was great when we were in the US. We managed to build up a pretty solid set of bookings, year after year. We were popular with the schools, because we usually did the plays exactly as written, but still made them fun and interesting."

"And you don't remember when Scott joined the group?"

Sienna frowned. "I'm pretty sure he was part of the group from the beginning," she said after a moment. "He might have joined after I did, but even if he did, he was in the first show. We did *Twelfth Night* and the girl I was rooming with went out with him a couple of times during the run."

"So you were travelling around, and you were staying in hotels?" Rockwell asked.

"Sure, hotels or motels or in dorm rooms or whatever cheap beds William could find," Sienna said. "Penny was in charge of booking shows and William was in charge of figuring out transportation and accommodations. Penny did great, moving us around the country, getting us performing in just about every small town she could find. Most of the places we played didn't have proper theatres, so we performed in high school gymnasiums or under tents in parking lots.

It didn't matter, because we all did it for the sheer love of theatre, not for fame or fortune."

Rockwell looked skeptical. "So you were one big happy group," he said. "And then what happened."

"Well, I wouldn't say we were all happy," Sienna answered. "Penny did a great job getting us shows, but a lot of people weren't very happy with William. We ended up staying in a lot of cheap and nasty motels or, even worse, in empty dormitories during summer breaks and things like that. There was some grumbling that we were doing a lot of shows and making a lot of money but William and Penny were pocketing it and not giving everyone their fair share."

"Right, so let me just check who all was with the company at this point," Rockwell said. "Clearly, you were there, and so were Ms. Jakubowski, Mr. Baldwin and Mr. Carson. What about Mr. Misnik?"

"Oh yeah, Adam was one of the founding members," Sienna answered. "He was the stage manager for all the shows. When I first started in the group, he was dating this girl called Beth, but they broke up after she caught him with me one time too many. Adam and I have been together ever since."

"What about all of the other people?" Rockwell asked. "The men and women in the long robes who wandered in and out of the show. How many of them came from the US with you?"

"Oh, none of them," Sienna answered. "But you've skipped ahead, you see."

"Sorry," Rockwell told her. Bessie watched him swallow a yawn and then had to fight back one of her own.

"Please, continue with the story," Rockwell told Sienna.

"Right, so after like four years or so, people were starting to complain a lot, and then William got us all together. We'd been all the way across the US from New York City, where we started, to Los Angeles. Now William made his big announcement. He wanted to take the troupe to England for a year." Sienna sighed. "I should have left when I had the chance."

"Why?" Rockwell asked. "What went wrong?"

"Well, William offered everyone a choice," Sienna continued, clearly determined to tell the story at her own pace. "They could leave the troupe and he'd give them enough money to get home, wherever home was, or stay and experience the 'next great adventure,' as he called it, with the group."

"And you chose to stay."

"I did. Obviously, William and Penny were going, and Adam decided to give England a try as well. The four of us were sort of the core of the troupe, and everyone expected me to go along. At the time it sounded like fun, anyway. Scott and Candy were just about the only ones from the rest of the group to sign up. Everyone else took whatever money they could get from William and took off."

"Candy was in the troupe?" Rockwell asked. Bessie could hear the surprise in his voice.

"Oh, yeah, just a minor player, like. Actually, she was our main little old lady. She's actually a very talented actress, if you don't mind that she did porn for a while. We never mentioned that when we did school shows." Sienna giggled.

"So when did she start managing Scott's career?"

"Oh, not long after she joined the group," Sienna explained. "Candy was always promising to use her connections to get this person or that person an audition somewhere. We'd all heard it so often that we'd stopped listening, but Scott believed her. She did manage to get him a few local commercials and voice-over work in some of the small towns we passed through, but nothing big."

Sienna sighed. "I guess we all should have believed her. She said she knew people in London, but she claimed to know people everywhere, and nothing much ever came of it."

"So the six of you set out for London when exactly?" Rockwell asked.

"Oh, not long ago," Sienna answered vaguely. "The thing is, apparently you need some sort of okay from the government to come and set up a theatre troupe in a foreign country. William didn't really do his research and then, when we were all set to come, we found out we didn't have the right piece of paper or something. Anyway, we were stuck in LA with virtually no money for five months while William did the paperwork. We all had to get part-time jobs to cover the cost of the nasty little apartment that we all crowded into. Well, actually, that isn't true. Scott and Candy stayed somewhere else. It was just me and Adam and William and Penny in this horrible little one-room apartment for what felt like years." Sienna shuddered and ran her hand through her hair again.

"Anyway, once the paperwork came through, we were on our way," she continued. "We had been rehearsing *Hamlet* in all of our spare time, so we decided to start with that. Unfortunately, once we arrived in London, we very quickly discovered that the UK doesn't have any shortage of talented theatre troupes performing Shakespeare. We did a few shows somewhere up north. I don't even know where we were, and then we settled into a squalid bed and breakfast in this appalling section of London and tried to work out what to do next."

"All six of you this time?" Rockwell asked.

"Yeah, all six of us. But only for a few days. Penny was working constantly, trying to get us bookings. That's when she managed to get us booked for this fortnight over here. Anyway, she found a little theatre in some scary corner in London and got us a single matinee performance there. William found a local amateur theatre group that was willing and able to supply the supporting players for the show. Scott was Horatio to William's Hamlet, and after the show, some big shot casting director appeared backstage and offered Scott a job on *Market Square*. Of course he took it and that was that."

"I thought he said something about giving William a week's notice?" Rockwell countered.

"Yeah, he offered, but William was so angry that the casting guy had picked Scott instead of him that he told Scott to just get out. It didn't really matter; because we didn't have any other shows booked anyway. Scott and Candy packed up their things and left that night."

"Candy went too?"

"Oh, yeah, she was the one who arranged for the casting guy to be there, even though William and Adam both keep claiming they had something to do with it."

Sienna leaned forward in her chair and lowered her voice. "I think she'd met him during her porn star days, but they didn't talk about how they knew each other."

Sienna sat back. "Anyway, that was about a month ago, and the four of us have been scrambling around London ever since, trying to figure out how to make ends meet. Apparently, we don't have permission to find other jobs, and we don't have enough money for plane tickets home, either. We were all hoping that this fortnight over here would earn us enough money to pay for flights back to the US, but with the low numbers at the show today, I'm doubting that it will."

"Why did you stop doing *Hamlet*?" Rockwell asked.

Sienna rolled her eyes. "After Scott left, everyone started arguing all the time," she answered. "We couldn't get *Hamlet* to work anymore, without Scott to play Horatio. Candy was brilliant as Gertrude, as well. Once they were gone, *Hamlet* fell apart and no one could agree on a different play, either. Adam has always fancied himself a writer. Somehow he managed to persuade William to let him write a script for the company that would give the four of us big parts and let us fill in the rest of the company with just about anyone. The people out there tonight were from some theatre group here on the island. We rehearsed with them for exactly twenty minutes this afternoon and then we went on."

And you could tell, Bessie said silently.

Rockwell managed not to say it. "You weren't expecting Mr. Carson to be here tonight, then?"

"No," Sienna said. "As far as I know, no one had seen or heard from him since he left. I think, if he'd called and told William he was coming, William would have told us."

"So his being here was a surprise. Why did he come?"

Sienna blinked and then shook her head. "I've absolutely no idea," she said. "Maybe he wanted to gloat over his good fortune."

"Was he the sort of person that would do that?"

Sienna shrugged. "I didn't think so, but then, I barely knew him. Maybe Candy wanted to gloat over his good fortune. She's definitely that sort of person."

Rockwell nodded. "Tell me about the knife," he suggested.

"About two years ago, when we were doing *Macbeth*, Penny found that knife in a little antique store somewhere in, oh, goodness, I don't know, Wyoming, maybe? It was cool because it was exactly the same as the prop 'jewelled dagger' that we were using in the show, but it was a real knife. She gave it to William for his birthday and he used to carry it around with him all the time."

"And he brought it to London with him?" Rockwell asked.

"No," Sienna replied. "That's the weird thing. He lost it about six months ago. We all joked about it, saying he shouldn't be bringing weapons to a foreign country anyway, but he was really upset. It disappeared from the apartment where we were staying in LA. For a long time he seemed to suspect Adam of taking it, but it never turned up, and I guess he finally decided that one of the other residents in the building must have taken it. It was probably the only thing in our apartment that looked like it had any value if anyone broke in, and the place was always such a mess, we probably wouldn't have noticed if anyone did."

"So as far as you know, no one has seen the knife in six months or so?"

"Until tonight," Sienna replied.

"So who wanted to kill Mr. Carson?"

Sienna shrugged again. "Probably all of us," she said flippantly. "We all hated him for getting the big break we've all always wanted."

"I thought you said you did theatre for the love of the art," Rockwell reminded her.

"Well, yeah, but getting a big paycheck would be nice, too," Sienna laughed. "Actually, doing it for the art is fine for a year or two, but I'm not getting any younger. I need my big break and I need it now. I just hope Candy will keep her promise and help me out. I don't think Adam's going to take me back, and besides, going back to a sinking ship doesn't really appeal."

"So you all hated Mr. Carson?"

"I didn't really hate him," Sienna replied. "Anyway, I was hoping he would help me, so I guess you can cross me off the list. William and Adam hated him, though. I'm not so sure how Penny felt about him.

She had a bit of a fling with him for a few months, but that was just because she was bored and William was chasing after some redhead. It didn't mean anything."

"When was that?"

"The fling with Penny? Oh, goodness, maybe a year ago? Maybe even longer than that. It was over before we started talking about going to London."

"Did William know about the affair?"

Sienna shrugged. "He must have. They certainly weren't discreet."

"So who do you think killed Scott?" Rockwell asked abruptly.

Sienna eyes opened wide. "Wow, I, um, that is, wow." She took a deep breath. "I guess I'd have to pick William if I had to chose someone. He really hated Scott for leaving and he seemed to blame him for a lot of the problems we were dealing with, even though most of them didn't have anything to do with Scott."

"During the second half of the show, did you see anyone stop to talk to Scott, or did you speak to him?" the inspector asked.

Sienna shook her head. "I waved at him once or twice as I walked past," she replied. "But once it got dark I couldn't even see where I was going, let alone worry about Scott. Walking off the super brightly lit stage into darkness was almost impossible. If it weren't for the flashlights I think I might just have wandered off into the sea."

Rockwell made another note and then nodded at Sienna. "I think maybe that's enough for tonight," he told her. "I didn't plan on spending this long with you as it is, but you've given me a lot of very helpful information. Thank you."

"You're welcome, I'm sure." She smiled up at him and then batted her eyelashes. "Are you single?" she purred.

Rockwell laughed. "No."

"What a shame," Sienna sighed.

"I'm going to have one of my officers take you back to your hotel now," the inspector told her.

"Oh, but what about Adam?" Sienna asked.

"I still need to talk to him."

"He's furious with me. Can't you take me into protective custody or something?" Sienna asked.

"Sorry, but you're going to have to work your own way out of this one."

Sienna sighed. "Can I keep your big strong policeman with me until Adam gets back and I've had time to beg for his forgiveness?"

"I suppose I can leave an officer with you until Mr. Misnik gets back to the hotel," Rockwell told her. He stood up, and Constable Wilson rose as well. The two men walked to the door with Sienna.

"Mr. Wilson, please escort Ms. Madison to Constable Johnson. Ask Johnson to drive Ms. Madison back to her hotel and stay with her until her partner arrives, then bring Mr. Misnik here."

"Yes, sir," Wilson nodded at the inspector. The pair left and Bessie was on her feet as the door shut behind them.

"That was fascinating," she told Rockwell. "I'm surprised you agreed to have an officer stay with her, though. She's trouble, that one."

"I'm sure Constable Johnson can handle it," Rockwell told her. "Jenny's an excellent officer, with ten solid years of experience."

Bessie laughed. "Won't Ms. Madison be disappointed?" she asked rhetorically. "But what did you think of the lovely Sienna?"

"I think she's bright and ambitious and probably only told the truth about half the time." He shrugged. "Right now I'm just trying to get a good first impression of everyone. I'm not expecting to solve the murder tonight."

"But what about…."

Bessie's question was interrupted by a knock on the door, and Bessie rushed back to her corner as Wilson walked back in with Adam in tow.

Rockwell ran through his warnings about recording and note-taking before casually mentioning Bessie's presence.

Adam just shrugged. "Whatever," he said in a bored voice. "I just want this to be quick. I'm tired. Live theatre is exhausting enough, but when you've poured your heart and soul into creating something and then you lay it all out on stage for people to watch, well, it's exhilarating and terrifying and a million other adjectives. I can't possibly explain it to you, but I'm desperately in need of rest."

"I'll try to keep this short, then," Rockwell told him. "Can we start with a brief history of Will's Comedy/Tragedy Players, please?"

Adam sighed, but he gave the inspector a brief rundown that was almost identical to the one Sienna had given, but with a much more positive slant to it. Rockwell took several notes during the recitation. Adam finished by explaining how the troupe had been forced to struggle on without Scott after he deserted them during their successful London run.

"Of course, we had to cancel a few shows," Adam told Rockwell. "We had to totally revamp the production after Scott and Candy took off. Although, I suppose I actually owe Scott a huge debt of gratitude. If he hadn't left, I might never have found the courage to offer my script to William. I was surprised and obviously delighted when he decided that we should perform it."

"But you weren't exactly thanking Scott tonight when you saw him," Rockwell pointed out.

Adam flushed. "Sour grapes," he said. "I'm not ashamed to admit it. We were all so angry when he got plucked from our midst and turned into a star. We all thought we were more talented than Scott, that's why he only ever had small parts in our shows, but he was suddenly on television five days a week. It was hard."

Rockwell nodded. "When did you find out that Scott was coming to the show tonight?"

"Oh, but I didn't know he was here until I saw him," Adam protested. "I certainly didn't stay in touch with him after he left."

"Did anyone?"

Adam grinned nastily. "I don't want to get anyone in trouble," he said. It was clear to Bessie that that was a lie.

"But I suspect he kept in touch with both Penny and Sienna."

"What makes you think that?" Rockwell asked.

Adam shrugged. "They both seemed rather too informed as to exactly how things were going for Scott," he said. "Penny had quite a hot and heavy affair with him before we came to London and I suspect Sienna was seeing him behind my back in the last month or so before we left, after he broke it off with Penny."

"Did William know about Scott and Penny?"

"That's a great question," Adam replied. "I wish I knew the answer. They were very discreet. I only found out because Penny told Sienna and she can't keep a secret, at least not from me."

"But you think she had an affair with Scott?"

"Well, yes, I mean, clearly she kept that a secret, but otherwise she's hopeless with secrets."

Rockwell raised an eyebrow and made a few notes before he continued. "Would Sienna have told William about Penny's affair with Scott?"

"Oh, no," Adam said insistently. "Her first loyalty would have been to Penny. As the two principal actresses in the troupe, they're very close."

"Weren't you angry when you suspected that Sienna was having an affair with him?"

Adam shrugged. "Sienna and I have a complicated relationship," he said. "We care about each other, but every once in a while one of us gets bored and seeks a little diversion elsewhere. It doesn't mean anything, of course. I would have rather she'd chosen to have her fling with someone outside the troupe, but we travelled so much that I suppose she never met anyone else."

"Tell me about the knife. Did you recognise it?"

"The one sticking out of Scott's body?" Adam asked. "It looked like the one that Penny gave William, oh, it must have been a few years ago now. It got lost a while back, though, so maybe it wasn't the same knife."

"It looked pretty distinctive," Rockwell commented.

Adam shrugged. "If it is William's, I've no idea how it got here. William accused us all of stealing it, but I always thought it was the apartment manager who took it. He was always wandering through out apartment, helping himself to our food and claiming that he was there to fix the pipes or something."

"But, presumably, he's back in the US?"

"Yeah, I guess," Adam shrugged again.

"So, who do you think killed Scott?" Rockwell asked.

"Penny would be my first guess," Adam replied promptly. "She wasn't happy when their affair ended, and she was really unhappy when Scott got his big break and didn't take her with him."

"Interesting, so you think she killed him just out of sheer anger at his good fortune?"

"Either that or maybe he promised her something and he didn't deliver," Adam shrugged again. "You asked for my opinion and that's it. It's just my gut feeling, I guess."

"Did you have any interaction with Scott during the second half of the performance?"

Adam laughed. "I was too worried about falling over or getting lost to spare a single thought for anyone in the audience. Well, aside from hoping that I was giving them my very best performance, of course."

"Well, thank you for your time, then," Rockwell told him. "I've sent Sienna back to your hotel. I assume you two are sharing a room. Is that going to be a problem?"

Adam laughed. "Because she quit the troupe tonight in the most dramatic way possible? No, it won't be a problem. I know she was just caught up in the excitement of seeing Scott again. I'm sure Candy filled her head with all sorts of nonsense. We'll be fine. I'll forgive her and we'll work it out. We always do."

Rockwell nodded. "I'm glad to hear that. You can go. Constable Wilson will escort you out and find someone to give you a ride back to the hotel. I'm sure I'll need to talk to you again, but that's all for now."

Adam nodded and got to his feet. "I really hope you enjoyed the show," he said politely. "I put my heart and soul into it, you know."

"It was certainly unique," Rockwell said. "But I'm too tired now to even remember what I saw."

"Maybe we can talk about it when I see you again," Adam said eagerly. "I really want to get as many opinions on it as I can. I know it probably needs some work and the more feedback I can get, the better."

"Yes, well, I'm no drama critic," Rockwell told him.

Rockwell stood up and pulled Wilson to one side for a quick conversation, then the constable escorted Adam from the room, while Rockwell sat back in his chair. As the door shut behind the men, Bessie jumped up, feeling far more full of energy than she should have.

CHAPTER 5

"*D*id you find him more trustworthy than Ms. Madison?" Bessie asked Rockwell, as she sat down in the chair Adam had just vacated.

Rockwell shook his head. "I don't trust anyone in this group," he replied. "They're all trained actors; the problem is, I don't know how good or bad any of them are at the craft."

Bessie laughed. "After tonight's show, I'd say they're all pretty bad."

Rockwell nodded. "Yeah, there is that," he agreed. "For now, I'm just gathering information. You, on the other hand, are supposed to be sleeping."

Bessie shook her head. "I'm far too interested in what everyone's saying to sleep," she said. "I'm afraid you're going to have to throw me out if you don't want me to listen."

"As long as you don't repeat anything you hear, I'll let you stay," the inspector told her. "And if anyone asks, you were asleep almost the entire time."

"Yes, sir," Bessie replied smartly.

A knock on the door stopped Rockwell from replying. Wilson walked back in with a tray of coffee cups.

"Where did these come from?" Bessie asked, as she eagerly took one.

"Mr. Costain made them for us in the staff space behind the ticket booth," the man told her. "There are biscuits, too," he added, pulling a packet of digestives out of his pocket.

The trio fell on the hot drinks and biscuits greedily, and within minutes there was nothing left but crumbs.

"I'll take the mugs and the tray back to Mr. Costain," Wilson said, getting to his feet. "Shall I bring the next person?" he asked Rockwell.

"Yes, I'll have Penny Jakubowski next, please," the inspector replied.

Wilson nodded and then left, pulling the door shut behind him. Bessie yawned deeply. "I shouldn't be more tired after all that coffee," she said, mostly to herself.

"I'm going to take advantage of the gap between interviews to go to the loo," Rockwell told her. "I'll be right back."

Bessie nodded. She wasn't in any hurry to get back to her corner behind the panels, so she got up and made a slow circuit of the small room. She peeked inside a couple of boxes, and discovered that the castle had hundreds of rolls of loo paper, two cases of ink for the printer that dispensed admission tickets and at least a dozen broken audio tour headsets. She briefly considered heading outside for some fresh air, but it was too dark to try to walk anywhere. She knew the castle grounds were uneven and she didn't want to risk a turned ankle. She was making another slow loop of the room when someone knocked on the door.

Wilson stuck his head in the door, and then Penny pushed it open and rushed inside.

"Oh," she exclaimed when she saw Bessie. "I didn't know you were with the police."

"I'm not," Bessie told her hurriedly. "The inspector has kindly allowed me to sit in here, in the corner, while I'm waiting. He's going to give me a ride home once he's done, you see."

Penny nodded. "But I'm ever so glad you're here," she exclaimed. "I really need someone to hold my hand. They said I can't have William in here with me. Will you please sit with me during my interview and help me?"

Bessie looked at Wilson, who found sudden interest in his shoes. "Well, I, um, that is," Bessie stammered.

"Oh, please," the other woman said, tears filling her eyes.

Bessie sighed. "If the inspector has no objection, I suppose I can," she said slowly.

"Oh, thank you," Penny replied, falling into Bessie's arms. Bessie stood helplessly as the woman began to sob. Wilson's attention shifted from his shoes to his fingernails as Bessie patted Penny on the back and muttered meaningless words at her. To Bessie, it felt like hours before Inspector Rockwell returned.

When he pushed open the door, he quickly assessed the situation and shook his head at Bessie.

"Ms. Jakubowski, please calm down," he said, taking Penny's arm gently. "Come and sit down and relax." He glanced up at the constable. "Wilson, can you go and find some water for Ms. Jakubowski, please?"

Wilson dashed away, looking grateful for the excuse to get away from the still sobbing actress. Bessie had been digging around in her handbag and she finally found a small packet of tissues. She offered one to Penny, who thanked her excessively for it.

"It's okay," Rockwell said, as they both sat down. "I just have a few quick questions for you and then you can get back to the hotel and get some sleep."

"I don't know if I'll ever sleep again," Penny moaned. "Every time I close my eyes, I see Scott lying there, so motionless, so…." she broke off, dropping her head into her hands and sobbing even louder.

Bessie exchanged glances with Rockwell and then sighed. Someone had to stop this nonsense and it didn't look as if the inspector wanted to jump in.

Bessie sat down in the chair next to Penny's and pulled her hands away from her face. "Enough," Bessie said sternly. "Pull yourself together."

Penny blinked a couple of times, staring at Bessie. "But I…."

"But nothing," Bessie interrupted. "You're an actress. You have to be able to control your emotions on stage. Control them now."

Wilson came back in with a bottle of water in his hand. Bessie took it and twisted off the cap. For a moment she was tempted to upend the bottle over Penny's head, but she resisted. Instead, she handed the drink to the other woman who took a hesitant sip. After a moment, she drank a bit more and then took a long and shaky breath.

"I'm okay now," she said. "I'm so sorry about that."

"It's been a very long day for everyone," Rockwell told her. "But if you can just answer a few questions, I can let you get some sleep."

"I'll try to be brave," Penny answered. "For Scott's sake."

She choked off a sob at the end of the words and had Bessie wishing she'd dumped the water over her after all.

"Right, I'm going to take notes and record this as well, if that's okay with you," Rockwell told her.

"It's fine, but I'd really like it if Mrs., er, um." She turned to Bessie. "I'm awfully sorry, but I've forgotten your name," she said with a helpless shrug.

"You can just call me Bessie," Bessie answered, deciding that informality would simplify things.

"Oh, right, well, please can I have Bessie stay with me?" Penny asked the inspector.

"I'm not sure I understand why you want her company," Rockwell answered.

Penny shook her head. "I'm sure you don't mean it, but you're awfully intimidating," she told him. "Bessie seems like such a kind and caring person. I'm sure I can be far braver with her holding my hand than I can be on my own."

Bessie wasn't sure what she saw flash over the inspector's face, but after a moment he simply nodded. "If you prefer, I suppose it will be okay if Bessie sits in on the interview."

"Oh, thank you," Penny said theatrically.

Rockwell asked Penny to tell him the history of the troupe, and her version was very similar to the others that Bessie had already heard.

Like Adam, she was far more positive about recent events than Sienna had been.

"How many shows did you do in London before you came here?" Rockwell asked after she'd finished.

"Oh, maybe just a handful," Penny answered airily. "Of course, once Scott left we were stuck, so it was just as well we didn't have a lot of shows lined up."

"And then you decided to try Mr. Misnik's play instead of sticking to Shakespeare?" Rockwell asked.

Penny looked down at the table and then around the room. "Well," she said finally, "I guess you could put it that way."

"What does that mean?"

"Well, as I said, we were stuck. We couldn't keep doing *Hamlet* unless we found at least a couple more strong performers, and we couldn't seem to agree on a different play. I thought *Romeo and Juliet* would be ideal, but no one else agreed with me." She sighed dramatically.

"Did you know that Mr. Misnik had written a play?"

"Oh, we all knew that. Adam was always talking about how he was going to be the next great playwright. William and I tried to encourage him, really. I mean, he wasn't hurting anything, writing in his spare time."

"So what made you decide to perform his play?"

Penny shrugged. "William makes those decisions," she said. "One day we were discussing what to do next and then the next day William was passing out scripts. Adam had written it just for our troupe, so it was perfect. There were four lead roles and the rest of the show can be filled in with amateur players who can be taught their parts in a matter of min... er, in a few solid hours of rehearsal."

"So Adam wrote the play after Mr. Carson and Ms. Sparkles left the show?"

"I guess so," Penny said with a frown. "I mean, I never really thought about it. He's been writing stuff for years. You'd have to ask him when he wrote it, I guess."

"What can you tell me about the knife?" Rockwell asked, changing the subject.

Penny's eyes filled with tears. "I just got a glimpse of it and the lighting was bad, but the knife looked like, that is, oh." She dropped her head into her hands again and began to cry.

Bessie rolled her eyes at the inspector and then pulled on Penny's shoulder. When Penny looked up, Bessie gave her an angry look. "You aren't helping Scott by crying," she said stoutly. "If you truly want to help him, you'll stop carrying on and focus."

Penny nodded. "I know you're right," she whimpered. "But it's so hard. I really cared about Scott."

"And you can cry all night about him if you want to," Bessie told her. "But for now, you need to stay strong and answer the inspector's questions."

"Okay," Penny said, taking a deep breath. "The knife looked like one of our prop knives, but if it had been, it wouldn't have hurt Scott. It also looked like a knife that I gave William a few years ago. That one was a real knife, but it disappeared about six months ago from our apartment in Los Angeles. If I could get a better look at it, I'd be more certain."

"Were they any distinguishing marks on the knife you gave Mr. Baldwin?" Rockwell asked.

"Our initials were engraved on the blade," Penny told him. "Sort of fancy-like and entwined. I actually designed the engraving and had it done by an expert."

"Did you have any interaction with Scott during the second half of the show?"

Penny shook her head. "Oh no, I was too busy," she began and then stopped. "I did," she said in a very quiet voice after a short pause. "I stopped once, on my way into the changing room tent, to say a quick hello. Scott didn't answer me. I just thought he was asleep."

Tears welled up again, but one stern look from Bessie seemed to get Penny back under control.

"He may well have just been asleep," the inspector told the actress. "Was it totally dark by that time or could you still see a little bit?"

"It was pretty dark," Penny answered slowly. "We all had flashlights. That sweet man from the castle was handing them to us as we came off stage and then collecting them back when we returned. I turned mine off as I was heading into the tent to change, and then I bent down next to Scott and whispered 'hi' or something, but he didn't reply. I didn't want to turn the flashlight on and risk annoying everyone else or upsetting his security guards."

"Okay, one last question," the inspector said in a tired voice. "Who do you think killed Scott?"

Penny blinked. "That's an easy one," she said with a small smile. "Candy."

Bessie was so surprised that she had to bite her tongue to keep herself quiet. The inspector looked shocked as well, but only for a moment.

"And why would Ms. Sparkles have wanted him dead?" Rockwell asked.

"Scott was getting ready to fire her," Penny said in a confiding tone.

"How do you know that?"

"Scott called me last week," she explained. "He told me how happy he was at *Market Square*, and that he'd been offered representation from one of the biggest talent management agencies in the world. He felt bad, but he was going to fire Candy and start using them. Candy was in over her head, anyway."

"I'm not sure how killing him benefits Ms. Sparkles," Rockwell remarked.

"She's his agent," Penny replied. "I'm sure she has a large life insurance policy on him, to protect herself from loss of future income. Scott's death will be a huge payday for her."

Rockwell made a few notes and then rubbed a hand over his face. "Thank you for your time tonight," he told Penny. "I'm going to send you back to your hotel now. I'm sure I'll have more questions for you very soon."

"Oh, that's it?" Penny said in surprise. She turned to Bessie. "I guess I didn't really need you after all."

Penny shrugged and then stood up and stretched. The action pulled the neckline of the very low-cut dress apart and Bessie wondered just how much more of Penny they were about to see, before the stretch ended and Penny glided towards the door.

"I'll see Mr. Baldwin next, please," Rockwell told Wilson, as he headed out with Penny.

"And hopefully, we'll see less of him than we saw of her," Bessie muttered under her breath.

Rockwell laughed for a long time, as Bessie did another slow circuit of the tiny space.

"This is outrageous," William said in a booming voice as the young constable led him into the room. "Do you have any idea what time it is?"

Rockwell gave him a tight smile. "I know exactly what time it is, and I also know that I am supposed to be off this weekend, spending time with my kids. Why don't you do us all a favour and just confess now and we can all go home?"

William's jaw dropped and he stared at the inspector for a moment, then he shook his head and began to laugh heartily. "Well done," he said through his laughter. "If I'd actually done it, I might just have been shocked into confessing. And you've managed to improve my vicious mood as well. I suppose I'd better behave myself now."

"I hope that I won't need more than few minutes of your time," Rockwell replied. "Please have a seat."

William sat down and leaned back in the chair, stretching his long legs out in front of him. He seemed to take up far more space in the small room than anyone else had. Rockwell sat down on the opposite side of the table, pulling out his notebook and flipping the recording device back on, after checking that William had no objection to either.

Bessie quietly slipped back into her corner as Rockwell asked William if he minded her being there.

"Why should I care?" William asked. "She seems harmless enough."

Bessie bit her tongue and slipped into her seat. Was it wrong to hope he was the murderer and that she would play a big part in catching him, she wondered, as she settled in to her chair. She wasn't sure why the remark rankled so much, but it set her on edge and now she focussed on him intently as Rockwell began his questioning.

Although Bessie had heard the background on the theatre troupe three times already, somehow William made it sound new and interesting. Bessie decided, after several minutes, that it was his voice that was so compelling. She listened carefully as he told the same story about the group's travels across the US and their decision to try their luck in the UK.

"Of course Penny was meant to arrange everything, and she rather let us all down," William said confidingly. "She didn't have the slightest idea what was involved in getting the right paperwork sorted out, and in the end, I had to step in and do all of it myself. It took some time, but California was lovely and I think it's safe to say that we all enjoyed our extended stay there."

Rockwell raised an eyebrow, but didn't comment. "And how have things been going in the UK?" he asked instead.

William shrugged. "We haven't had as much success as I'd hoped for, of course. We did some shows in a little town called Bolsover up north and then had a single booking for London. Again, I hate to put the blame on Penny, but I can't be expected to do everything, can I?"

"And Penny booked the fortnight over here?" Rockwell checked.

"Oh, yes, I suppose that's something. Of course, we had to change plays before we came over."

"Yes, tell me about that," the inspector invited. "What led to the change in plays and why *Much Ado About the Shrew?*"

Bessie noticed William cringe as Rockwell said the name of the play. Interesting, she thought.

"Well, once Scott and Candy left we had a bit of a dilemma," William replied. "I love Penny to bits, but she's rather overconfident in her own abilities sometimes. She wanted to do *Romeo and Juliet*, which is a lovely play and one I would have enjoyed performing myself, but Penny simply wouldn't listen when I suggested that Sienna should play Juliet."

"Who would have played Romeo?" Rockwell asked the very thing Bessie had been wondering.

William laughed. "Oh, yes, quite the double standard, I agree. I would have played Romeo, of course, as lead actor in the company. But I do think I've aged rather more, um, gracefully, shall we say, than my darling leading lady."

Bessie bit back a snort of laughter. She had no idea how old the man was, but the idea of him playing the teenaged Romeo was just as bizarre as imagining Penny as Juliet.

"So the company couldn't agree on a play?" Rockwell dragged the conversation back on track.

"No, we couldn't. Adam's been writing his own plays since before I met him and he'd been nagging for ages for me to give something of his a try. When it became clear that time was running out, I reluctantly gave in."

"And how do you think the performance went tonight?"

Bessie leaned forward in her seat, eager to hear what the director thought of his show.

"I was very disappointed in tonight's show," William said, sighing. "Very disappointed indeed. There is so much talent in our little group, but I don't think it was properly showcased tonight. We were tragically under-rehearsed, especially with the members of the cast that we added once we'd arrived. The whole thing felt rather confused and unfinished, and one of the reasons I'm so eager to get away tonight is so that I can start arranging for additional rehearsals."

Rockwell nodded. "I'm sure that will help," he said. Bessie didn't agree.

"Anyway, before I forget, I would like to offer you and your friends complimentary tickets to a show later in the run," William said. "I would be delighted if you would all come back and give us another chance."

He reached inside his robe and pulled out a small bag. While Rockwell protested, he dug around inside the bag and then smiled at the inspector. "I've a number of tickets for Sunday's matinee, if that appeals to you. Otherwise, I'll make arrangements for tickets to be held for you for whichever performance you'd like."

"I can't possibly accept," Rockwell told him. "Although I appreciate the gesture."

"Well, then, perhaps your friend can accept them instead?" William suggested. He stood up and walked over to Bessie, handing her a small stack of tickets. "I'd love to see you all again on Sunday afternoon," he said, bowing to Bessie. "I can promise you a much more thoroughly rehearsed performance."

Bessie looked over at the inspector for guidance, but he was taking notes and missed the look. Bessie shrugged. "Thank you," she said. "I'm not sure if we'll make it or not, but I do appreciate the thought."

William nodded and then returned to his seat. "We must be nearly finished," he suggested.

Rockwell nodded. "Just a couple more things. What can you tell me about the knife?"

"The one stuck in Scott's back?" William asked. The inspector nodded. "That was just a harmless prop knife," William told him. "I assume whomever killed Scott put it there for dramatic effect. It couldn't have had anything to do with Scott's death."

"It wasn't a prop knife," Rockwell replied.

William shook his head. "I knew it," he exclaimed. "One of them stole my knife. Who was it?"

"So you think it was your knife?"

"It must have been," William said excitedly. "It was a gift from my beloved Penny and one of them stole it from me."

"When did you last see it?"

"Before tonight?" William asked with a wry grin. "Let's see. I guess it disappeared from our apartment in California about six months ago or more. I kept insisting that one of them had taken it, but they all denied it and I couldn't prove it, of course. If I knew who'd done it, I'd kill them."

Rockwell raised an eyebrow as William flushed and then gave a forced laugh.

"Obviously, I wouldn't really kill them," he backtracked. "But I loved that knife. It was very special to me. I was devastated when it went missing."

"Who could have stolen it?"

"Well, any of the rest of the troupe," William said. "Penny wouldn't have, obviously, because she gave it to me. I always thought Adam had done it, but after a while I had to stop arguing with him about it or it would have torn the troupe apart."

"Would you include Candy and Scott as possible thieves?"

William looked shocked. "There's an interesting idea," he said. "Maybe Scott stole the knife himself and then someone used it on him. What divine justice."

"So Scott could have taken it?" Rockwell confirmed.

"Oh, he and Candy both had plenty of opportunity to take it," William replied. "They had keys to our apartment, even though they didn't stay with us. We used it as a rehearsal space, and they were in and out of it all the time."

"Did you talk to Scott at all during the second half of the show?"

William shook his head. "I had no interest in ever interacting further with the man," he said haughtily.

"Just one last question, then. Who do you think killed Scott?"

William sat back in the chair and looked thoughtful for a moment. "Are you absolutely certain it wasn't just an unfortunate accident?" he asked.

"Absolutely," Rockwell replied.

William sighed deeply. "I hate to say it, but I think Adam is the most likely candidate, then."

"Why?"

"He was the most hurt that Scott was the one that got plucked from obscurity and made it into the big time. The truth is, Adam was never the best actor in our troupe, and Scott was starting to score bigger and bigger parts in our shows. Scott was, as much as I hate to admit it, very talented. Sooner or later, Scott was going to replace Adam as second lead, and Adam knew that. One of the reasons he was so focussed on writing scripts was so that he had something to fall back on, you see."

"But with Scott gone, Adam must have felt like his place was more secure. Why kill the man?"

"Jealousy?" William suggested questioningly. "It wasn't just professional jealousy, either. If Scott hadn't done so already, he was about to replace Adam in Sienna's affections, or at least in her bedroom."

"Again, with Scott gone, surely that was no longer an issue?"

"Ah, but Sienna was leaving with Scott and Candy after the show," William reminded Rockwell. "Adam is crazy in love with Sienna. He'd do anything to keep her."

"Including murder?"

"I wouldn't have said yes twenty-four hours ago," William said in a sad voice. "But, well, now things have changed. Anyway, if it was my knife that killed Scott, well, I always thought Adam took it."

The inspector made a few more notes and then thanked the man for his time. He was sent on his way with the constable.

"One more to go," he commented to Bessie as they waited for Candy Sparkles.

"They really are an unlikeable bunch of people," Bessie commented.

"Planning to come to the matinee on Sunday?" Rockwell said, teasingly.

"I might," Bessie replied. "Assuming you don't shut the whole show down."

Rockwell shrugged. "I need to talk to the Chief Constable about that, but I think we can simply shift the stage to a different location here and the shows can carry on. I want the troupe on the island, and at least if they're performing, they're busy and I know where they are."

Bessie made her way back to her corner as Wilson escorted Candy into the room. She picked up a strange scent that she'd noticed earlier, but ignored. It smelled like a combination of suntan lotion and cut flowers that had been kept a few days past their best. Bessie wrinkled her nose and then settled into her seat as Rockwell ran through the preliminaries with Candy. The woman readily gave her consent for Bessie to remain.

"Bessie and I are old friends," Candy laughed throatily. "I don't have any secrets from her."

"Can you give me a brief rundown of the history of the theatre troupe and your involvement in it?" Rockwell began. Bessie could hear the repressed sigh in his words. Candy's version of events was much the same, although Bessie could detect quite a bit of bitterness and unhappiness this time around.

"I was in New York, trying to find work managing young talent, when someone suggested I join this new theatre troupe that was going to travel all across the US," she explained. "I knew William from way back and I was just stupid enough to think it sounded like fun."

"But it wasn't?"

"Oh, sometimes it was," Candy said, flipping her hair. "I mean, when I was knee-deep in naked men during my heyday, I often dreamt of being asked to do Shakespeare and suddenly I got to do it seven days a week and twice on Sunday. I really enjoyed the acting, and I was good at it as well. But we made an absolute fortune for the troupe and I never saw more than a pittance of the money."

"So why did you come to the UK with them?" Rockwell asked.

"I have friends here," Candy said, with a sexy smile. She slid her sunglasses off and even from her distant seat, Bessie could see that Candy's eyes were a luminous blue. Coloured contact lenses, Bessie decided, as Candy leaned forward in her seat and focussed all of her attention on the inspector.

"Old and very dear friends," she said softly. "I couldn't afford to come over on my own, but this way the troupe paid my way. Once we were settled, I made a few phone calls." Candy licked her lips and leaned forward a bit more, giving both Bessie and the inspector a stunning view of her plentiful cleavage.

Constable Wilson dropped his pen. He banged his head on the table as he rushed to pick it up from the floor. Bessie shook her head. Clearly he'd had an eyeful as well.

"Sorry, sir," the constable said as he sat back up, his face beetroot red.

"And you managed to get Mr. Carson a part on television," Rockwell said, ignoring the young constable.

"Scott was hugely talented," Candy told him. "He didn't really need me, but luckily he hadn't realised that yet."

"And if he had, you would have been out of a job."

Candy shook her head. "He signed a long-term contract with me. If he wanted out, he'd have had to pay me a small fortune."

"What happens now?"

"I had insurance on his life, of course. Not a huge amount, but enough to get me back to the US and support me while I figure out what to do next. Nowhere near as much as I'd have earned if he'd kept working, though."

"What did you think of the show tonight?"

Candy threw back her head and laughed heartily. "It was appalling," she finally gasped out, struggling to get her breath back. "I'm not just saying this, but I always thought that Scott and I were the most talented people in the troupe, and tonight's show sort of proved that."

Rockwell nodded. "What can you tell me about the knife?"

"It looked like a prop knife. If it was real, then it was probably the one that Penny gave William a few years back. He said he'd lost it, though, so I don't know how it suddenly turned up here."

"Did you talk to Scott during the second half of the show?"

Candy shrugged. "Once it got dark, I fell asleep," she said in a sheepish tone. "I can't believe someone murdered Scott right next to me. It's a scary thought."

The inspector made a note and then nodded at Candy. "Last question, who killed Scott?"

Candy shrugged. "That's all I've been thinking about all night," she said. "And my favourite candidate is Sienna."

"Really?" Rockwell said. "I thought Scott was going to get her an audition on his show?"

"Yeah, but I've had lots of time to think about this, and I still think it was her. She probably didn't bother to mention it to you, but she and Scott had an affair a while back. Scott and I didn't have any secrets; I guess I was sort of like a big sister to him. Anyway, she was devastated when he ended it with her, and angry. The sort of angry that just gets bigger and bigger over time."

"Angry enough to stick a knife into him?"

Candy shrugged. "'Heaven has no rage like love to hatred turned, Nor hell a fury like a woman scorned.'"

"Is that Shakespeare?"

"No, it's William Congreve, from *The Mourning Bride*. I thought it was apt."

"Indeed," Rockwell made another note and then ran a hand over his face. "Thank you for your time," he said to Candy. "I'm sure I'll need to talk to you again before this is all over, but I think that's more than enough for tonight."

"Scott and I were only planning to stay one night," she told him. "And I really need to get back to London to sort everything out. You aren't going to make me stay here, are you?"

"I'm sorry, but I am going to ask you to remain on the island for the foreseeable future," Rockwell replied. "I'll do my best to wrap everything up quickly."

"I'm sure you will," Candy purred, standing up slowly. She looked at Rockwell and licked her lips again. "Maybe, if you have more questions, you could come and visit me at my hotel," she suggested. "I'm sure it would be much more comfortable than this little room."

"We have interview rooms at the police station," Rockwell said smoothly. "They're much more comfortable than this room as well."

Candy laughed huskily. "The offer remains open," she said suggestively. "Any time, day or night."

Rockwell flushed. "Thank you for your time," he said, motioning to Wilson to escort the woman out.

As the door shut behind the pair, Rockwell blew out a long breath. "Let's get out of here," he suggested to Bessie.

"What a lovely idea," Bessie replied, with a tired nod.

CHAPTER 6

*A*t the door, Rockwell turned on his torch. The lights outside the small building only illuminated a small area around it. Within a few steps, Bessie found that she was holding onto the inspector's arm. They slowed their pace and Bessie peered anxiously at the small section of ground they could make out in front of them by the light of the torch.

"Inspector Rockwell, sir," Wilson's voice hailed them from behind another torch. "Constable Jenkins is going to take Ms. Sparkles back to her hotel. What did you need me to do next?"

"How are Hugh and Gary getting along?" Rockwell asked.

"Constable Kewin finished about half an hour ago," Wilson reported. "I believe that Constable Watterson is talking to the last of the audience members now."

"Can you please walk Miss Cubbon towards the ticket booth and then keep her company for a few minutes, while I get reports from both of them?"

"Of course, sir," Wilson replied. Rockwell headed towards the stage, where Bessie could see a swarm of people still hard at work in the VIP section.

Wilson offered his arm to Bessie, and the pair made their way towards the castle entrance. They stopped just short of the ticket booth, where Bessie could see Hugh taking careful notes as he spoke with a man she didn't recognise.

"You won't remember me," Constable Wilson said to Bessie.

"Of course I remember you," Bessie said in reply. "You're Paul Wilson. You grew up in Ramsey, but your uncle ran the chippy in central Laxey and you used to spend a lot of time there. He had the best fish and chips I've ever tasted. What ever happened to him?"

"Ah, Uncle Kevin retired and moved to a small town in Derbyshire."

"Why Derbyshire?" Bessie asked.

"He reckoned it was about the centre of Britain," the young man explained. "He said after spending his entire adult life selling fish, he wanted to be as far from the sea on all sides as he could get."

Bessie laughed. "I remember every Bonfire Night, you and your brothers would put a 'Guy' in the shop doorway and get everyone to give you a penny before you'd let them in."

The man laughed. "We made a surprising amount of money doing that," he told Bessie. "Of course, there were five of us, so once we'd split it five ways, it never seemed like much. Mostly, we ended up spending it on fish and chips, anyway."

Bessie laughed. "I can't believe your uncle made you pay for your food."

"Only on Bonfire Night," Wilson told her.

Bessie laughed again. "If you speak to him, please tell him I said hello."

"Oh, aye, I will," he assured her. "Anyway he's coming over for a spell next month. He wants to be here for the Tynwald Day celebrations."

"I'll have to watch out for him if I go, then," Bessie said.

The pair stood silently for a while. Bessie watched as people came and went from the crime scene, torches bobbing along with them. After a while, she recognised Inspector Rockwell's tall form talking to one of the men who was dressed all in white. After a few minutes, Rockwell headed back towards Bessie and Wilson.

"Are you okay for five more minutes?" Rockwell checked in with Bessie.

"Of course," she replied, feeling as if that was about all she could manage.

Rockwell walked over to the booth and knocked on the door. Hugh let him in and Bessie watched the short exchange. After a few moments, the stranger emerged and headed out of the castle grounds, escorted by yet another uniformed man.

Only a minute or two later, Rockwell and Hugh came out as well. Henry rushed up from near the castle entrance.

"How are things going?" he asked in a tentative voice.

"Ah, Henry, I think I'm just about done here for tonight," Rockwell told him.

"Oh, good," Henry said with a sigh.

"Unfortunately, while I'm just about done, I don't think the crime scene folks will be finished for several more hours," Rockwell added.

Henry's face fell. "I see," he said gloomily.

"We've finished with the storage room and the ticket booth, anyway," Rockwell told him. "You can lock those back up. I wish I could tell you when the others will be done, but they have a lot of ground to cover and they're working by artificial light, so it takes a little bit longer sometimes."

Henry nodded. "I've rung my boss at MNH, and he's on his way," he said. "Once he gets here, I'll probably head for home, unless anyone needs me."

"Did someone take your statement?" Rockwell asked.

"I did," Hugh answered for Henry. "I talked to both him and Bob before I started on the audience."

"Thanks," Rockwell said. "That was smart on your part."

Hugh flushed at the unexpected praise.

"Now, let's all get out of here," Rockwell suggested. "There's nothing else we can do until I get the crime scene reports anyway, and that won't be before tomorrow afternoon."

"And we all need some sleep," Bessie added.

Hugh nodded. "I talked to Grace a little while ago," he told Rockwell. "She decided to stay with Doona tonight and help with the kids. She said they all ate too much popcorn and then the kids fell asleep in front of the telly."

"Good to know, thanks," Rockwell said. "You have your car here, right? Are you okay to drive back to Laxey or should I have someone take you?"

"I'm okay," Hugh said after a moment's thought. "I had some coffee about half an hour ago, so I'm actually getting my second wind. I'll put the windows down and turn up the radio. I'll be fine."

"I'll follow you anyway," the inspector told him. "That way we can look out for each other."

"Fair enough," Hugh agreed. "Is Bessie going with you?"

Rockwell glanced at Bessie and nodded. "Bessie and I have lots to talk about," he told Hugh. "And she'll help keep me awake."

Wilson was working the overnight shift, so he made his way back towards the crime scene to get new instructions while Henry headed into the ticket booth to straighten everything out for morning. Bessie, Hugh and Rockwell made their way out of the castle, carefully following the limited light from the two police torches.

Moments later, Bessie sank down in the comfortable seat in the inspector's car and shut her eyes.

"Aunt Bessie? You need to do up your seat belt."

Rockwell's voice seemed to be coming from far away and it took Bessie a moment to realise that she fallen asleep as soon as she'd sat down. She quickly buckled her seat belt, blushing in the darkness.

"I should have had more coffee," she said, a bit too loudly.

"We all should have," Rockwell replied. "Hang in there. Home isn't too far away."

He started the car and switched on his headlamps, and then waited. After a moment, Hugh's car drove slowly past them. The inspector pulled out behind the younger man.

"So, I suppose I should thank you for an interesting evening," Rockwell said as they drove slowly through Peel.

Bessie tried to laugh, but the sound that came out was closer to a sob. "I'm starting to think I've brought some sort of curse on myself," she told the man. "I keep stumbling over murders. It's getting quite ridiculous."

Rockwell patted her arm. "Bad things happen, even in beautiful places like the Isle of Man. And bad people are everywhere. You've just happened to get caught up in a rather unfortunate string of dreadful situations."

"Tonight was meant to give us all a break from all of the nastiness that's been taking place," Bessie told him.

"Unfortunately for Scott, someone else had other plans."

Bessie sighed. "Are you sure it isn't me?" she asked. "Maybe I forgot to wave to the little people or something."

"If it makes you feel any better, Henry seems to think he's the one who's cursed," Rockwell said with a chuckle. "And, to be fair, he has been around when most of the bodies have turned up."

"So maybe, if I stop going anywhere that Henry is, we'll both have better luck," Bessie said, frowning as she heard the bitterness in her voice.

"Bessie," Rockwell said in a serious voice. "I know that this all feels overwhelming and awful right now, but you know it has nothing to do with you, right? Sometimes good people get dragged into bad situations, just because they're in the wrong place at the wrong time. I am really sorry that it seems to be happening to you a lot lately. But I am glad that I've been able to meet you and become your friend, so it isn't all bad."

Bessie smiled. "Every cloud has a silver lining," she agreed.

"Is that Shakespeare?"

"Actually, I think it's a paraphrase from Milton, but I could be wrong," she shrugged. "Anyway, let's don't worry about me. Who killed Scott Carson?"

Rockwell sighed. "That's tonight's big question. Although I'm also wondering who on earth thought *Much Ado About the Shrew* was going to be a success, as well."

Bessie laughed. "It was pretty awful," she said. "In fact, it was nothing but awful."

"Oh, I don't know, there were a few not entirely awful moments."

"Really?" Bessie said. "I must have missed those."

Rockwell laughed. "The first minute or so wasn't too bad," he suggested.

Bessie thought about it. "I suppose it wasn't," she agreed. "Because nothing was happening. It definitely all went downhill after that."

"I'm tempted to go on Sunday afternoon and see if it's improved any," Rockwell said.

"I was thinking the same thing," Bessie replied. "I don't suppose it could get any worse."

Rockwell laughed. "I think you're tempting fate," he teased.

The inspector drove carefully across the middle of the island, following Hugh, who stuck meticulously to the speed limit.

"So, who do you think killed Scott?" Bessie asked, echoing the question the inspector had put to each of the suspects earlier.

Rockwell shook his head. "At this point, I'm trying to keep an open mind," he told Bessie. "Every one of them had a motive of some sort, although some seem stronger than others."

"And I suppose they all had the opportunity," Bessie added. "I mean, once it got dark, any one of them could have slipped over and stabbed Scott on their way in or out of the dressing room tent."

"As could a number of other people," Rockwell pointed out. "We're going to have to try to track down as many audience members as we can. It isn't outside the realm of possibility that someone from the audience or someone from the cast of extras was able to sneak up and kill Scott. With the bright lights facing the stage, the whole VIP section was pitch-black by the end of the show."

Bessie nodded. "But what sort of motive would any of them have had?"

"No idea," Rockwell replied. "But we have to investigate every possibility."

"The knife will probably narrow things down, though, won't it?" Bessie asked. "I mean, if it is the one that William lost six months ago, there aren't too many people who had access to it."

"Did you see Scott move once he got settled on the ground?" Rockwell asked Bessie.

Bessie frowned. "I wasn't really paying attention," she said after a moment. "I think he probably changed position at least once or twice, but I was focussed on the stage and what was happening there. Besides, every time I glanced in his direction, I ended up getting distracted by the people going in and out of the tent. They were tripping and stumbling all over the place."

Rockwell nodded. "I'm sure I saw him sit up for a short while, but I wasn't really watching, either. I'm surprised that his two bodyguards didn't see anything, though."

"They didn't strike me as the brightest of men," Bessie said. "Besides, they were both wearing dark glasses the whole time. I doubt they could have seen much of anything."

"Hugh took their statements. They both claim that they didn't see anything. Apparently they're both actors, rather than trained bodyguards. They're called Carl and Ed, and from what they told Hugh, they were hired by Candy to make Scott look important. Neither one of them ever worked any type of security before today."

"Wonderful," Bessie sighed.

"Hugh's interviews with the audience members didn't really tell us anything, either, although I didn't expect them to."

"No one saw anything?" Bessie asked.

"Apparently not. There were only about a dozen people left by the time Scott's body was found, and several of them told Hugh that they only stayed because they'd fallen asleep."

Bessie laughed. "I can believe that," she said.

"If they're to be believed, none of them knew who was in the VIP area, and Hugh reckoned none of them really cared, either."

"They might have, if they'd known it was a famous soap star," Bessie suggested.

Rockwell shrugged. "According to Hugh's summary of their statements, everyone saw people coming and going at the tent, but no one noticed anyone doing anything that looked like a person stabbing someone."

"It was too dark to see anything properly," Bessie said with a sigh.

"Did the other constable learn anything interesting from the rest of the cast?"

The inspector laughed. "Apparently he got an earful about the show from every one of them," he told Bessie. "They'd all signed up to do *Hamlet*, apparently, and they'd been rehearsing for months. Suddenly the group turns up with a different play and expects them to learn it in less than twenty-four hours. Kewin said he has about ten pages' worth of complaints about every single person in the company."

"Oh dear. I don't suppose any of them noticed anything suspicious?"

"Obviously, I have to sit down and read each report in full," Rockwell told her. "But according to Kewin's summary, they were too busy to notice what was going on at the changing room tent. They didn't have any costume changes and they were all told to stay away from where the, quote, 'lead actors,' end of quote, were getting ready."

"How nice," Bessie said sarcastically.

"Indeed. Anyway, none of them admitted to knowing who was in the VIP area. Obviously, we need to check into everyone's background, but at the moment we don't have anything to tie any of them to Scott or anyone else in the group."

The pair fell silent for a short while, as Rockwell drove steadily towards home.

"So, come on then," Rockwell said eventually. "Who do you think killed Scott?"

"Maybe they were all in on it together," Bessie suggested. "That's why they're all blaming one another now, so that everything gets confused."

"I know they're all actors, so I could be totally wrong, but I don't think they like each other well enough to agree to a plot like that."

Bessie laughed. "You could be right," she said. "Everyone was so quick to blame everyone else for the things that have gone wrong for them. I'd almost feel sorry for them, after all their problems, except none of them are at all likeable."

They'd reached the outskirts of Douglas now, and Hugh drove carefully around the town, heading for the coast road to Laxey.

"Did you enjoy your first TT, then?" Bessie asked as they made their way past the event's Grandstand. She was referring to the annual motorcycle road race that brought thousands of bikers and spectators to the island.

"It was different," the inspector replied. "I put in a lot of extra hours and spent a lot of time in different parts of the island, but overall I enjoyed it."

"What did your wife and the kids think?"

"Sue took the kids back to Manchester," Rockwell said. "They were off school for the fortnight anyway, and Sue's mum needed to have a bit of minor surgery that, luckily, got scheduled right in the middle of the period, so it all worked out for the best."

"They seem like terrific kids," Bessie told him.

"Ah, thanks. They have their moments, but I'm proud of how they handled things tonight. It was a pretty ghastly situation for them to be in."

"Are you going to go to Doona's after you drop me off?" Bessie asked, aware that she was probably being nosier than she should.

"Yeah, she said she'd wait up for me," Rockwell told her. "I'll probably just check on the kids and then head home. My rental flat is only on the next street from hers. If the kids are asleep, I'll leave them there and they can walk home when they wake up tomorrow."

"When is Sue due back?"

"She's flying back in the morning. She wasn't best pleased when she heard about what happened tonight. Once she heard, she decided to switch her flights, so hopefully she'll be here by lunchtime."

"That should make the kids feel better, anyway."

"Yeah," Rockwell sighed. "I don't get near enough time with them, you know, and now, left alone with them for the weekend, everything's blown up in my face."

It was Bessie's turn to pat his arm. "You're doing a vital job and I don't know anyone who could do it better," she said softly.

He glanced over at her. "Thanks," he said.

A moment later, Hugh's indicator went on, and he turned down the small lane that led to his flat. "I've been trying to persuade Hugh to buy a little place of his own," the inspector told Bessie. "House prices just keep rising and if he doesn't get on the property ladder now, he may never manage it."

"You need to have a word with Grace," Bessie suggested. "I'm pretty sure she has a lot more influence on young Hugh than anyone else."

Rockwell nodded. "I hope so. She's a lovely girl."

"She is. I just hope she can put up with his job."

"Yeah, me too," Rockwell said, with a hint of some suppressed emotion.

Bessie might have asked him what was wrong if they hadn't pulled up to her cottage just then.

"I'll just come in and check the place over," the inspector told Bessie.

Bessie shook her head. "Don't be silly," she said. "It's nearly morning. Anyone who might have broken in and stolen my things is long gone and tucked up in bed."

Rockwell shook his head. "I'll just do it anyway," he told her firmly. "If nothing else, because if I don't, Doona will never forgive me."

"I don't need mollycoddling," Bessie said stoutly, as she climbed out of the car.

"I'm not mollycoddling," the inspector said with a laugh. "I'm just hoping to find a stray biscuit that's trying to escape."

Bessie shook her head. It was nice of him to pretend that he was really after a biscuit, but she knew he was being as overprotective as Doona had become. Really, she was a fully-grown woman and she could look after herself.

Inside, it only took the inspector a few moments to walk through the cottage.

"No scary monsters lurking behind your curtains," he reported cheerfully as he rejoined Bessie in the kitchen. "Did you find any errant biscuits?"

Bessie handed him a chocolate digestive and smiled to herself as his eyes lit up. Maybe he wasn't pretending as much as she'd thought.

She locked the door behind him, glancing at the kitchen clock. She'd expected a late night, but nothing as late as this. It was nearly four and she usually got up around six. She shook her head. No alarm for tomorrow for sure. Of course, she couldn't turn off her internal alarm that rarely failed to have her up within minutes of six, but she would try.

She put away the biscuit packet and checked her phone. The message light was blinking. She pressed play and grabbed a pen and paper in case she needed them.

She needn't have bothered, though, as the messages were all from nosy friends who had somehow already heard that she's found another body. They'd all ring back in the morning. Bessie knew that for certain. She also deleted the message from Dan Ross at the *Isle of Man Times;* she had no interest in talking to the newspapers about her evening.

She turned the ringer off on the phone, her one concession to her age. She'd decided a few years back that she was too old to be running down stairs in the middle of the night when some double-glazing salesman decided to ring and try to sell her new windows. She turned the volume down on the answering machine as well, since it was likely she'd get a call or two before she was up in the morning.

Double-checking that all of her doors were locked up tightly, Bessie headed upstairs. She quickly slipped into her favourite night-gown and ran a brush through her hair, grateful that she kept it short so it needed very little attention. She brushed her teeth with good intentions but little enthusiasm. It was all she could do to keep her eyes open. She glanced in the mirror and smiled. She so rarely wore makeup that she hadn't even considered any today. It wouldn't hurt, therefore, if she skipped washing her face.

She turned off the bathroom light and crawled into her bed, which felt a hundred times more comfortable than normal. Switching off her bedroom light, she fell into a sound sleep within seconds.

CHAPTER 7

*B*essie wasn't sure what woke her the next morning. She was just suddenly awake. She sat up in bed and looked at the clock. It was quarter-past eight, the latest she'd slept in a long time. An unexpected noise stopped her as she began to climb out of bed. She listened intently. Someone was banging on the cottage door.

I wonder if they'll go away if I go back to sleep, she thought to herself. Another loud round of banging more or less answered that question. She sighed and then got out of bed and pulled her bathrobe around herself.

She was halfway down the stairs before she was awake enough to wonder who could possibly be at her door. Perhaps it's just some unhappy child who has "run away" to visit me, Bessie thought. Bessie loved children, but she'd never had any of her own. Instead, she acted as a sort of honourary aunt to just about every child in the village of Laxey. Many of them used her house as a sort of refuge from their parents when they argued. Bessie was always sympathetic and always had biscuits or cake as well. It was unusual for anyone to turn up this early on a Saturday morning, however.

Now she pulled open the door and blinked in the bright sunlight.

"Oh, thank heavens you're at home," Penny Jakubowksi gasped. "I just don't know where else to go."

Bessie's jaw dropped as Penny pushed past her into Bessie's cottage and then burst into tears. She threw herself into Bessie's arms and wept while Bessie stood helplessly. Bessie muttered a few "there theres," but Penny seemed beyond listening, so instead Bessie entertained herself by trying to come up with the name of a favourite author starting with each letter of the alphabet. She was stuck on X when Penny finally stopped crying.

"Oh, I am sorry," she told Bessie, pulling a tissue from the pocket of the voluminous dress she was wearing. "I didn't mean to fall apart like that."

"But why on earth are you here?" Bessie asked, knowing that it was probably a rude question, but feeling justified under the circumstances.

"Everything is just so awful now," Penny said, tears welling up in her eyes again. "I needed to get away, you see, and I remembered how kind you were last night when I needed a friend. I asked around and it seems that everyone on the island knows Bessie Cubbon and where she lives. Please, can I just stay for a little while? An hour or two away from everyone else will do me the world of good."

Bessie was shaking her head before she'd given the question any real thought. She didn't want to spend any time with the woman who was so prone to hysteria.

Penny wasn't paying attention, though. She was looking around Bessie's kitchen. "I could make you breakfast," she offered, opening Bessie's refrigerator. "I make a mean omelet." She poked around inside of it. "You have eggs and cheese and ham. I can make you a breakfast you won't forget in a hurry."

Bessie wavered. While she didn't fancy spending time with the woman, an omelet sounded lovely, and she certainly didn't feel like going to all the trouble of making one herself.

"I can wait outside while you get dressed or whatever," Penny offered eagerly. "I don't blame you for not wanting to leave me alone in the house. I'd be the same way in your shoes."

Bessie glanced down at her bare feet and then shrugged. "Why don't you take a walk on the beach?" she suggested. "It's a beautiful morning and the beach shouldn't be too crowded yet. It gets busy once the families in the rental cottages down the way get moving, but they all seem to sleep late on a Saturday morning."

"That's a wonderful idea," Penny agreed eagerly. "I'll take a short walk and then, once you're dressed and ready, I'll make us both a delicious breakfast."

"Okay," Bessie found herself agreeing. She showed Penny out the back door for her walk, and then she rushed back upstairs and raced through the shower. Even though she was hurrying, she took a moment to think about Matthew, her lost love, as she covered herself in her favourite rose-scented dusting powder. That was one morning ritual that she never forgot. She dressed quickly and then glanced in the mirror. A dash of lip-gloss and quick comb of her hair completed her morning routine.

Penny's face had been done up perfectly, and Bessie realised that the other woman's heavy eye makeup hadn't budged in spite of Penny's lengthy crying jag. As Bessie patted her hair into place, she wondered at the elaborate tangle of curls and plaits that Penny's hair was styled in this morning. It must have taken her ages, Bessie thought. Didn't the woman ever sleep?

As Bessie headed back downstairs, she decided that this morning called for a pot of coffee. She set it brewing before she headed out to look for her unexpected guest. Penny was sitting on the large rock that sat behind Bessie's cottage. At high tide it was surrounded by water, but at the moment it sat on dry sand. Penny was staring out to sea. Bessie walked up next to her and then cleared her throat.

"Oh, there you are, my darling," Penny said. "I'm ever so jealous of you and this amazing view. I think your life must be positively idyllic."

Bessie smiled at her. "I love my life," she said. "My little cottage by the sea suits me perfectly."

"But don't you get lonely?" Penny asked. "I assume you must be a widow?"

"I never married," Bessie told her. "And no, I don't get lonely. I have many dear friends and I have my books. After all these years on my own, I think I'm rather too fond of my own company. I'm quite happy this way."

Penny shook her head. "I've been with William forever," she told Bessie. "I can't imagine not having a man in my life."

Bessie bit back a dozen replies before she settled on a neutral one. "Well, everyone is different. That's what makes the world such a fascinating place."

"William and I met when I was sixteen," Penny said, looking back out to sea. "We met doing community theatre. It was *Romeo and Juliet.*"

"And you were Juliet to his Romeo," Bessie guessed.

Penny laughed. "Ah, wouldn't that have been romantic? Unfortunately, no. I was merely an attendant to Juliet, and William was Gregory, a servant to the Capulets." She shrugged. "We were both still learning our craft in those days."

"And you've been together ever since?"

"Oh, yes. I had just turned sixteen and William was somewhat older. He swept me off my feet and I've never been interested in anyone else."

"Sixteen is very young," Bessie commented.

"He was so handsome in those days," Penny sighed. "Not that he isn't still handsome," she added hastily. "But in those days he was stunning. He was actually dating the girl playing Juliet when I first met him, but once our eyes met, that was the end of that."

"Poor Juliet," Bessie said.

Penny laughed. "She ended up falling for her Romeo. Last I heard they were married with four kids and still doing community theatre. William and I had bigger dreams, of course."

"I don't know. Being happily married with children and still pursuing your passion sounds pretty good to me."

Penny frowned. "But she gave up on becoming a star," she said with a dramatic sigh. "I guess it's just different for some people, but I need to perform. Applause is like oxygen for me."

Bessie shrugged. "I'm happy with a simple life. But then I've never even tried acting. Maybe I'd get hooked if I gave it a try."

"We could give you a part in the show," Penny offered. "We can always use more extras. You'd be fabulous, I'm sure."

Bessie laughed. "Thanks for the offer, but I think I'm strictly audience material," she told the other woman. "I do have to say, though, that that was the most interesting offer I've had in a long time."

Penny laughed. "Well, the offer's open if you change your mind," she promised. "Just let me know and I'll tell William to find you a part."

Bessie's stomach growled, interrupting her intended reply.

"Is that time for breakfast, then?" Penny asked brightly.

"Yes, please," Bessie replied.

The coffee was ready when they returned to the kitchen, and Penny's mood brightened even further after her second cup. Bessie helped her find the equipment she needed and then sat down at the table and watched her work.

"I've done a lot of short-order cooking over the years," Penny told Bessie as she cracked eggs. "Pretty much any small town you end up in has a diner or two that can use an extra cook for a week or so. It's a great way to supplement the rather meagre payments actors get for performing."

"I thought your troupe was quite successful," Bessie said.

"Oh, this one was," Penny answered. "At least while we were touring the US, we were. I didn't do any cooking for, I don't know, five years, maybe. Well, except for meals for me and William, and sometimes the rest of the troupe as well. But I didn't need a second job. We did okay."

"What made you decide to come to the UK, then?"

Penny shook her head. "That was all William," she said. "He's always had this crazy idea about performing Shakespeare's works in their home country. He'd been talking about it since I met him. I guess, when we'd gone all the way across the US, he felt like it was the perfect time."

"And you came with him," Bessie said.

"I love him," Penny said. "It may have been a crazy scheme, but part of being in love with someone is supporting them in their crazy schemes, you know? Besides, if I let him go without me, he would have just found someone else to take my place. We were all hoping this trip might be our big break."

"And for Scott, it was."

"Yeah," Penny sighed. "He was really talented," she said softly.

Bessie watched as Penny deftly shredded cheese and then chopped a slice of ham into small pieces. She heated a pan and then swirled butter around in it. The kitchen filled with wonderful aromas as Penny added the eggs and then the ham and cheese to the hot pan.

A few minutes later, Penny slid the gorgeously browned omelet onto two plates. Bessie topped up her coffee and grabbed a fork. Penny had been right. She wouldn't forget this breakfast in a hurry.

"This is delicious," she told Penny as she ate. "You're a good cook."

"If the acting thing doesn't work out, I always said I'd love to open my own restaurant." Penny laughed bitterly. "Who am I kidding?" she asked. "The acting thing isn't working out, not even a little bit. And I haven't two cents to my name to put towards buying a little restaurant, either." She sighed deeply.

"I would have thought you'd have made some decent money during your years of travelling," Bessie said innocently.

Penny shrugged. "We made some money, but the travelling part isn't cheap. We spent almost every penny on hotel rooms and meals. Whatever was left over went to paying for things like props and costumes. Oh, everyone in the group got a small salary as well, but mostly mine went to pay for makeup and extra costume pieces that the group's budget didn't cover. By the time we got to LA, we were pretty much broke, and then we had to stay there for half a year while William sorted out the paperwork for the trip."

"Plane tickets are expensive as well," Bessie remarked.

"They really are," Penny agreed. "We all worked at least part-time to help pay for our apartment and other expenses while we were in LA, and William made sure to put away little bits here and there until he'd saved up enough to pay for our flights here. Unfortunately, now we don't have any money for flights home, but maybe the two weeks over here will help."

"I certainly hope so," Bessie told her. "What will you do when you get home?"

Penny shrugged. "I don't even know where I'll go," she said sadly. "I suppose I'll go wherever William wants to go, but at the moment I have no idea where that is."

"Where would you go, if it were up to you?" Bessie asked.

"Maybe New York," Penny said. "I don't know. I suppose anywhere William can find work."

"What about you? Don't you want to find work?"

"Oh, sure," Penny said indifferently. "But really, if William's happy, I'm happy."

Bessie drew a breath and forced herself to count to ten. "And does William feel the same way about your happiness?" she asked.

"I'm sure he loves me," Penny said, avoiding answering the question directly.

"It must be difficult, all that travelling. When you get back to the US, do you think you'll stay in one place for a while?"

"I'd like to," Penny answered. "I'd like to settle down and buy a little house and just be like a nice normal couple for a little while before we go back to chasing fame." She laughed. "I can hear William's voice in my head, saying 'boring,' even as I speak."

"It doesn't sound boring to me," Bessie told her. "It sounds lovely."

"William isn't the settling down type," Penny said. "He's too creative. He gets bored too easily. His mind is always working and he needs new stimuli or he gets frustrated."

"Really?" Bessie said, cutting herself off before she added the 'perhaps William needs to grow up a little bit' to her reply.

"But it's so invigorating being with such a brilliant man," Penny told her enthusiastically. "He makes every day a new adventure. I'm never as happy as when I'm with him."

Bessie gathered up the breakfast dishes and put them on the counter to avoid commenting.

"Shall I do the dishes, then?" Penny offered.

"I'll get them later," Bessie told her. "Let's go out and sit on my rock and chat, shall we?"

"I'd love that," Penny replied.

Outside, there was a cooling breeze blowing off the sea that made the warm morning feel comfortable. The two women sat side by side on the large rock and watched the waves silently for a moment. Further down the beach the sand was beginning to get crowded with families with small children making sandcastles and collecting shells and rocks, but behind Bessie's cottage it was still empty and quiet.

"He cheats on me, of course," Penny said conversationally.

"Of course, because he always needs new stimuli," Bessie said sarcastically.

The sarcasm was lost on Penny, however. "Exactly," she said. "It doesn't mean anything. It's just about new experiences."

Bessie nodded and carefully considered her reply. "You could do better," she said finally, unable to find a better way to express what she was thinking.

"Oh, no," Penny said, shaking her head. "William's perfect for me. He really is."

"Except for the cheating part," Bessie suggested.

"Well, yeah, I mean that really upsets me when it happens, but it doesn't happen often."

"Really?" Bessie could hear the skepticism in her voice.

"Oh, well, not all that often," Penny said, not looking at Bessie. "I mean, when we had the troupe and there was a continuous stream of pretty girls in and out of the chorus, well, he used to chase after them all, but once the group split up, he calmed down a lot."

Bessie nearly bit her tongue in half trying not to say what she was thinking. "I'm surprised you put up with that," she said finally. "You're a beautiful woman. There must be plenty of men out there who would be honoured to spend time with you."

Penny shrugged. "Like I said, I'm in love with William; I have been since I was sixteen. Anyway, he's been much better lately. I think he and Sienna might have had a bit of a fling, but she's really Adam's problem, not mine. William and Candy used to get together once in a while as well, but they'd dated years ago, so that was just friendly-like."

Bessie stood up abruptly and gasped as she stepped into cold seawater. The tide was on its way in and she hadn't noticed that the rock was slowly being surrounded by water. She was glad she hadn't bothered with shoes as she splashed up the sand, taking a few steps towards her cottage.

"I'm sorry," she said to Penny. "But I can't just sit here and listen to you try to justify the appalling way that William treats you."

Penny shook her head. "You just don't understand," she said tearfully.

"No, I suppose I don't," Bessie agreed. "And nothing you can say will get me to understand, so I don't think we should discuss it any further."

Penny shrugged. "Please don't be mad at me," she said to Bessie. "You're just about the closest thing I have to a friend right now."

Bessie sighed deeply. This woman needed a lot more than just a friendly shoulder to cry on, and Bessie didn't feel up to the job. "What about Sienna?" she asked.

Penny climbed down from the rock carefully, making sure to keep her very high heels out of the water. She walked carefully back up the beach, following Bessie, who'd turned to head for home once Penny had left the rock.

Bessie opened the cottage door, and Penny followed her back inside. They took their seats at the table and Penny sighed.

"Sienna is a friend, I guess," she said, finally answering Bessie's question. "But it's hard to be friendly with someone that you know would steal your boyfriend if given the opportunity."

"No offense to William," Bessie said. "But I'm sure Sienna could do better as well."

Penny laughed, a harsh and brittle sound. "But William runs the show, you see," she told Bessie. "And little Sienna wants to be a star more than she wants to breathe."

"Couldn't she do better than being the second lead actress in a small travelling theatre group, then?" Bessie asked.

"Our Sienna is lovely to look at," Penny said harshly. "But she can't act her way out of a paper bag and she can't carry a tune if she had to do so to save her life. She's second lead because she's sleeping with the stage manager and for no other reason. That's why she's been chasing after William. She's after my job and she won't ever earn it based on her acting ability."

"Do you think Scott would have helped her become a star?"

Penny shrugged. "He might have, if he thought there was something in it for him. Oh, not sex," she added, when she saw the look on Bessie's face. "Scott and Sienna had a fling ages ago, and when that finished Scott wasn't interested in getting back with her again."

"Does everyone in the company sleep with everyone else?" Bessie demanded.

Penny shook her head. "It really wasn't as bad as it sounds," she said defensively. "I've never been with anyone other than William." Penny blushed brightly as she spoke.

"Should I ask why you're blushing?"

"Oh, I, well, the thing is, about a year ago, maybe more, I got Scott to agree to pretend to have an affair with me. I thought maybe it would shake William up a bit and get him to, well, I really wanted him to propose, but I would have been happy if he'd just stopped chasing other women. I wanted him to see how it felt, you see."

Bessie didn't see at all, but she kept her mouth shut.

"Anyway, we snuck around a bit, meeting for lunch in out-of-the-way places and that sort of thing, but William either didn't catch on or chose to ignore it. After a little while I got bored with the pretense and we dropped it."

She looked around the room as if she were suddenly worried she might be overheard, and then leaned in towards Bessie. "I think Scott might have been gay," she whispered. "We spent a lot of time alone together in hotel rooms and he never once even tried to kiss me, let alone go any further."

Bessie nodded and refrained from pointing out to Penny that perhaps the man simply hadn't been attracted to her. Obviously the thought had never crossed Penny's mind, and she didn't want to be the one to put it there.

"Anyway, I said Scott had a thing with Sienna, but I always

wondered if it was just to make Adam jealous and nothing really happened with them either."

"You could ask Sienna," Bessie suggested.

Penny made a face. "We're not that close," she replied shortly.

"What about Candy?" Bessie couldn't help but ask.

Penny giggled. "You know, for a former porn star, she was quite a prude off-camera. I know I said that she and William used to get together once in a while, but I'm not sure if that was about sex or just about friendship. Beyond that, I don't think she was sleeping with anyone in the group, and I never saw her picking up guys anywhere on our travels, either. Of course, she's much older than the rest of us, which matters a lot to men."

"What about Adam?"

"Oh, he'd sleep with anyone if he could," Penny said casually. "But he doesn't get all that many opportunities. Sienna keeps a very close eye on him."

"Do you still think Candy killed Scott, then?" Bessie asked.

"Oh, did I say that?" Penny asked. "I mean, I guess so. I don't like her because she broke up our happy little family, so I don't mind thinking of her as a murderer. It's much more uncomfortable thinking that someone from our little group might have done it."

"Indeed," Bessie said.

An insistent buzzing noise interrupted what she was going to say next.

"Oh, that's my phone," Penny said, digging through her pockets. Bessie watched as she dug out a huge pile of tissues, a hotel room key, a small wallet and, finally, a large mobile phone.

"William insisted that we all get these as soon as we arrived in the UK," Penny told Bessie as she stared at the still ringing device. "I'm not sure how it works, actually."

After several seconds, Penny finally stabbed at a button with one of her well-manicured fingers. "Hello?" she said cautiously into the phone.

Bessie could make out William's thunderous voice, but couldn't hear his actual words.

"Yes, yes, I know," Penny said. "I'll be there. I'm only a short distance away. I'll grab a taxi now."

There was a long pause while Penny listened and then, "What do the police want with me? Really? But I already told them everything I know. Anyway, I'll be back soon."

Penny pulled the device away from her ear and stared at it again. After a moment, she closed her eyes and punched a button. "Hello?" she said into it.

"I guess that's done it," she said with a shrug as she tucked the phone back in her pocket. "But I have to go," she told Bessie. "Apparently the police have been looking for me. Anyway, we're having rehearsals all afternoon to try to get the play into proper shape before tonight's performance."

"Well, good luck with that," Bessie said.

"Oh no," Penny gasped. "You must never wish an actor luck. That's bad luck."

"I'm sorry," Bessie told her.

"You should say 'break a leg,'" Penny told her solemnly.

"Okay, well then, break a leg," Bessie said, feeling a bit ridiculous.

"Thank you," Penny replied. "And thank you for your time this morning. I feel so much better now than I did when I got here. You're an excellent listener."

"I'm glad I could help," Bessie told her sincerely. She didn't like the woman or the way she lived her life, but she sympathised with her in the difficult situation where she now found herself.

"I walked down from the little shop at the top of the hill. That's where the taxi left me," Penny told Bessie. "If I walk back up, will I find a taxi there?"

"Probably not," Bessie told her. "But I can ring for one for you." Bessie quickly rang her favourite service, and they promised to have a car there in minutes.

"You're in luck today, Miss Cubbon," the dispatcher told her. "Mark is just dropping someone off at the Wheel, and I can have him come straight to your cottage from there."

"That's wonderful," Bessie replied. "I'm not going anywhere. This is for a friend, but I appreciate the quick service." She disconnected, feeling glad she wasn't the one in need of a taxi. She didn't like Mark and she wasn't in the mood to listen to his misogynistic nonsense this morning.

After Penny left, Bessie washed up the breakfast dishes and tidied her small kitchen. The answering machine light was blinking, but she didn't feel in any hurry to listen to its nagging messages.

Only after she was happy that the kitchen was tidy did she sit down and press play. As expected, nearly every message was a virtual repeat of one that had been left the previous evening. It seemed everyone on the island had heard about Scott Carson's death now, and they all wanted the latest news from Bessie, who'd been unfortunate enough to be there when it happened.

Bessie noted a few names of people she'd take the time to ring back, the ones that occasionally rang just to say "hi" rather than waiting to pester her only when they thought she might have something interesting to discuss. The rest she deleted without guilt.

She worked through the return phone calls until lunchtime. Everyone seemed excited by the idea that she'd actually meet someone as famous as Scott Carson. His untimely death just added to their curiosity.

"I think I must be the only person on the island who didn't know who he was," Bessie complained to Doncan Quayle, her advocate, when she returned his call, which had been full of genuine concern.

Doncan laughed. "*Market Square* is one of those popular culture shows that everyone knows a little bit about, even if they never actually watch it."

"I don't know anything about it," Bessie disagreed.

Doncan just laughed again. "I suppose I should say most people rather than everyone," he conceded. "It's been on the air for thirty-odd years, though. I'm sure if you had a television you'd have caught an episode or two in that time."

Bessie chuckled. "I don't think I've missed anything," she replied.

Lunch was a bowl of tomato soup from a tin, with some of the extra loaf of crusty bread she'd bought but not ended up taking for the previous night's picnic. After her delicious breakfast, Bessie wanted to keep lunch light.

She spent an hour after lunch doing some necessary cleaning around her cottage, promising herself a night of reading if she finished all the little jobs she'd been putting off. The phone rang as she was putting the vacuum cleaner away.

"Bessie? It's Doona. How are you feeling after last night's, um, excitement?"

"I'm fine," Bessie assured her closest friend. "I'm tired, but I'm planning to have an early night."

"Maybe not too early?" Doona asked. "John was wondering if you'd mind if we came over to talk things through. He's hasn't taken your formal statement yet, either."

"John? Oh, you mean Inspector Rockwell." Bessie was going to have to start calling him John one day, she supposed. She regarded him as a good friend now.

Doona laughed. "Yes, Inspector Rockwell," she agreed. "We'll invite Hugh as well, if you're happy to have us all over."

"Oh, of course I am," Bessie replied. "What time are you planning on getting here?"

"I'll have to ring John to confirm everything," Doona told her. "He's taken the kids home just now. I think Sue was due back around one o'clock. Anyway, for now let's say six, and I'll bring dinner and a pudding."

"Even better," Bessie replied.

They agreed on Chinese takeaway, with Doona promising a surprise for pudding.

"I'll ring you back if there's any change. Otherwise we'll all see you at six."

Bessie was glad now that she'd taken the time to clean. Since she didn't need to worry about dinner, she grabbed her latest book and curled up to get lost in someone else's imagination.

The knock on her door startled her several hours later. Reluctantly, she put a bookmark into the book and hurried to let her visitors in.

CHAPTER 8

Moments later, Bessie's cottage was filled with the spicy sweet smell of Chinese food. Doona carried in a large box full to overflowing with small white takeaway containers, and Rockwell followed with a second box, equally full. Hugh was just climbing out of his own car, but he leaned back in to grab a foil-covered pan from his passenger seat before heading towards Bessie, who was holding the door for everyone.

"My goodness, it all smells gorgeous," Bessie said, as Doona set out boxes all along Bessie's counter.

"I said I'd bring pudding," Hugh said, waving the pan he was carrying. "It's still warm if you want to pop it in the oven until we've eaten."

"What did you bring?" Bessie asked curiously.

"It's an apple crumble," Hugh answered. "Grace has been getting me to try more cooking, and it was one of the first things she showed me how to make. It's dead easy and it tastes really good."

"It smells wonderful," Bessie told him as she opened her oven door. She set it on a very low temperature so the crumble would stay lovely and warm.

"Oh, I've left the rest in the car," Hugh said, shaking his head. He dashed out and was back before Bessie could reply.

"Vanilla ice cream," he told the others, as he handed Bessie the plastic bag with the container of ice cream in it. "I thought it would make a nice change from custard, especially on such a warm day."

"What a wonderful idea," Bessie said enthusiastically. She loved ice cream, but rarely bought it for herself.

"You didn't look very happy to see us when we arrived," Doona told her friend. "Are you sure you're feeling okay?"

Bessie laughed. "I was lost in Montenegro with Archie and Nero Wolfe," she explained. "They were sneaking up on this, oh, but you don't need to know the details. Suffice to say, things were very intense and I felt a tiny bit grumpy that I was interrupted."

Doona laughed. "I feel as if I should apologise, although we did warn you we were coming."

Bessie shook her head. "I should have set an alarm for just before six so that I could get my brain back here before you arrived. Anyway, let's eat. I'm starving. I didn't eat nearly enough lunch."

Everyone filled their plates with rice and bits of this and that. Bessie made sure to balance every spicy dish with another more mild choice, and she smiled as she watched Hugh piling on the spicy choices. "I suppose the ice cream will help cool down your stomach," she told him once they'd sat down.

"I love spicy food," Hugh told her. Then he laughed. "Okay, I just love food," he admitted.

The foursome ate happily for several minutes, talking about the weather and the new car Hugh was considering buying, all avoiding any mention of the events of the previous evening. It wasn't until Bessie had served up generous helpings of apple crumble with huge scoops of ice cream on top that the uncomfortable topic finally came up.

"So, Bessie, I need your formal statement," Rockwell told her. "Maybe we could do that quickly after pudding?"

"Of course," Bessie was quick to agree. So while Doona and Hugh tackled the washing up, Bessie sat down with the inspector and gave her statement. As Rockwell had spent the evening with her, he needed little more than a broad outline of the night.

"Obviously, I'm very interested in your impressions of everyone and that sort of thing," he told Bessie. "But that doesn't belong in a formal statement."

"You might be interested in my morning as well," Bessie told him. "Ms. Jakubowksi dropped in for a visit."

Rockwell's jaw dropped, and Doona spun around from the sink. "What did you just say?" Doona demanded.

Bessie laughed. "Ms. Jakubowski dropped by. She said she needed to get away from everything for a little while." Bessie shrugged. "I think she just needed a shoulder to cry on and I don't think she'd have found one in the troupe."

"I was looking for her this morning," Rockwell told Bessie. "When she finally turned up at the hotel, she just told me that she'd been seeing the island. She never mentioned visiting you."

"Well, she certainly didn't ask me to keep her visit a secret," Bessie replied. "Not that I would have, anyway," she added hastily.

"I didn't specifically question where she'd been," the inspector said. "But I'm not happy that murder suspects are dropping in to visit you," he told Bessie.

"She just needed someone sympathetic to talk with," Bessie replied.

"And you're a good listener," Doona said. "Some days you were the only thing that kept me sane during my divorce."

"Did she say anything that you think might be relevant to Scott's murder?" Rockwell asked.

"I have no idea," Bessie said. "She talked a lot about William and how much she loves him. She said she'd pretended to have an affair with Scott to try to make William jealous, but it didn't work. She said she thought Scott might be gay."

Doona burst out laughing. "That man was not gay," she said emphatically. "He spent half an hour chatting me up last night. I think I would have known if he were gay."

"He was an actor," Rockwell pointed out.

Doona opened her mouth to argue further, but Bessie held up a hand. "It really doesn't matter at this point," she said firmly. "Whatever his inclinations, according to Penny they never had an affair, although she wanted William to think that they had."

"That's just crazy," Hugh interjected from where he was busily drying dishes. "Why would you want your boyfriend to think you were cheating on him?"

"From what she said, she was hoping to give him a taste of his own medicine," Bessie replied. "Apparently, he cheats quite regularly, or at least he did when the troupe was travelling around the US."

"And she puts up with it? That doesn't make sense." Doona said angrily. "When my ex-husband cheated, I was done."

"She says she loves him," Bessie replied.

"I think I need to have a chat with that girl," Doona said. "She could do so much better."

"I told her that, but I don't think she was listening." Bessie sighed. "Don't forget, he's not just her boyfriend, he's also her boss. He runs the troupe and makes all the casting decisions. Maybe it has something to do with fame or something."

Rockwell held up a hand. "We could debate about what's going on in Penny's head all night," he said. "But I don't think that will get us any closer to figuring out who killed Scott. I'd like to focus on that, and if I'm honest, I don't think I'm going to last much more than another hour or so. I'm out on my feet."

Bessie nodded. "The inspector is right," she told the others. "We all need a good night's sleep tonight."

"Please, Bessie, you really do have to start calling me John," Rockwell told her.

Bessie nodded. "I'll try," she said. "I was raised that policemen deserve our respect, and calling you by your first name feels too familiar, that's all."

"But we've been friends for months now," the inspector argued. "At least in the privacy of your own home, I'd like you to call me John."

"Okay," Bessie said. "John," she added, feeling a little bit foolish.

John gave her a big smile in reply as Doona and Hugh sat back down at the table with them. Bessie had set a pot of coffee brewing and now she got up and poured drinks for everyone.

"Does anyone want anything else?" she asked before she sat back down. "I've a brand-new box of those lovely chocolate-covered biscuits that you can only get in Douglas, if anyone has room."

Doona laughed. "I haven't got any room left, but I'll still have just one, or maybe two."

"I could probably find room for a few," Hugh added.

Bessie pulled the box of biscuits out of the cupboard and piled several of each of the varieties onto a small serving plate. She passed around small plates to everyone and everyone took a few biscuits to go with their coffee.

"I'd rather have tea with these," Bessie said with a sigh as she looked at her plate. "But tea would probably put me to sleep."

"Okay, then," Hugh said briskly. "Motive, means and opportunity, let's go."

Everyone exchanged glances, before John finally spoke.

"As far as opportunity goes, I'm going to say that everyone in the troupe had plenty of opportunity. Scott was lying on the ground very close to their tent, and it wouldn't have taken much more than a few moments for someone to stop, bend down, and stick the knife in."

"But no one could see anything. It was really dark. How did they manage to stab him in just the right place? And why didn't Scott make any noise? And...."

The inspector held up a hand to stop Bessie's flow of questions.

"It was really dark. That's what gave the killer cover, of course. But the main members of the cast all had torches. Henry passing them out at the side of the stage. You must remember watching them bobbing back and forth between the stage and the tent?"

Bessie nodded. "I kept trying to ignore them, because they were distracting, but I do remember seeing them. Even by torchlight, the killer got lucky. They could have missed hitting anything vital and just hurt Scott."

"You mustn't repeat this," John told her. "But it wasn't a single stab wound. The killer had a couple of goes, presumably trying to make sure they completed the job."

Bessie put her half-eaten biscuit back on her plate, suddenly far less hungry. "Why didn't Scott make any noise?"

"We're still waiting on toxicology reports," the inspector said. "It's possible that there was something in the wine that knocked him out, but we won't know for sure for a few days. It's also possible that he made some noise but no one heard him. With all the people coming and going and the action on the stage, it's possible any sounds were simply drowned out by everything else that was happening."

Bessie shook her head. "Poor Scott," she said sadly.

"Anyway, for the time being, I have a couple of constables from Peel digging around into the backgrounds of good local folks that made up the rest of the cast for the show. The Peel office is also checking out the audience members and trying to chase up everyone who was there but left before the body was discovered. They're looking for anyone who might have had any sort of motive for killing Scott, although I don't think either the audience or the extras actually had the opportunity to get to him."

Hugh nodded. "I've been going over it all in my head," he told the others. "I think at least one of us would have noticed if anyone from the audience had come up towards the VIP section during the show. And they wouldn't have been able to get to the stage and come out towards the tent, either. Henry was keeping an eye on things there."

"I know I was bored enough that if anyone came up towards us I would have noticed," Doona said. "And I would have welcomed the distraction."

"What about the extras?" Bessie asked. "I mean, I doubt they knew Scott, but they certainly could have come out from the stage to the tent, couldn't they?"

"Again, Henry was keeping an eye on them," the inspector replied. "Or rather, he was keeping an eye on the main cast members. He was passing out torches and keeping track of them, and he's certain that no one other than the four main cast members came past him towards the tent."

"And none of them passed their torch back with blood-covered and shaking hands?" Doona asked.

John shook his head. "We suspect that the killer wore gloves, although we've not found them. But there was so much going on last night in the dark, anyone could have tucked them in a pocket and then thrown them in the sea or something. We haven't found any costumes with blood on them, either."

"That should rule out Candy, though," Bessie said thoughtfully. "She didn't have a chance to put on gloves and then hide them again. We would have noticed if she had."

"Maybe," John said. "But we aren't totally ruling her out just on that point."

"I talked to the two bodyguards," Hugh said. "I think I would have noticed if either of them had bent down towards Scott at any point, and I didn't."

"No, I didn't see them move," Bessie said. "They were sort of big immovable objects in my peripheral vision. I think I would have noticed if one of them bent over low enough to stab Scott."

"I didn't see them move, either," John added. "And I'm certain I would have noticed."

Doona shrugged. "I didn't see them move either, but this is boring. Let's talk about motive."

Hugh laughed. "What about means?" he asked.

"That is another point that seems to narrow down the suspect list," John replied. "The knife was definitely the one that Penny gave William years ago. She identified it for us this afternoon."

"So it had to be one of the cast," Doona said, snapping a biscuit in half.

John shook his head. "We're keeping an open mind," he told her. "It is just about within the realm of possibility that someone from the audience or the extras snuck into the tent and found the knife where someone had hidden it, and then stabbed Scott. I think that's extremely unlikely, but I never discount any possibility until it's proven impossible."

"Yeah, well, you have to do that. You're the one investigating. I'm just sitting on the sidelines and it seems to me that the knife proves that it was one of the main cast members," Doona said defiantly.

"I'm fine with that as a working hypothesis," John replied.

"As long as you're including Candy in the list," Bessie added. "She wasn't one of the cast members, but she certainly could have taken the knife."

"Scott could have taken the knife as well," John added. "Although it doesn't seem terribly likely, since he ended up stabbed with it. I think it's far more likely that the killer had the knife."

"So that brings us to motive," Doona said. "And here's where it all gets interesting."

Bessie sighed. "I think it's all terribly sad," she said. "They seem like a group of very unhappy people who've joined together to make each other even less happy."

John patted Bessie's arm. "If you'd rather we just call it a night now, we can all go and you can get some sleep," he said softly. "Figuring this out is my job, not yours, after all."

Bessie shook her head. "If you think I might be able to help in any way, I'm happy to talk it all through. Finding Scott's killer is the most important thing right now."

"Okay, then," the inspector said slowly, watching Bessie's face intently. "Let's talk about motives for the five main suspects."

"It seems to me that Sienna was better off with Scott alive," Bessie began tentatively. "He was offering her a chance to leave the troupe and try her luck with Candy as her agent. I can't see any reason why she'd kill Scott."

"And yet Candy picked her as the murderer," John reminded Bessie. "Candy seemed to think that Sienna was still hurt because Scott dumped her."

"She didn't act like she'd been dumped and badly hurt last night," Doona said. "She was all over him, and he didn't seem to mind."

"Which rather seems to give Adam a strong motive," Hugh chimed in. "He had to have been furious when Sienna announced she was leaving."

"But she didn't announce that until after the show," Bessie pointed out.

"Maybe she said something to Adam earlier?" Hugh shrugged.

"Anyway, maybe he was still angry about the affair Sienna had with Scott in the past."

"William seemed to think Adam had the best motive," John said. "He suggested that Scott was on track to replace Adam in the troupe as well as in Sienna's affections."

"But surely none of that mattered once Scott left?" Doona asked.

"Or maybe, when Scott turned up out of the blue, that was the last straw for Adam and he just snapped," Hugh said, with a touch of melodrama.

"William did say that he always suspected Adam of stealing the knife," Bessie remembered.

"And speaking of William, he had a very similar motive for killing Scott," John said. "Allegedly, Penny had an affair with him as well."

Bessie shook her head. "But Penny said it never happened," she said. "Apparently, she and Scott were just pretending, to make William jealous."

"It doesn't really matter whether they had an affair or not," John pointed out. "What matters is whether William believed that they were having an affair or not."

"But surely he didn't steal his own knife," Doona said.

"No, but maybe he got it back somehow and didn't bother to tell anyone. Maybe he found out that Scott had it, and he got it off him and stabbed him with it," Hugh suggested.

"That's a lot of maybes," Bessie pointed out. "And we aren't even sure if William even suspected that Penny and Scott were having an affair. Penny said he never gave her any hint that he suspected."

"Can we think of any other possible motive for William?" John asked.

"Professional jealousy?" Bessie suggested. "I think everyone in the troupe was jealous of Scott's big break."

"Seems a bit of a stretch to murder him over that, though," Doona said. "I mean, it isn't like *Market Square* is going to offer William Scott's old job or anything."

"But maybe he just couldn't stand that Scott was so happy and so famous," Hugh said. "Some people are like that. They hate to see other people happy."

"He was certainly not pleased to see Scott," Bessie said. "But I didn't get the feeling any of them were, except maybe Sienna."

"Penny seemed happier, once she talked to him for a bit," Doona offered.

"Yeah, but only after Scott offered to help her and William," Hugh pointed out.

Bessie shrugged. "That just leaves Candy to discuss. Like Sienna, I think she was better off with Scott alive, wasn't she?"

"Did someone say that Scott was going to fire her, though?" Doona asked.

"Someone said it, but I don't know how you could prove such a thing," Bessie answered.

"And didn't she have a big insurance policy on his life?" Doona added.

"She did admit to having insurance on his life," John replied. "But she also claimed to have a contract with him that meant he couldn't fire her. We need to find out how much the insurance is worth to get a better idea of her possible motives."

"It seems like he was sleeping with everyone else. Did he sleep with Candy?" Hugh asked.

"We aren't sure that he actually slept with any of them," John said. "Penny denies that they were having an affair. Sienna keeps saying she barely knew the man. Candy said he was like a little brother to her. We're looking into what was going on in London and on the set of *Market Square* now to find out if he was seeing anyone there."

"What does that have to do with anything?" Bessie asked.

"If he had a serious girlfriend in London, it might suggest that he wasn't really interested in getting back together with Sienna, assuming they were ever together in the first place," John tried to explain, and then shook his head. "I suppose it's all part of trying to see the bigger picture," he told Bessie. "It might not have any relevance at all, but we won't know for sure until we try."

Bessie nodded. "So are we any closer to figuring out who killed Scott?" she asked.

Everyone looked at her with tired eyes. "I don't think my brain is up to figuring that out right now," Doona said with a sigh. "I keep fantasising about my pillow."

Hugh laughed. "I'm not quite there yet," he said with a frown, "but I'm pretty tired."

John nodded. "At the moment, they all seem equally likely, or unlikely, if you prefer," he said. "I think after we've all had some sleep, we'll be able to see things more clearly."

Bessie stood up and started to gather up coffee mugs and plates. Everyone else jumped up to help and they had Bessie's kitchen tidied up in no time.

"I'm not comfortable with the idea that murder suspects are visiting you," John told Bessie as the group headed towards the door.

"It isn't like I invited the woman," Bessie said. "She just turned up on my doorstep."

He frowned. "I want you to promise me that you'll ring me if she comes back," he told her sternly.

"I'm not sure how I can do that without being rude," Bessie said with a frown. "I mean, I can't very well open the door and say, 'Oh hi, come in while I ring the police and tell them that you're here,' can I?"

Doona laughed. "That would be awkward," she agreed. "How about if you say 'Hi, come in. Let me ring Doona and invite her over. I know she'd love to see you.' Would that work?"

Bessie nodded. "I suppose I could do that," she agreed.

"And that doesn't just apply to Penny," John added. "If any of the suspects turn up on your doorstep, you ring Doona right away, okay?"

"Okay," Bessie sighed.

"Promise?" he asked, looking into her eyes.

"I promise," Bessie said with a deep sigh. "Honestly, you're starting to fuss over me almost as much as Doona. Thank heavens Hugh is more sensible."

Hugh flushed. "I was just thinking that maybe I should stop over on your couch for a few nights, just until we work out who killed Scott," he admitted sheepishly.

Bessie shook her head. "Out with you all," she said mock-sternly. "Leave me alone and let me get some sleep."

"What happens next?" Doona asked as she picked up her handbag. "I mean what's everyone doing tomorrow, and are we going to meet up again tomorrow night to try talking it all through again?"

"I'm going to spend most of tomorrow going over everyone's statements," John replied. "I'm hoping I can find something we've missed, some little discrepancy or oddity that can point me in the right direction."

"I spent the day today working," Hugh said. "I was thinking I might spend at least some of tomorrow with Grace. She's still really upset about being a witness to murder."

"And understandably so," Bessie replied. "I think she's a lovely girl," she told Hugh, who blushed at her words. "Make sure you take good care of her."

"Oh, yes," Hugh replied. "I'm trying to do just that."

Bessie smiled at her friends. "Anyone who wants to is welcome to join me tomorrow afternoon," she said. "I have tickets for the matinee performance of *Much Ado About the Shrew.*"

Doona groaned. "I really don't want to have to watch that again," she said.

"I think it might be quite interesting to see it again," Bessie told her. "They've been rehearsing, apparently. Anyway, I can't see how it could be any worse, and it means I can check out all of the suspects again."

John was frowning. "I'm not sure I'm happy for you to be spending time with the suspects," he said seriously.

Bessie laughed. "You can't mean that," she told him. "I'll be in the middle of Peel Castle, surrounded by dozens of other people."

"So was Scott," the inspector said soberly.

"But it was dark," Bessie argued. "And he seems to have had quite a few people who didn't like him. Tomorrow's show will be in broad daylight, and I'll be surrounded by friends. Or at least as many friends as want to come with me?"

She ended the last sentence as a question, which made everyone smile.

"I'll come," Doona said, sighing. "Maybe I'll be able to follow the show more now that I've seen it once."

Hugh snorted with laughter. "I doubt it," he said gloomily. "But I'll come as well. I'll ask Grace if she wants to join us, but I doubt she'll say yes."

"I don't blame her one bit," Bessie said. "And I do understand if you'd rather spend the day with her."

"And miss out on the fun?" Hugh laughed. "Something exciting always happens when you're around," he told Bessie.

Bessie frowned. "That has rather been the case lately," she said. "But tomorrow may well be uneventful and boring."

"Famous last words," the inspector said gloomily. "Just in case it isn't either of those, I'll come as well."

The foursome agreed that the two o'clock start time meant they didn't need to bring much in the way of a picnic.

"I'll bring a couple of packets of biscuits, and we can buy tea from the vendors, assuming they're still there." Bessie said.

"They're still there," John confirmed. "And I didn't mention it, but they are all being looked at as possible suspects. As far as we can tell, though, they all packed up and left as soon as the interval was over, while there was still just enough light for them to see by."

"I can't see any of them having any sort of motive," Bessie said. "They're all long-term residents of the island."

"Everyone has to be considered," John reminded her. "But they come very low on my list."

With the arrangements made for the next day, Bessie let her friends out and then locked up her little cottage. She switched off the phone's ringer and checked that the volume on the answering machine was as low as it could go. Upstairs, she changed out of her clothes, crawling into her favourite nightgown with a small sigh of satisfaction.

Bessie couldn't remember the last time she'd been so happy to crawl into bed, unless you counted the previous night. She set an alarm for seven, just in case her internal alarm didn't wake her. She turned off her light and nestled down under the covers. After a couple of minutes of tossing and turning, she sat back up and switched on the light. She quickly reset her alarm for eight and then smiled to herself as she turned off the lamp again. Snuggling under the covers for the second time, she was asleep almost before she had time to think.

CHAPTER 9

*B*essie's eyes opened just seconds before her alarm began to ring. She switched it off and then cautiously stretched. Pushing back the covers, she climbed out of bed and looked at herself in the small mirror that was on the wall across from her. She felt a million times better than she had the previous morning. It was amazing what a good amount of sleep could do.

If she could have whistled, she would have done so in the shower, but since that was a skill she'd never quite managed to acquire, she hummed to herself instead. She dressed quickly and made herself a light breakfast. A nice long walk on the beach left her feeling happy with the world, in spite of the crowd she had to negotiate her way through.

It was really only crowded in front of the section that ran behind the new cottages that had been built recently as holiday homes. Bessie was pleased to see them busy. Thomas Shimmin, who owned them, had spent a lot of money making them nice, and he needed them to be full to capacity during the fairly short summer season. By October, they would be empty again and they would remain so until spring. As it was still only June, most of the families on the beach were busy with quite small children. The schools wouldn't break up for the summer until sometime in July. Then the beach would feel even busier as families with school-aged children crowded on to them.

Bessie pushed on, past the crowds, walking towards the home she still thought of as the Pierce mansion. Doncan Quayle was in the process of trying to get the property sold, and while he wouldn't give her any details, he'd mentioned that he had several showings over the last few weeks. She was still hoping that whoever bought it would live in it full-time, rather than using it as a holiday home the way the Pierces had. She paused at the base of the cliff that ran up to the house, wondering if anyone would mind if she slipped up the steep steps and had a peek at the house.

Glancing at her watch, Bessie decided against being nosy for today. She needed to get some lunch before too much longer so that she'd be ready for Doona to collect her at one o'clock. That would give them plenty of time to get to the castle for the two o'clock show. It wasn't like they needed to worry about fighting their way through crowds to find a good place to set out their blankets. Bessie couldn't imagine that there would be a sudden rush to see *Much Ado About the Shrew*, not after the disastrous opening night.

Back at home, Bessie curled up with her friends from the previous evening, finishing the Nero Wolfe book she'd read many times before. With Wolfe and Archie safely back in New York, she made herself some lunch. The picnic hamper looked quite empty with just a few packets of biscuits in it, so Bessie found herself adding some sandwiches and the rest of the box of pork pies from the packet she'd opened for the picnic for the first performance of the play. A few packets of crisps and a shop-bought chocolate Swiss roll helped fill in the gaps.

Doona arrived in the passenger seat of John Rockwell's car, but she quickly swapped it for the back so that Bessie could have the front.

"I don't mind a bit," she insisted when Bessie tried to argue. "I was just keeping John company in the front, since he was nice enough to drive."

"No point in wasting petrol," John replied easily. "I was coming from my flat anyway, which is practically next door to Doona's house.

It isn't far out of the way to drop you ladies off after the show before I head back to Ramsey."

"How are the kids?" Bessie asked. "I hope they weren't too upset by what they saw."

"They're doing okay," John assured her. "Actually, Thomas now wants to be a forensics specialist and Amy wants to be an actress, so I think the only one who's truly upset is Sue."

Everyone laughed, and the group made their way across the island in good spirits.

"What are you doing for Tynwald Day?" Bessie asked the inspector as they drove past Tynwald Hill.

"I hadn't thought about it," John admitted. "I just have it marked as a day off in my diary."

"It's your first one on the island," Bessie protested. "You should attend the ceremony and then stay for all of the fun."

"There's fun?" he asked.

Bessie and Doona laughed. "It's an all-day festival," Bessie explained. "After the ceremony, which is fascinating, if not exactly fun, there's all sorts of things to do and see. They'll be live bands and demonstrations by martial artists and Manx folk dance groups and choirs. There's a whole tent devoted to Manx businesses. They pass out their brochures and free pens and things with their names on them. Manx National Heritage will have a big display as well. And then, at the end of the night, there's a huge fireworks display."

"I didn't realise there was that much to do," John answered her. "I think I'll have to check it out. If Sue and the kids are here, I'll have to drag them along. Sue might take advantage of the long weekend to take the kids to see her mother, though. She's doing better, but still isn't back to her old self."

Bessie thought about asking for more details, but it not only felt like prying, she really didn't like hearing about the various ailments that affected older people. She was blessed to be in good health herself and she tried to avoid thinking about all the things that could go wrong with her somewhat past middle-aged body.

"I think we shall have to make a day of it," Doona said brightly.

"Hugh said he's going to try to get there and Grace is planning to come. It should be fun."

"It's not another occasion to pack a picnic, is it?" John asked.

"You can," Bessie answered. "But there will be loads of food vendors and all sorts of delicious things to try. I usually just eat my way from one of the food carts to the next, buying just a little bit from each vendor."

"That sounds like a plan," Doona said from the back.

"It does indeed," the inspector replied. "I think I'm going to like Tynwald Day."

"You can try your hand, or rather your feet, at a bit of folk dancing as well," Bessie told him. "They always let people from the crowd join in and that way you can burn up all those extra calories."

"Um, maybe not," John laughed. "But I'll be happy to cheer you and Doona on if you want to give it at try."

"Maybe we should just watch this year," Doona said.

"We'll see," Bessie told them both.

The inspector turned the car down the steep hill past the House of Mananan, heading for the causeway to Peel Castle. As they came around the corner, Bessie gasped. Cars were backed up all along the road, trying to get into the car park next to the castle.

"What's going on?" she asked.

"I've no idea," John replied.

They sat in the traffic jam for several minutes, inching forward a little at a time as, presumably, the person at the front of the queue found a parking space at the other end. It was only a few minutes before two when John finally reached the small car park. It was jammed full of cars, parked every which way. Many of the drivers would be trapped until most of the cars around them left. John pulled forward, following the road around the castle to the end. The entire length was clearly marked "no parking."

John pulled up at the very end of the causeway and parked. He pulled a "police vehicle" sign from his glovebox and set it on the dashboard. Cars that had followed him along the road now had to turn around and head back down the road, past the castle and the full car park, to try to find parking further away.

"I don't think anyone will ticket drivers if they park along here today," John remarked as he helped Bessie from the car. "But I'm not telling anyone else that."

Bessie shook her head. "But where are they all going?" she asked. "The castle is the only thing down here."

She got her answer only a few minutes later as she, John, and Doona made their way to the castle entrance. A long queue of people snaked down the stone steps to the road below.

"This is crazy," Doona muttered, looking at the crowd of people carrying picnics, blankets, and folding chairs.

"Why are they all here?" Bessie asked the inspector. "I'm sure Henry said they'd had nothing but cancellations."

John shrugged. "Maybe no one could find anything else to do on a sunny Sunday afternoon?"

"Can I have your attention, please?" A loud voice shouted down from the castle entrance. "Can you please quiet down and listen?"

The crowd grew quieter as everyone turned their attention to Bob, from Manx National Heritage, who'd appeared at the top of the stairs.

"Thank you," he said with a nervous-looking smile. "Um, I'm sorry to tell you all this, but the afternoon showing of *Much Ado About the Shrew* is now completely sold out. Unless you already have tickets, I'm afraid I can't let you in. We have some limited availability for next weekend, but you'll need to ring the ticket office on Monday to purchase those tickets. Thank you."

There was a great deal of grumbling among the crowd, but after a few moments, where Bob kept apologising profusely, people began to accept that they weren't going to be able to get in and they started to disperse.

"That might clear out some of the mess in the car park," John said quietly.

"I just hope Hugh's already here," Bessie replied. "Otherwise he's going to get caught in the mass exodus."

A few minutes later, Bessie and her friends were the only people remaining on the stone steps.

"Bessie," Bob said, "of course you and your friends are welcome, with or without tickets."

Bessie shook her head. "I keep telling you not to give me any special treatment," she replied. "Anyway, we do have tickets. I wouldn't have stayed otherwise."

Bob nodded. "Of course you wouldn't have."

"But what's going on?" Doona demanded. "I thought everyone cancelled their bookings."

Bob shrugged. "After the mess on Friday night, we almost cancelled the rest of the run, but then last night people started lining up before five o'clock for the show. By seven, when the show was due to start, we were turning people away. From what I can gather, everyone's heard how appalling the show is and they all want to see for themselves."

"Some of them probably want to see where Scott Carson, off the telly, was murdered as well," the inspector suggested. "Some people are fascinated by ghoulish things like that."

The trio followed Bob up the steps and into the castle grounds. Bob carefully shut and locked the entrance door, to which a sign saying "Sold Out" had been posted.

Bessie was surprised, as they crossed the grass, at how much had changed since Friday night. The stage had been moved some considerable distance from where it had been, and Bessie tried not to stare at the section of grass that was marked off with police tape in a now empty section of the castle grounds.

"Your friend Mr. Watterson arrived around half one," Bob told Bessie. "Henry and I thought we might as well put you all back in the VIP section again."

Bessie would have protested, but she relished the idea of having the best possible view of proceedings, especially in light of the huge crowd that was packed tightly across the grass. Bessie was most interested in who went in and out of the changing room tent during the second half.

There were several large groups in the VIP section already, but Hugh had claimed a fairly large section of the grass for them right next to the new, light blue, changing room tent. Although they were in a completely different part of the castle grounds, they were sitting roughly where Scott and Candy had been on Friday night in relation to the tent.

"We've wired up lights in there now," Bob whispered. "Of course it won't matter today, since it's the middle of the afternoon, but it helped last night, I can tell you."

It was already time for the show to start, so Bessie and her friends quickly spread out their blankets and settled in.

Hugh gestured to a collection of Styrofoam cups with lids in front of him. "I got everyone hot milky tea," he said. "And I brought back a bunch of sugar packets in case you prefer yours sweet."

Bessie and the others thanked him, and Bessie was quick to add a packet of sugar to hers and take a big drink. It was delicious and strangely comforting in the midst of the unexpectedly large crowd.

"I don't care," the shrill voice cut through the ambient noise. "You're mean and hateful and I can't wait to get away from you."

Bessie was almost certain the voice belonged to Sienna. But who was she arguing with?

"By all means, go," was the reply. Adam's voice sounded amused by Sienna's words, rather than angry. "Just remember what I said," he added, his tone sharpening. "The next time you go, you won't be welcome back."

"Ha," Sienna laughed. "The troupe needs me."

Adam chuckled. "Girls like you are a dime a dozen," he said in a dismissive voice. "I could pick any half-decent looking woman out of the extras and she could do your part tomorrow."

"But you need me," Sienna said, her voice sounding pleading now.

Adam laughed harshly. "Any girl in the extras could replace you in my life tonight."

The tent flap snapped open and Sienna appeared in the opening. She looked as if she was about to cry. She was dressed in an elaborate costume for the first act and she blinked out at the large group in the

VIP section. Nearly everyone within earshot had been hanging on every word of her exchange with Adam.

Adam came up behind her now and smiled smarmily.

"Oh, dear, we should have been rehearsing a bit more quietly, shouldn't we, darling?" he said to Sienna, slipping an arm around her waist. "We certainly don't want to spoil the show by shouting out our best lines before it even begins."

Sienna blinked a couple of times before she nodded slowly. "Sorry," she said softly. "I didn't realise there were so many people out here."

"Everyone back in the tent," William's voice boomed out from the small enclosure. "It's nearly show time. No more rehearsing, it's time to perform."

Bessie exchanged looks with Doona.

"That wasn't part of the show on Friday night," Doona whispered.

"No, it certainly wasn't," Bessie agreed. "It will be interesting to see if they try to add it in somewhere, though."

Doona giggled. "Surely Adam won't be rewriting the script during a performance?"

"I wouldn't put anything past this group." John leaned in to add his thoughts.

They all laughed and Bessie passed around a packet of chocolate digestives while they waited for the show to start. They would enjoy the rest of the hamper's contents during the interval.

A few minutes later they could see the steady stream of extras beginning to make their way from behind the stage towards it.

The first half didn't seem much different from Friday's show to Bessie. She supposed that the transitions between scenes were somewhat smoother, and the extras seemed a little bit more confident in their roles, but for the most part it was still something of a confusing mess.

"I'm not sure the extra rehearsals have helped much," Doona whispered to Bessie as the main cast members disappeared into their tent and the extras wandered back off the stage towards their larger one that had been moved behind the new stage location.

"It was less disorganised," John said with a shrug. "At least I think it was."

Bessie laughed. "I still didn't really follow what was going on," she said with a shrug. "I wonder what everyone else thought."

"I'm going to go and try to find out," John said. "I'm going to wander through the crowd and see what people are saying."

"That's a great idea," Hugh said enthusiastically. "I think maybe I'll go walk around the different vendors and see what's being said over there."

Doona and Bessie both laughed. "Why don't you grab yourself a little snack as well?" Doona suggested with a wink.

"Oh, aye, I might just," Hugh replied.

"So what do you want to do?" Doona asked Bessie after the men left.

"I think I'm going to stay right here," she answered. "I don't want to miss anything exciting that goes on in the tent."

"Good point," Doona said. "Do you mind if I leave you for a short while? I really need to stretch my legs a bit."

"Off you go," Bessie told her. "I'm going to get up and have a stretch as well, but I'm going to stay here."

"Okay, I won't be long," Doona told her friend. "You stay here and don't go in the tent, no matter who invites you."

Bessie rolled her eyes at her overprotective friend. She got up slowly, stretching muscles that were unaccustomed to sitting on the ground for such long periods. She noticed a folding chair that one of the others in the VIP section was using. Surely they couldn't be all that expensive, she thought. I'm going to have to look into buying one. She frowned at herself.

It could be argued that such a purchase would be another concession to her age. She looked around and noted that nearly everyone sitting on chairs was middle-aged or younger. Several small children even had their own little chairs. She added a chair to her mental shopping list.

"Bessie, wasn't it?" The deep voice came from behind her. Bessie turned and looked at William Baldwin.

"Yes, that's right. How are you today, Mr. Baldwin?"

"I'm well, thank you," he said with a small bow. He was wearing jeans and T-shirt and Bessie was surprised at how different he looked in the casual clothes. "Are you enjoying the show more today?" he asked.

Bessie smiled graciously. "I can tell that you've been rehearsing," she replied. "And I'm looking forward to the second half." She didn't say the "being over" out loud.

"Well, I do hope my Penny wasn't too much of a bother yesterday morning," he told Bessie. "Sometimes she gets silly ideas in her head."

"She was no bother at all," Bessie replied. "I think she just needed to get away from everyone for a short time. You've all been travelling together for years. Sometimes it's helpful to have someone different to talk with."

"I suppose," William shrugged. "Anyway, I hope you enjoy the second half." He bowed again and then headed purposefully towards the stage.

Before Bessie had a chance to wonder what he had really wanted, Penny herself was engulfing her in a hug.

"Oh, Bessie, I'm so happy you came," she said exuberantly. "We've had such a wonderful turnout and I'm so thrilled to be performing in front of such a lovely crowd."

"They were turning people away at the gate when I arrived," Bessie told her. "And I'm sure Bob said there aren't many tickets left for next weekend, either." Penny was wearing a black T-shirt and black trousers, and Bessie wondered if she wore them under her costume to make changing between scenes easier.

As they spoke, Bessie glanced around and realised that a slow but steady trickle of people were exiting the castle. Maybe Penny wouldn't notice, she thought.

"How are you finding the new location for the stage?" she asked Penny, hoping to distract the woman.

"Oh, it's fine," Penny answered airily. "I don't pay that much attention to the little details."

"And the new tent has lighting in it, I was told."

"Yes, it does, which is a huge help for costume changes once it grows dark," Penny told her. "Oh, I need to go and check on the blocking for the next scene. I hope I have time to chat later."

Penny was gone before Bessie could frame a reply. Bessie watched her disappear behind the stage. Deciding it was time to have a snack, Bessie sat back down on the blanket and dug into her hamper. She was sorry she hadn't asked anyone to bring her back some tea, but at least she had plenty of biscuits, or would do until Hugh got back.

A moment later Sienna and Adam emerged from the tent and headed towards the stage. They appeared to be arguing, but they were doing so very quietly and Bessie couldn't hear a single word. They weren't in costume either, and Bessie shook her head at how very short Sienna's shorts were. As she watched them disappear behind the stage, she noticed someone else joining them. What was Candy doing at the show, and why was she hanging out by the stage?

Bessie's friends were back before she'd had time to eat more than a couple of biscuits. Doona brought her a huge container of tea, reminding Bessie once again why the two were such good friends.

"So, what's everyone saying about the show?" Bessie asked, after she'd thanked Doona profusely.

"I think it's safe to say no one is hugely impressed," John answered. "Several people I talked to were packing up to head home. Apparently, half the show was enough for them. I got the feeling from the ones that were sticking around that they were just waiting for something to go badly wrong."

"Like what?" Bessie asked.

"Many of them heard about all of the wardrobe problems with the first show. I think they were all hoping for mismatched shoes and shirts on the wrong way around."

"But that only happened because it was dark," Bessie said.

"I got the impression that most people were expecting the whole thing to be a good deal funnier, perhaps unintentionally funny, but funny nevertheless." Hugh said. "One guy I know was packing up and he said it was just too boring."

"The people I talked to said they were just confused," Doona added. "They couldn't follow the plot, although one of my friends said she was just happy to sit and watch Adam, even if she didn't understand a thing he said."

Everyone laughed. "I suppose a lot of my friends are just hanging around to watch Sienna," Hugh said. "I'm sure her costumes are shorter today."

Bessie nodded. "I think you're right. And I think she's been on stage more today as well. I wasn't specifically noticing who was doing what on Friday, but it seems to be that we've seen more of Sienna this afternoon than we did then."

"But if he gave her a bigger part, what was she fighting with Adam about?" Doona asked.

"Maybe about what she did to get the bigger part?" Bessie suggested, nodding towards the back of the stage where Sienna and William had just appeared.

The two were deep in conversation, with William's arm draped over Sienna's shoulders. As they walked back towards their tent, he kept a firm hold on the pretty young actress.

"That looked very cosy," Doona hissed, after the pair disappeared into the tent.

"And Penny isn't pleased," Hugh said. They all looked up and watched as Penny dashed from behind the stage into the tent. Her eyes were red and swollen and she held a huge wad of tissues in her hand. Adam followed not far behind Penny, his own face a picture of indifference.

"I'm sure I saw Candy behind the stage earlier," Bessie told the others. "I wonder what she was doing there."

She didn't have to wonder for long, as just then Candy emerged from behind the stage and headed straight for the VIP section.

"Bessie, my darling, how lovely to see you here again," she said as she reached the roped-off area.

Bessie returned the quick and superficial hug that Candy bent down to give her, pulling back rapidly as she breathed in the alcoholic fumes that the other woman was emitting.

"Maybe I could sit with you to watch the rest of the show?" Candy asked, dropping to the ground between Bessie and Doona. "I arrived too late for the first half and ended up standing outside the locked castle door until the interval. It wasn't until people started leaving that I was able to get in."

"Why bother?" Doona asked. "I would have thought you'd have better things to do."

Candy laughed heartily. "You don't mince words, do you?" she said to Doona. "I was torn, really, between coming and not. In the end, I wanted to see how much they'd managed to improve things over the last two days. I'm still interested in helping little Sienna along, as well. I wanted to see her work again, especially in the context of all the stress she must be under."

"Any special reason why Sienna would be under more stress than the others?" John asked.

Candy shrugged. "She has to think that Adam killed Scott, doesn't she? That must put a damper on their relationship."

"I thought you suspected Sienna," John said.

"Oh, I don't know." Candy waved a hand. "Sienna, Adam, William, Penny, spin the wheel, flip a coin, throw a dice. It could have been any of them." She laughed again. "Except only one dice is called a die, isn't it? That's ironic." Candy's drunken laughter echoed around them for a moment. Bessie finally interrupted.

"Candy, are you okay?" she asked with genuine concern.

"Oh, I'm drunk, I suppose," Candy answered. "But I took a taxi here. I didn't drive. I just can't seem to find anything to do with myself except drink wine and get maudlin. I didn't realise how much I cared about Scott, you know? He was a good kid and we were having fun together. He was going to go far, he was, and he was going to take me with him. Now I'm back on my own. And you know what?"

Candy leaned in close to Bessie and whispered. "I'm almost ready to consider axing, ax, I mean, asking William for my old job back."

Bessie held her breath until the woman swayed back away from her. Candy smelled as if she'd been bathing in wine as well as drinking it.

"Do you think the troupe would take you back?" Doona asked.

Candy shrugged. "I'm not sure I want to go back," she said. "That's why I wanted to see the show again. It sucked big time on Friday night. I need to know if they've improved it. You saw the first act was it any better?"

Bessie and her friends exchanged looks.

"No," Hugh blurted out. He blushed. "That is, I still didn't understand what was going on."

Candy nodded. "That's what I thought on Friday. I thought maybe I just drank too much wine and that's why I was confused."

"You seem to have drunk more today," Doona suggested.

Candy laughed again. "You're right about that, sister. But I don't have time to sober up. The troupe is only here for another week." She laughed again, and then the laughter turned into a coughing fit. After several minutes, Bessie started to worry. Doona offered Candy a bottle of water, and after a few sips the coughing finally petered out.

"Three packs a day for twenty years," Candy gasped out.

The sound of voices stopped anyone from replying. The supporting cast members had returned to the stage while Bessie and her friends had been focussed on Candy. Now they all turned their attention back to the show.

Twenty minutes in, Bessie felt like just walking out. The second half remained as confused as it had been on Friday, even if the extras all knew their cues perfectly. Bessie let her mind wander. She tried to think back to the night of Scott's murder. As she watched the four lead actors take part in each short scene, only to disappear back into their tent to reemerge in different costumes for another, Bessie tried to remember the comings and goings from Friday.

"They're doing things in a different order," Doona hissed to Bessie. "Dare I say, it's even more confusing now than it was on Friday?"

"They've changed the running order of the scenes," Candy said, shaking her head. "It barely made sense on Friday. This is madness."

Bessie shifted on the grass, trying to find a more comfortable position. She glanced back towards the audience behind them. Several people were standing up and packing up their things in spite of the performance going on in front of them. While it was rude, Bessie sympathised.

A few moments later, Bessie watched as Penny carefully climbed the wooden stairs to the small balcony that was perched on the edge of the stage. She remembered the scene from Friday; it had been lifted from *Romeo and Juliet* almost exactly as written and had been the one small part of the show that she's actually felt she'd understood. Whatever else she thought of Penny, the woman had poured her heart and soul into Juliet's balcony scene.

William appeared and began the famous scene. The audience seemed to grow quieter and more attentive as if everyone suddenly felt like they could understand what was happening. William was overly dramatic, though, and Bessie couldn't help but feel that his Romeo wouldn't have attracted Juliet in the slightest. She watched Penny, wondering what the woman was feeling as she perched on the tiny balcony.

"O Romeo, Romeo," she began.

Bessie gasped. "But that's Sienna," she whispered to Doona.

"What's she doing up there?" Candy barked out loudly.

A sudden loud cracking noise cut off the conversation. Bessie and the others watched helplessly as the tiny balcony seemed to shake, and then the entire structure crashed down onto the stage below.

Sienna's scream echoed across the castle grounds.

CHAPTER 10

*I*nspector Rockwell was halfway to the stage before Bessie even fully registered what was happening. Hugh was only a step behind. Doona quickly got to her feet and started giving orders.

"You two stay here," she told Bessie and Candy.

Bessie watched as Doona grabbed Bob and said something to him. Bob nodded and rushed off towards the front of the castle. People all around the site had risen to their feet and now stood watching the scene on the stage unfold.

John was clearly giving the orders on the stage, and Bessie noticed that Hugh had his mobile out. She wasn't anywhere near close enough to actually see it, but she imagined that she could tell that he'd pushed a single number three times over. It wouldn't be long before the emergency services began to arrive.

The robed members of the local theatre group made their way off the stage and back to their tent. That left Penny, William and Adam helping John and Hugh to rescue Sienna from the wooden rubble. Bessie could see blood on Sienna's head as she was pulled out of the wreckage. She gave the audience a weak wave, which generated a huge round of applause from everyone.

John and Hugh carefully stretched her out on the stage and then John stepped to the edge.

"Ladies and gentleman," he said loudly. "I'm afraid that's going to have to be the end of the show for today. I'm going to ask you to bear with me for a short while. Obviously, the Isle of Man Constabulary, of which I am a part, will have to investigate this accident. Therefore, I will ask you all to remain where you are until you've had a chance to give a statement to an officer."

A generally disgruntled murmur went through the crowd, but no one said anything loudly enough for Bessie to hear.

The inspector turned back to Sienna, and only a few moments later Bessie could hear sirens. It wasn't long before several uniformed officers arrived, along with a pair of ambulance men pushing a stretcher. John came off the stage to issue instructions to the newly arrived officers, while the paramedics took charge of Sienna.

Within minutes, they were wheeling her away over the rough ground towards the castle entrance. Penny, William, and Adam watched from the stage, all three looking stunned.

As officers began to take statements from the audience, Doona came back over to Bessie and Candy.

"John's going to set up in the storage room again. He wondered if you'd like to join him?" she said to Bessie.

Bessie got up slowly. "I would, indeed," she said. "Especially if he has a chair for me."

Doona laughed. "We need to get you a little folding chair for these sorts of things," she told her friend. "I think I could do with one as well."

"What am I meant to do?" Candy asked in a dull monotone.

Bessie looked at the woman, who appeared to be almost in shock.

"Can you wait here for a bit?" Doona asked her. "I'll have someone bring you a cup of tea. I'm sure Inspector Rockwell is going to want to talk to you."

Candy shrugged. "That's fine," she said.

Bessie followed her friend through the crowds towards the little storage room. Doug, from MNH, was there with his keys to let her in.

"Where's Henry today?" Bessie couldn't help but ask.

"He's having a much-deserved day off," Doug told her. "Bob and I thought we could handle things. Jack's here somewhere, as well. He's from the maintenance team."

"Henry will be glad he missed this," Bessie said.

"Aye, he will," Doug agreed. "He was plenty shook up by what went on Friday night, you know. At least today he wasn't anywhere near here when things went wrong."

"You can just wait here for John," Doona told Bessie. "I've got to go and help sort out the interviews with the audience. There's quite a few more of them today than there were Friday night, even if a lot of them did sneak away during the interval."

Bessie and Doug set up the small table and chairs in the same way that they had been set up on Friday evening. Bessie thought about moving the panels back into place with a chair for herself behind them again, but decided against it. All of the main cast members knew her by now. If they didn't want her in the room, they could tell the inspector that, but she wasn't going to stay out of sight in a corner.

Once Doug was happy that the room was set up the way the inspector would want it, he left Bessie there and headed out to see what else needed doing.

Bessie sank down into one of the chairs. She'd brought along one of her larger handbags and now she dug inside it for a book. There were at least two in there, and she let fate chose for her by simply pulling out the first one she touched.

She'd brought her picnic hamper with her as well, so now she helped herself to a handful of custard creams and settled in to read. It was nearly an hour before the inspector finally joined her, and Bessie was absorbed in imagining what might happen if she, too, simply turned up at CIA headquarters and offered her services as a spy.

Of course, she'd reasoned to herself, it would make more sense if she applied at MI-6, the British Intelligence service. Otherwise, she totally agreed with her book's heroine, though. Why didn't spy agencies hire the elderly, who had an entire life's worth of experiences behind them, and a great deal of extra time on their hands?

Bessie didn't have a husband or children to worry about. She could travel the world, carrying out missions, and hardly anyone would even notice she'd gone. With nothing else to do in the tiny storage room, Bessie had set the book aside and given the notion some semi-serious thought. By the time John joined her, she'd decided that she would miss her little cottage by the sea too much to leave. She was just rejoining the action with the fictional elderly spy when the inspector opened the door and walked in.

He looked exhausted, and Bessie handed him a chocolate Bourbon biscuit as he sat down, before he even spoke. After a surprised look, the man ate the biscuit as if he hadn't been fed in months. Bessie pulled out the packet and handed it to him. About half the container disappeared before the inspector spoke.

"Thank you. Those really hit the spot," he told Bessie. "I didn't realise I was hungry, but clearly I needed something."

"I have digestives and custard creams if you fancy anything else," Bessie replied. She smiled to herself as she watched him think about it.

"No, better not," he replied eventually, patting his flat stomach. "Anyway, we have a lot to do and I need to get around to Noble's to talk to Sienna as soon as I possibly can, as well."

"How is Sienna?"

"Better than she might have been," John said with a sigh. "She was conscious and her vital signs were good when she left here, anyway. The paramedics think she may well have a broken leg and a concussion, but it could have been much worse. She fell a pretty long way and she landed in a pile of broken wooden beams. She could easily have been killed."

"Did she tell you anything useful before they took her away?" Bessie asked.

"No, not really," John told her. "She was pretty shaken up."

Bessie frowned. "I'm guessing that you don't think it was an accident."

"No," John said. "I don't think it was an accident. From what I could see, it looked as if someone pulled a number of nails out of at least one of the main support beams. It's possible they did more than that. There's an accident investigation team on-site at the moment, inspecting everything. There were a crowbar and a hammer behind the stage, right next to the steps for the balcony. Anyone could have used them to pull out the nails."

"Why were they there?" Bessie asked.

"No one is sure," John sighed. "Jack, the maintenance man on duty, swears that all of the tools and equipment were put away before the show started, but Bob remembers Jack working on a loose step right up until two o'clock. It's possible he left the tools there when the extras began to take to the stage. Regardless, the tools were kept in an unlocked closet behind the ticket booth. Anyone could have simply walked in and taken what they wanted. I can't see anyone stopping a member of the cast from borrowing a hammer. Bob said the entire cast has been on the site since ten this morning."

"What about the audience or the extras?" Bessie asked.

John shrugged. "As with Scott's murder, we aren't ruling anyone out at this early stage. The extras have to be more likely than the audience. Doug was on duty next to the stage, at least during the show and the interval, and I think he would have intercepted any audience member that might have wandered back there. Unfortunately, he was on the opposite side of the stage from the balcony, and he doesn't think he saw anything significant."

"Presumably the extras were all over the place back there, though," Bessie said thoughtfully.

"They were," John agreed. "I'm hoping at least one of them might have noticed something significant, but I'm not sure that any of them had any reason for wanting to hurt Sienna."

"Are you sure Sienna was the target, though?" Bessie asked. "On Friday night the Juliet role was played by Penny."

John rubbed a hand over his eyes. "Maybe I will have a few custard creams," he said eventually. After he'd eaten a handful of biscuits, he continued. "In answer to your question, no, I'm not sure Sienna was the target. It's also possible that someone was just trying to disrupt the show, with no clear target."

"Surely if it was one of the players, they were putting themselves in danger as well, though," Bessie said, thinking hard. "The people on stage were at risk for getting hit with flying bits of debris, and anyone standing under the platform might have been really hurt."

"A few of the extras did sustain minor injuries," John told her. "Just cuts and bruises, but, as you say, it could have been worse."

Bessie sighed. "I'm trying to remember who was on stage when it happened. William was there, but he was about as far away from the balcony as you could get."

"Did you get the feeling he was trying to stay away from the balcony?" John asked.

Bessie shrugged. "I'm pretty sure he stood in the same sort of place on Friday," she said. "He was meant to be Romeo, watching Juliet from afar, right?"

John nodded. "I thought the staging was about the same as Friday, also, but I wanted your impression."

"I don't think either Penny or Adam was on the stage during the scene," Bessie said thoughtfully.

"No, they were both backstage when the accident happened," John confirmed. "I suppose, on some level, that makes them the most likely suspects."

"What about Candy?" Bessie asked.

John nodded. "She's also a possibility. She was definitely behind the stage between acts."

"But what possible motive could she have had for hurting Sienna?"

"Penny might have been the target," John reminded her.

Bessie sighed. "I can't see any reason why Candy would have wanted to hurt Penny, either."

"Neither can I," John sighed. "I think we'd better get on with questioning everyone."

The inspector went to the door and asked the constable stationed there to start bringing the main cast members in to him, one at a time.

"I want to leave Candy for last. I'm hoping she might be closer to sober by then."

Bessie nodded.

"I think I'm going to have to ask you to wait outside," John continued. "The Chief Constable is on holiday at the moment, so I just might be okay with letting you sleep in the corner during the first round of interviews, but I don't think I can risk having you in here for another round."

Bessie opened her mouth to protest, but the door opened and the constable ushered Adam into the room.

John frowned. "I asked for William Baldwin first," he said to the constable.

"I'm afraid I rather insisted on being first," Adam said, before the policeman could speak. "I'm absolutely desperate to get to the hospital to be with Sienna, you see."

"No one is going to be seeing Sienna tonight," John told him. "She'll be under police protection for at least the next twenty-four hours."

Adam nodded. "I think that's wonderful," he said in a relieved tone. "I'm glad she'll be protected, but I want to be there, just so she knows I'm there, even if I can't see her."

"You sound very devoted for a man who was threatening to replace her with an extra before the show," the inspector remarked.

Adam flushed. "We weren't getting along before the accident. I'll admit to that. She quit the troupe on Friday night and then had to beg for her place back after Scott's death. But she still wasn't happy. She kept telling me that she'd be gone as soon as Candy sorted everything out for her. Sienna had, or rather has, big dreams, and she isn't going to let me stop her from achieving them."

"Let's sit down, "John suggested. "I need to get a formal statement."

Adam sighed and sank into a chair. John took a seat on the opposite side of the table and waved the constable into a chair next to him.

"Miss Cubbon, if you'd like to wait outside," he began.

"She can stay," Adam interrupted. "I just want to get it over with as quickly as possible and find a taxi. I thought I'd run back to the hotel and pack Sienna a bag. I'm sure she'll be wanting her own nightclothes and things."

"I'm sure she will," John agreed.

Bessie sank into a chair near the door, and tried to look inconspicuous as John began.

"When did you find out that Sienna was going to be playing Juliet in that scene today?"

Adam looked surprised. "When did I.....oh, but that's genius," he told the inspector. "I never even thought of that, but you're right. No one wanted to hurt Sienna. Someone was after Penny."

"I didn't say that," John pointed out.

"No, but it's obvious. No one knew that Sienna was going to do that scene until the very end of the interval. William called us all together backstage with a few changes just before we were due to go back on. He rearranged a few of the scenes and he put Sienna into the Romeo and Juliet skit. As soon as the conversation was finished, we all headed into the tent to get changed. No one would have had time to do anything to the balcony after that. Penny must have been the target."

"Did William normally make changes like that in the middle of a show?" John asked.

"No," Adam shook his head. "Not normally, although this show hasn't been anything like normal for us, so it's hard to be certain. You can't really rearrange scenes if you're doing straight Shakespeare, can you? And you usually don't change lead actresses halfway through a show, either."

"Any idea why William made the changes?"

"He's trying to persuade Sienna to stay with the company, and if that means making Penny unhappy, well, that's a step he's obviously prepared to take."

"How unhappy was Penny?"

"She was devastated," Adam said with a sigh. "I'm sure she's convinced that William is going to replace her with Sienna, both personally and professionally."

"Is he?" John asked.

Adam shrugged. "He might be thinking about it, but I'd like to think I'll have some say in the outcome. I'm not giving up Sienna without a fight. Oh, I don't mind if she starts getting bigger parts in the shows. She's worked hard for the group; she deserves them. But I'm not going to just stand by and let William worm his way into her bed, that's for sure."

"So who do you think tampered with the balcony?"

Adam shook his head. "Are you sure it wasn't just an accident?" he asked plaintively.

"I'm positive," John assured him.

"If there had been more time after William's announcement and before the second half started, I think I'd suspect Penny, but as it happened, Penny had to be the target. The only person who could benefit from something happening to Penny is Candy."

"Candy?" John's face revealed nothing. Bessie knew that if Adam looked at her, he'd see shock written all over hers.

"Yeah, Candy," Adam repeated. "She's trying to get her old job back, you see. I guess if you're a manager and your only client dies, you suddenly find yourself without any income. She wants to rejoin the troupe, and if something happened to Penny, William would have no choice but to hire her."

"Killing Penny seems a bit drastic," the inspector replied. "I mean, surely she could just ask William for a job?"

Adam shook his head. "She probably didn't mean to kill Penny," he argued. "She was probably just trying to get her out of the show for a little while. Penny and Candy have a sort of love-hate relationship, because Candy had an affair with William when she first joined the troupe."

"Well, that's one theory," John said. He asked Adam a few more questions, pinning down everything the man had done that day, which Bessie found incredibly dull. Really, it seemed that Adam had done nothing but eat and rehearse for the entire day until time for the show.

"And you're certain you didn't see anyone doing any work on the balcony today?" John double-checked as the interview wrapped up.

"I'm certain," Adam replied. "But I probably wouldn't have paid any attention to anyone if they had been hammering or sawing or whatever. The crew moved everything yesterday from the old location to the new one and they were adjusting things all day yesterday and then again this morning."

John nodded. "If you think of anything that might help, please get in touch," he told the man.

Adam nodded. "Can I go see Sienna now?" he asked anxiously.

"You can certainly go to Noble's," John answered. "But, as I said, no one will be seeing Sienna tonight, except, hopefully, me."

"What did you think of all of that?" the inspector asked Bessie after Constable Clague had escorted Adam from the room.

"I just don't see Candy being that desperate," Bessie said.

"I'm not sure she was sober enough to do any carpentry," John said. "Although she is an actress. Could she have been pretending to be drunk?"

"She certainly smelled drunk." Bessie gave a small shudder as she remembered. "And I'm pretty sure it wasn't just her clothes."

The knock on the door interrupted the conversation. The young constable ushered William into the room.

"I must say, I am getting quite tired of seeing you," he said to the inspector in a crisp upper-crust British accent.

"Likewise, I'm sure," John muttered under his breath as he stood up to greet the man. "I'll try to keep this short," he said out loud. "Please have a seat."

After checking that William didn't care about Bessie's presence, the inspector walked the man through his day, checking that he hadn't seen anyone near the balcony at any time.

"I suppose there might have been," William said. "I can't say I pay all that much attention to the crew and the extras. Really, Adam handles most of that sort of thing." He waved a hand dismissively. "I'm running the troupe. I have far more important things to worry about."

"When did you decide to give the Juliet role to Sienna?" John asked.

"Oh, heavens, last night. Penny was terrible last night. She missed her cue and then she garbled up her lines. I almost fired her on the spot, but, well, we've been through a lot together, so I decided to simply cut her part."

"When did you tell her?"

"I told everyone between acts. I called all of the principal actors together and told them that I was rearranging things slightly and swapping Sienna into Penny's place in the balcony scene. I had to rearrange the scenes in order to give Sienna time to change into the Juliet costume, you see."

"I'm surprised Sienna was ready to take on the part. Surely there were lots of lines for her to learn?"

"She's been Penny's understudy for years," William replied. "We often run rehearsals where Sienna would stand in for Penny, just to change things up. I knew Sienna was more than ready to take on the scene."

"So who do you think tampered with the balcony?"

William shrugged. "I should think it's obvious," he said. "Adam wants to keep Sienna with the troupe at all costs. He didn't know I was going to be expanding Sienna's role; he was targeting Penny, of course. I assume he thought if he could get Penny out of the way, Sienna could move into the starring role and then she wouldn't want to leave anymore."

"Killing Penny seems extreme," John said.

"Oh, I'm sure he didn't want to kill her," William answered. "He just wanted her out of the show for a short time. I'm sure he thought that Sienna would get rave reviews once she took over Penny's job and then I wouldn't be able to put Penny back into the lead role again once she'd recovered."

"Where does Candy fit into all of this?"

William shrugged. "I haven't the faintest idea," he said. "I know she was here today, but I don't know why."

"It's been suggested to me that she wanted her old job back."

"Really?" William sounded shocked. "What an interesting idea."

"Would you take her back?"

"I simply don't know," William said, still sounding surprised. "I mean, the thought never occurred to me. I'll have to think about it. Of course, now, with Sienna out of the show, we are rather desperately in need of some talent."

The inspector asked a few more questions, but William had nothing useful to add to his statement. After Clague showed him out, John sat back in his chair.

"I need a couple of digestives now," he said with a sigh.

Bessie nodded and handed him the biscuit packet. After John took a few, she grabbed one herself.

"None of them are shy about accusing others, are they?" Bessie asked.

"It's interesting that no one seems to think what happened today was a murder attempt," he said in reply.

"Do you think it was a murder attempt?" Bessie asked.

"I'm keeping an open mind," John replied. "The bigger question, for me, is whether it's tied to Scott's murder. No one we've talked to yet seems to think it is, but it certainly could be."

"There can't be two people in the troupe with murder on their minds, can there?" Bessie asked.

The inspector didn't get to reply. Instead, Penny swept into the room with the constable almost chasing behind her. She was back in her basic black T-shirt and trousers with black trainers on her feet.

"Oh, thank goodness," she gasped, rushing towards Inspector Rockwell. "I thought you'd never get around to me, and I'm so scared." She sat down across from the inspector and took his hands in hers.

"Someone tried to kill me," she said in a quavering voice. "I've never been so frightened in my life."

John cleared his throat and then looked at Bessie. She nearly chuckled at the desperation she saw in his eyes.

"Penny, please calm down," Bessie said, leaning over to rub her back gently. "Take a deep breath and just relax. Whatever happened tonight, you're completely safe in here."

Penny looked over at Bessie and then blinked back the tears that welled up in her eyes. "Bessie, thank you so much for being here," she said. Penny let go of John's hands to grasp Bessie's tightly. "But what can I do? I'm so scared."

"Why do you think someone was trying to kill you?" John asked, his voice clipped and professional now that Penny had released his hands.

"Well, who else could they have been targeting?" Penny asked, letting go of Bessie's hands to wave hers in the air. "I was supposed to be on that balcony, not Sienna."

"When did you find out that Sienna was doing the part tonight instead of you?" the inspector asked.

"Just before the second half started," Penny said quietly. "Just before we were due to go on."

"I've been told you were quite upset," John told her.

"I guess you could say that," Penny replied with a shrug. "I should have seen it coming. It's exactly the sort of thing that William does. It's all about what's best for the troupe and he won't let emotions get in the way of what he thinks is best. Sienna was threatening to leave, and by giving her a bigger part, he was hoping to keep her. Intellectually, I understand why he did it, even if emotionally I'm devastated."

Now that she'd calmed down, the inspector ran her through her day. Like the others, Penny didn't recall seeing anything out of the ordinary during the day.

"Just one last question, then," John told her. "Who do you think tampered with the balcony?"

Penny flushed and looked down at her lap where she had been wringing her hands throughout the conversation.

"I'm not sure I feel comfortable speculating," she said softly.

John exchanged glances with Bessie, who picked up on his cue. "Penny, John just wants your opinion. You know these people. They're your family. He's got to try to work this out from the outside looking in. You're on the inside and you must have some thoughts about who might have done it. Nothing you say is going to get repeated outside of this room, and you might just help the police work out not only who sabotaged the stage, but who killed Scott."

Penny nodded at Bessie and then covered her face with her hands for a moment. When she pulled her hands away, she lifted her chin and inhaled sharply. "The only person I can think of that might have done it is Sienna," she said, gazing into Bessie's eyes.

"Why Sienna?" Bessie asked, doing her best to hide her surprise.

"She wants my job and my boyfriend," Penny answered. "Getting rid of me would get her both things."

"Surely if she'd damaged the balcony, she wouldn't have been willing to go on it," John suggested.

"She probably thought it would just shake and scare me or something. I'm sure she didn't expect it to collapse," Penny argued. "Anyway, from what I could see, she's barely got a scratch on her. It could have been, maybe should have been, a lot worse. She must have realised what was happening and braced herself or something."

"Thank you for your time," John said. "You're free to go now."

"But what about protection?" Penny gasped. "You can't send me back out there without any protection. Someone tried to kill me."

"You said yourself you thought Sienna did it," John pointed out. "She's safely tucked up in hospital. She won't be able to get anywhere near you for at least a couple of days."

"But what if it wasn't her?" Penny asked, tears beginning to flow down her cheeks. "What if it was someone else?"

"Would you like to suggest anyone in particular?" the inspector asked.

"Oh, no," Penny said, swiping ineffectually at her tears. "I can't imagine why anyone else would want to harm me in any way."

"Then you should be absolutely fine," John suggested.

"I'm just so frightened," Penny sobbed.

Bessie sighed. "I have a friend that runs a small hotel in Douglas," she told Penny. "Let me see if he has any rooms for tonight." She pulled out her mobile and made the quick phone call. When she put the phone down, she gave Penny a reassuring look.

At Bessie's request, the inspector tore a small sheet of paper from his notebook for Bessie to write on. "Here's the address," she told Penny, handing her the slip. "I'm sure Inspector Rockwell will have a constable escort you back to your hotel and then wait while you pack a few things. My friend, Harry, is expecting you. You'll be safe enough tucked up there for the night. Maybe things will look brighter tomorrow."

Penny's thanks went on long enough to start annoying Bessie, and it seemed to her like hours before the woman finally left.

"She thinks William tried to kill her," the inspector said, as the door finally shut behind her.

"It certainly seems that way," Bessie agreed. "And she must know that we suspect as much."

"It was kind of you to help her out. I hope it won't be too costly. I can't see Penny paying for the stay with your friend, and I can't see her moving out in a hurry."

Bessie shrugged. "Harry is a very good friend. He'll give me a good deal on Penny's room, no matter how long she stays."

"But will he still be your friend after Ms. Drama Queen descends upon him?" John asked.

Bessie laughed. "Oh goodness, I hadn't thought of that," she said.

Moments later Constable Clague was back again, this time with a seemingly sober Candy in tow.

"I have a terrible headache," Candy announced as she sat down across from the inspector.

Bessie offered her tablets, but Candy demurred. "I took some of my own stuff a little while ago; it just hasn't kicked in yet," she told Bessie. "But thank you anyway."

John ran her through her day, which didn't take long, as Candy had spent much of it sleeping.

"I wanted to get here for the whole show," she said, "but I overslept and then, after I'd had some lunch, it was already nearly two. By the time I arrived the door was locked."

"A lot of people came to see the show today," John said.

"Yeah, but luckily for me, not many of them wanted to stay for the second half," Candy said, laughing. "As soon as the first act was over, the door flew open and I was in."

"Why were you backstage between the scenes?" the inspector asked.

"I wanted a quick word with everyone. I'm trying to figure out what I want to do with the rest of my life. I wanted to get a feel for how everyone was feeling towards me."

"You're thinking of rejoining the troupe?"

"Well, I'm not sure what else to do," Candy said frankly. "Scott was my ticket out, you know? Oh, I have a few connections here and there, but what I don't have is another client with his star power. Say what you like about the man, he was hugely talented."

"What about Sienna?" John asked.

Candy shook her head. "Look, I offered to help her out, and I think I could have landed her a few little jobs here and there, especially with Scott's name on my books, you know? But she can't act to save her life. She's pretty and she's ambitious and that can take you quite a long way if you have the right connections, but I reckon her chances at the big time died with Scott, just like mine did. I'm just trying to find a way to hold on now until I can collect the insurance money from Scott's death. They won't pay out until there's an official verdict on what happened to him."

"So who do you think tampered with the balcony?"

Candy shrugged. "My best guess would be William," she said. "I think Sienna was driving him crazy, demanding a bigger part and threatening to leave every two seconds. I think he fixed the balcony and then offered Sienna the lead role, knowing the balcony wasn't safe."

"Do you think he was trying to kill her?"

"Oh, good heavens, no," Candy laughed until she began to cough. "Sorry," she said when she could breathe again. "No, I don't think he wanted to kill her. I doubt he even wanted to hurt her. I suspect he just wanted to shake her up a little bit. I bet he figured the balcony would creak and shake while she was on it and she'd decide she didn't want to be the star after all, that's all."

"It's a theory," John said noncommittally, writing something in his notebook.

As the door shut behind Candy, he let out a huge sigh. "Sometimes I think I should have been a postman," he told Bessie.

She laughed. "You would have found it boring after a few weeks," she replied.

"Maybe, but some days…." he trailed off, flipping through his notebook aimlessly.

"You need a good night's sleep," Bessie suggested.

"Yeah, and a holiday," he grumbled back. "Let's get out of here."

They quickly tidied up the room as much as they could and then headed out. Hugh and the other constables were still working their way through the audience, the extras and the vendors, and the inspector left Bessie on her own so he could have a chat with Hugh.

"Okay, Hugh's going to handle things here," he told Bessie when he rejoined her. "And he's going to make sure Doona gets home safely. Let's go."

"You have to get into Douglas and talk to Sienna, right?" Bessie asked. "Why don't I just wait here and get a ride home with Hugh when he's done?"

"That could be hours," John replied. "I'll run you home. You don't need to sit around here all night."

Bessie protested a bit more, but John wouldn't change his mind. They made their way back to his car and then headed out of Peel towards Laxey.

"I never took your statement," John said tiredly as he drove.

"I don't have anything interesting to put in it," Bessie told him.

"But I do need a formal statement from you," he said with a sigh. "Is it too much to ask that you come by the station tomorrow sometime?"

"I'd be happy to," Bessie assured him. "I'll come in the morning and then maybe I can take you and Doona to lunch, Hugh too, if he's around."

"That sounds good," John agreed. "I'll put you in my diary for eleven and then plan on lunch at midday."

"I'll ring Doona's answering machine and let her know," Bessie said. "I suppose I'll ring Hugh's as well."

"No need," John assured her. "He's meeting me later tonight to go over everything. I'll tell him then."

Plans in place, Bessie settled back to enjoy the view as they made their way to her cottage.

At home she felt restless, but she forced herself to curl up with her book and read through the rest of the spy story she'd started at the castle. After all the biscuits she'd eaten through the afternoon, she wasn't terribly hungry for dinner. She reheated some soup that she's tucked in her freezer some weeks earlier and toasted a few slices of bread to go with it.

After dinner, she took a walk on the beach, enjoying how different it felt to when she normally walked early in the morning. She smiled and nodded at several families that were making sandcastles and splashing in the sea. Encouraged by their actions, Bessie slipped off her shoes and walked to the water's edge, thinking she'd enjoy the coolness of the water on her feet. She quickly changed her mind as what felt like ice-cold water washed over her toes.

Laughing at herself, she headed further up the beach, enjoying the way the warm sand squished under her bare feet. The water would be warmer in July and August, and she would, no doubt, try again, but she sternly told herself that there would be no more walking in the sea this month.

She pulled an old favourite off her bookshelf when she got back home and took herself upstairs to get ready for bed. Snuggling down under the covers, she read until she couldn't keep her eyes open any longer. She slept soundly and, as far as she could remember the next day, dreamlessly.

CHAPTER 11

On Monday morning Bessie woke up close to her normal time of six. She took a quick shower, patted on her favourite powder, dressed, and then made herself tea and cereal. She was out the cottage door for her walk before seven and had the beach almost entirely to herself.

She waved to a fisherman who was sitting on the low wall that ran along one section of the beach. He'd turned around as she'd shut her cottage door. Now he waved back and then turned back to watch the day's calm sea.

Bessie walked past the new cottages, glancing in where curtains were open. She was appalled at the mess she saw in most of the rooms. It's a wonder there's any sand left out here, she thought, as she walked past yet another cottage where she could see trails of sandy footprints stretching from the patio doors into the cottage interior.

One cottage was neat as a pin, and Bessie wondered if it was empty. It would be strange for there to be a vacancy at this time of year, but last-minute cancellations did happen. Once again, when she reached the Pierce mansion, she thought about climbing up for a good look around.

A light rain, almost more of a mist, changed her mind. The narrow wooden stairs were quite steep, and having fallen down them once, she wasn't in a hurry to repeat the experience. She turned towards home, quickening her pace a bit in light of the weather.

As she reached the cottages, she again found herself peeking inside where curtains were open. No one seemed to be awake in most of the cottages, although she did spot one exhausted looking woman rocking a crying baby. In another she saw a toddler in his pyjamas eating cereal right out of a box. A carton of milk had tipped over on the table, and she watched for a moment as it dripped steadily every time the child bumped the table. The pile of clothes under the table didn't look clean anyway, so the fact that milk was spilling on them probably didn't matter much, she thought. As she passed the single tidy cottage, she was shocked when she glanced through the glass patio door and met the eyes of someone looking out.

After a moment's indecision, Bessie squared her shoulders and waved to the stranger. It was no good pretending she hadn't been looking, and if the cottage inhabitants wanted privacy, they needed to learn to pull their curtains shut. It was a public beach, after all.

She needn't have worried. Her nervous wave was returned, and the occupant also gave Bessie a cheery look. Bessie slowed her pace as the cottage's inhabitant slid open the patio door.

"Good morning to you," the other woman called.

Bessie returned the greeting, studying the woman as she emerged from the cottage. Bessie would have put her somewhere in her mid-sixties. She had grey hair and bright blue eyes, and was tending towards plump. About Bessie's height, she was dressed in casual and comfortable clothing, and her bright smile made the drizzly morning suddenly feel warmer.

"Please tell me you're the owner of that adorable little cottage down there," the woman said. "Joan and I have been wanting to meet you."

Bessie wasn't sure what to make of that, but she admitted to ownership of her home.

"Oh, you must pardon me," the other woman laughed. "I think my manners have deserted me. When I'm on holiday I'm simply not myself. I'm Janet Markham. My sister, Joan, and I have been holidaying on the island for years, but this is our first stay in Laxey. We love our little hired cottage, but we're both mad jealous of yours."

Bessie laughed, delighted by the friendly woman. "I'm Bessie Cubbon, and I love my little cottage as well," she told Janet. "It's been my home since I was eighteen."

"Oh, my," Janet sighed. "How very fortunate you are."

Bessie nodded. "I quite agree with you."

"But Joan will never forgive me if I don't ask you what your cottage is called. I mean, we've both tried reading it out from the sign by your door, but I'm guessing it's Manx, so we're probably pronouncing it all wrong. And we're both desperate to know what it means, as well."

Bessie nodded. "Treoghe Bwaane," she replied, confident of her Manx pronunciation of that much, if little else, in the difficult Celtic tongue. "It means widow's cottage," she told the other woman.

"Oh, are you a widow?" Janet asked. "I am sorry."

"Actually, I'm not," Bessie told her. "I never married. The cottage already had its name when I bought it."

"Really?" Janet beamed at her. "Neither Joan nor I ever married, either. We were both schoolteachers in our local village school until we retired. Now we have more time to travel, although neither of us wants to go too far from home. I've no interest in getting on a plane, and Joan shares that sentiment."

"Janet, to whom are you speaking?" The voice startled both women. From behind Janet, another woman emerged. If Bessie had seen them in a crowd of thousands, she could have instantly identified them as sisters. Joan appeared to be a few years older than her sister, and was a few pounds lighter, but otherwise there was little difference between the pair.

After Janet performed the necessary introductions, Joan shook her head.

"My sister never has mastered her manners," Joan said with an affectionate grin. "Imagine keeping you standing out in the rain to chat. Do you have time to come in for a cuppa?"

Bessie glanced at her watch and nodded. "Maybe just a quick one," she said.

An hour later she emerged from the small holiday home stuffed full of tea and homemade biscuits. It seemed that Joan baked nearly every day, wherever they were.

"That's why this cottage has been so good for us," Janet explained. "We can self-cater to our hearts' content."

Bessie made her way home feeling as if she'd made two new friends. The sisters had only arrived on Saturday for a fortnight-long stay, and Bessie was looking forward to having a chance to see them again. I just need to work out who killed Scott first, she thought to herself.

Back in her own snug home, she had little time left before she had to report to the police station. The light rain had blown over, and the sun was shining a short time later as she climbed into the taxi she'd ordered. Her favourite driver, Dave, greeted her cheerfully.

"Mark was pleased with you the other day," he said to Bessie during the short journey. "He said he came out to your cottage and picked up some gorgeous actress."

"Yes, well, Penny's an actress at any rate," Bessie replied with a shrug.

Dave laughed. "I'd rather drive you any day," he told Bessie gallantly.

At the station, Doona made Bessie a cup of tea while she waited for Inspector Rockwell to finish a phone call.

"I won't offer you biscuits, because we're going for lunch later," Doona told her.

Bessie thought about arguing, but the biscuits she'd eaten with the Markham sisters had been quite filling and very tasty. Doona only ever stocked plain digestives at the police station, otherwise the young constables would eat them all every time her back was turned. She had a hard enough time keeping the unexciting digestives away from them.

"Ah, Bessie, thank you for coming in." The inspector greeted her with a smile a moment later. "Come on back and let's get your statement sorted, shall we?"

Bessie sighed as she sat down on the hard chair in the inspector's office. "I feel as if I've done this an awful lot lately," she complained.

"Let's hope this is the last time," John replied. He took her back through everything that she'd done the previous day, starting with breakfast.

They walked slowly through her entire day.

"Why do you have me start with breakfast?" Bessie asked. "Nothing relevant happened until I got to the castle."

"But once you start running through your day, you get into a rhythm," John explained. "By taking me through the ordinary parts of your day, you start to talk without really thinking about it. Then, when we get to the difficult parts, you're used to giving me what I need."

"I suppose so," Bessie said doubtfully.

The inspector laughed. "Well, that's what they taught me in CID training school, anyway," he told her. "It may not be true, but I've found over the years that I like to work that way, regardless. If nothing else, you can learn a lot about a person if you find out about the minutiae of their lives."

"I can certainly believe that," Bessie said. "I'm afraid to ask what you learned about me the first time you interviewed me."

John grinned. "I learned that you are very smart and you don't like to waste your time," he said. "And that you have an encyclopedic knowledge of the good people of Laxey."

Bessie laughed. "That makes me sound a bit nosy," she protested.

John smiled. "Should we get on with your statement, then?" he asked, changing the subject.

"I don't think I've helped at all," she said when they'd finished. "I wasn't in the right place to see anyone sabotaging the balcony and besides, you were sitting next to me the whole time."

John nodded. "I wasn't expecting anything new from you," he assured Bessie. "But every word helps build up the bigger picture. Remember, it isn't just me that reads these statements. There is a section of CID in Douglas that spends all of their time analysing active cases. They'll read your statement along with mine and Hugh's and Doona's, and compare them to what was said by everyone else in the VIP area, and then the audience as a whole. They'll look for discrepancies and patterns and that sort of thing."

Bessie nodded. "I just wish I could have helped more."

"You've done your fair share," John told her. "Now, we have a few minutes before lunch. I shouldn't discuss Sienna with you, but you sat in on the all the other interviews, so I can't see what it will hurt."

"You were able to see her last night, then?"

"I was. And, interestingly, she's requested that no one else be allowed in to see her, at least for now."

"How did Adam take that news?" Bessie asked.

"He wasn't pleased, but I told him it was doctor's orders, rather than letting him know that Sienna didn't want to see him."

"That was nice of you," Bessie remarked. "Why is she refusing to see people?"

John shrugged. "I couldn't work out if she's genuinely afraid of someone or if she's just wanting some space for a little while."

"After travelling with the same people for so many years, I have to say, I'd be in favour of some peace and quiet."

"Agreed. I didn't get the feeling that she was worried that someone might try to hurt her again, but she's an actress, so she might have been deliberately misleading me."

"Penny was the only one who seemed to think what happened was a murder attempt," Bessie remarked.

"And Sienna's with the majority on that point. She didn't think anyone was trying to kill anyone," John told her.

"So what did she have to say? Did she have any idea who might have done it?"

John held up a hand. "I'll save her suspicions for last," he told her. "Her basic statement was much the same as the others. She didn't know William was going to give her Penny's part until just before the second half started, but she knew all of the lines and cues from rehearsals."

"It still put a lot of pressure on her, changing things at the last minute like that."

"From what she said, she was delighted. I think she'd been making quite a few threats about leaving before the show started," John said.

"Did she say anything else interesting?" Bessie asked.

"Not really. She didn't see anyone doing anything with the balcony. She said that if she had, she certainly wouldn't have climbed up on it. Apparently it felt somewhat wobbly to her as she climbed up the stairs, but she just assumed it was badly constructed. It never occurred to her that it might be dangerous."

"So who does she think damaged it?" Bessie demanded.

"Penny," John replied.

Bessie's jaw dropped. "But that doesn't even make sense," she said, shaking her head. "Penny thought she was going to be up there. Why on earth would she put her own life in danger like that?"

"Sienna thinks Penny thought she wouldn't get hurt too badly when it fell, and that she would garner lots of sympathy from William. She reckons Penny was hoping William might propose if he was suddenly confronted with the thought that he could have lost her."

Bessie sighed. "It seems far-fetched," she said. "But if a woman is prepared to pretend to have an affair with someone, thinking that will help with her relationship, maybe she is capable of putting her own life in danger for the same reason."

John shrugged. "I can't imagine doing either, but Sienna seems to believe it."

"It's interesting that she didn't tie the accident to Scott's murder, either," Bessie said thoughtfully. "None of them seem to have made that connection."

"No, they haven't," John agreed. "And as you said earlier, aside from Penny, they all insisted that whoever tampered with the balcony wasn't trying to kill anyone, no matter who the target might have actually been."

"So, does that mean that the two incidents aren't connected?" Bessie asked.

"I'm not a huge fan of coincidence, especially in the middle of a murder investigation," John replied. "At the moment, I'm investigating the two crimes separately, but I'm looking for connections that I think must be there, somewhere."

A tap on the door saved Bessie having to admit that she felt completely clueless. Doona stuck her head in.

"It's nearly lunchtime," she said cheerfully. "I've booked us a table at *La Terrazza,* and we don't want to be late."

"Oh, goodness," Bessie exclaimed. "That does sound good. I think we were just about finished, weren't we?" she asked the inspector.

He laughed. "If we weren't already, we would be now," he said. "I couldn't possibly make us late for lunch."

The trio exited out the back of the station, climbing into the inspector's car for the short journey towards the waterfront.

"I just heard that Andy Caine is doing all the puddings at *La Terrazza* until the end of the summer," Bessie told the others. "He's accepted a place at a culinary college in Leeds, starting in September, but for now he's baking cakes and pies for *La Terrazza.*"

"Is Anne still working there as well?" Doona asked about Andy's mother.

"No, Andy's insisted that she quit both her jobs and just take it easy for now. I saw her in Shopfast last week and she said she's going to start job hunting as soon as he goes off to school. Apparently she doesn't need the money now, but she's bored out of her mind just sitting around at home."

"She's earned a bit of a break," Doona said.

"She has indeed," Bessie agreed. "She's also thinking of taking a few classes at the college here on the island. She never even finished her A-levels, and that's always bothered her. Andy just wants her to be happy, so he's offered to pay for whatever classes she wants."

"I'm so very pleased for them both," Doona told Bessie. "Sometimes good things happen to good people."

"They do," Bessie agreed. "Maybe not as often as we'd like, but they really do."

The restaurant was busy and Bessie was glad that Doona had

thought to make a booking. Hugh was already at the table, working his way through a plate of garlic bread, when they arrived.

"I'm sure you got that for us all to share," John commented as he sat down and took a piece.

"Oh, um, sure," Hugh stammered, flushing. "Please, help yourself," he said to Doona and Bessie with a marked lack of enthusiasm.

Bessie laughed. "You and John eat it," she told the man. "I'll order another plate of it for me and Doona to share."

Their waitress, Debbie, was a young woman who had spent some time in Bessie's spare room, so she was quick to take their order and very attentive.

"I'm sure I never thanked you for all those nights when you listened to my stupid teenaged drama," the girl told Bessie. "The least I can do to make up for it is make sure you have excellent service."

Bessie laughed. "I'm sure you did say 'thank you,'" she replied. "Otherwise, I wouldn't have let you come back."

Debbie laughed. "All my friends at uni say I'm ever so polite," she answered. "I'm sure you were a good part of that."

Bessie enjoyed having a chance to catch up with her young friend, even if the conversation was constantly interrupted by Debbie's work responsibilities.

In the middle of a busy restaurant, the foursome wasn't going to be able to discuss Scott's murder anyway, so no one was bothered by Debbie's frequent visits. Andy Caine stopped by as well.

"I suggest the shortbread," he told them with a chuckle. "I'll admit it. I've shamelessly stolen Aunt Bessie's recipe, but I make it fancier by plating it with a scoop of homemade vanilla ice cream and a warm caramel sauce."

"Sold," Hugh said with a laugh.

In the end, they all tried the suggested pudding and they all cleared their plates, in spite of the garlic bread and generous servings of Italian favourites they'd already eaten.

"We should do this more often," Bessie said as they slowly made their way out of the restaurant. "I don't think I'll need to eat again for a week."

"I should be okay until dinner time," Hugh said with a grin, making everyone laugh.

The inspector asked Hugh to give Bessie a ride home, as he had to get back to the station for a meeting. Doona rode back with him, sure she wouldn't be in too much trouble over her long lunch hour, since she'd been with the boss.

Back at home, Bessie decided that she needed to take another walk. She felt too full to just sit and read, and the cottage was tidy enough for now. The beach was busy, but Bessie didn't mind dodging sandcastles and rugby balls as she walked along it. She didn't see Joan and Janet anywhere, but they had mentioned heading out to Castle Rushen for the day, so presumably that's where they were.

This time, when she reached the stairs to Thie yn Traie, the Pierce family mansion, she decided to climb up and have a peek. The stairs felt a bit wobbly, but she made it safely to the top and then stood blinking in the bright sunlight.

She'd forgotten how large and how ugly the house was. From the beach, she could only see the wall of windows that faced out towards the sea. Now she looked at the many wings that jutted out from the main house, making the entire structure look like an unfortunately beached octopus.

She glanced around but didn't see anyone, so she walked forward slowly. She'd spent some time inside the mansion, but had only ever been in a few rooms. Now curiosity had her wanting to peer in as many windows as she could. Before she could make it to the closest windows, however, she was interrupted.

"Bessie? Bessie Cubbon? Is that you?" The voice surprised her and she quickly turned towards it. Someone was walking down the drive towards her, but with the sun behind him, she couldn't see who it was.

She stood still, waiting until he came closer. She was too old to be trying to run away and besides, she wasn't doing anything wrong, really. Maybe she was trespassing a little bit, but it wasn't like she was planning to do any damage to anything.

It was still a relief when the man got closer and she recognised him. "Robert Clague, I'm awfully glad it's you," she admitted.

"What are you doing up here?" he asked.

"I was just being nosy," Bessie said with a shrug. "I was inside once or twice, but I wanted another look before it was sold and someone new moved in."

"It looks pretty much the same, I'd imagine," Robert told her. "The family is selling it fully furnished. They didn't want to keep anything that might remind them of the island."

"That's so sad," Bessie said. "Especially after their many happy years here."

"I suppose after what happened it's understandable," Robert said.

"Of course it is," Bessie agreed. "Anyway, what are you doing here?"

"Manxman Security is guarding the property until it's sold. There are a lot of curiosity seekers and the like, and the family would rather not have nosy people poking around the place and taking pictures."

Bessie blushed. "Oh, dear," she said quietly.

Robert laughed. "Anyway, we've someone here twenty-four hours a day, seven days a week at the moment. Apparently a sale is practically agreed, though, so I suppose we'll be gone soon, unless the new owners are super security conscious as well."

"I don't suppose you know anything about the buyers?" Bessie asked hopefully.

"Unfortunately, no, I don't," he told her. "You should ring your advocate. He's handling everything."

"And he won't tell me anything until it's all public knowledge," she replied.

"I suppose that's how it should be," Robert suggested.

"Yes," Bessie agreed with a laugh. "It's just frustrating."

"Anyway, if I had a key, I'd let you have a wander around, but I don't," he told her apologetically. "But feel free to walk around and look in windows, if you'd like."

Bessie blushed again. "That's okay," she said. "I suppose I should get home and do something useful with the rest of the day. It was great to see you again, though."

"You too," he told her. He gave her a quick and unexpected hug, and then turned to walk back towards the small guardhouse that was just inside the gate. Bessie was quick to head back towards the stairs, embarrassed at having been caught snooping.

She was halfway home before the sheer ridiculousness of the situation hit her. She burst out laughing, shocking a couple of small children who were building a sandcastle near her feet. Apparently it was her day for embarrassing herself, she decided, as she quickly made her way home. No doubt Robert thought she was a nosy little old lady, and goodness only knew what those children and their parents thought of her.

Safely back in her little cottage, Bessie decided that she needed to lose herself in someone else's imagination and forget all about her awkward afternoon.

Having thoroughly enjoyed spending time with an elderly spy, she now turned to another favourite. This time the lady in question was the widow of an enterprising criminal who had left his lovely wife with a notebook full of contacts for whatever emergencies might arise. Bessie quickly forgot herself in the other woman's fictional world, which seemed to be suddenly full of unexpected calamities. The knock on her door was something of a shock.

Bessie walked to the door slowly, giving her mind time to refocus on the real world. It wasn't until she reached the door that she thought to wonder who it might be. It would be unusual for any of her young visitors to come over on a school night. The caller knocked again, while Bessie stood there, feeling uneasy.

She sighed and pulled the door open, annoyed with herself for her timid behaviour. Whomever she'd been expecting, it wasn't who she found there.

"Ah, so Penny was right about how to find you," Candy said with a huge smile. "I'm so glad I found you at home."

CHAPTER 12

*B*essie stared at her visitor with John Rockwell's words ringing in her ears. She needed to ring Doona; she'd promised she would.

"Candy, what an unexpected surprise," she said. "I was just going to take a short walk. Would you care to join me?"

Candy laughed throatily. "Don't want me in your house?" she asked. "I guess I can't blame you, with a murderer running around loose."

Bessie wasn't sure how to reply. "Not at all," she said hesitantly. "That is, I try to take a walk every day." And I've already had two today, she added, but only to herself.

"Fair enough," Candy said. "Hey, here's an idea. While we're walking, why don't you bring your phone and call your friend the police inspector? I bet he'd love to hear that I'm visiting."

Bessie sighed. "Actually, I'm going to ring my friend Doona," she told Candy. "She worries about me rather too much since someone tried to kill me."

Candy laughed again. "You call whomever you want," she told Bessie cheerfully. "I'm harmless. I just needed a break from all the drama."

"I can understand that," Bessie said dryly.

Candy laughed until a coughing fit started. Bessie went into the kitchen and fetched her a glass of water, leaving Candy on her doorstep, coughing violently.

"Oh, that's much better," Candy said after several swallows. "Okay, grab your phone and your keys and let's walk. I'll wait for you on the big rock out back. Penny told us all about it."

Candy was gone before Bessie replied, quickly disappearing behind the cottage. Bessie shut the door and then, after a moment's hesitation, locked it as well. Doona and the inspector are making me paranoid, she grumbled to herself as she headed to the phone. If she was quick, she could ring Doona now and save herself from having to ring her in front of the other woman.

Doona was still at the station, so Bessie was able to reach her right away.

"It's Bessie. Candy's just turned up at my door," she told her friend.

"Stay outside with her," Doona said, sounding anxious. "I'll be there as soon as I can."

Bessie slipped on her shoes, tucked her phone in a pocket and grabbed her keys. She let herself out her back door, locking it behind her. Candy was, as promised, sitting on the large rock. The tide was coming in and Bessie was careful to avoid the cold water as she approached the rock.

"Penny was right," Candy said quietly when Bessie reached her. "It's idyllic here."

"Thank you," Bessie said.

"I suppose those little cottages are expensive?" Candy asked, gesturing towards the cottages along the beach.

"They're holiday homes," Bessie told her. "I've no idea how much they cost to hire, though."

"Whatever it is, I'm sure I can't afford it," Candy said with a sigh.

"I was fortunate to buy my little place many, many years ago," Bessie said. "I couldn't possibly afford to buy anything now. Prices on the island have gone crazy in the last few years."

"How long have you had the cottage?"

"I bought it when I was eighteen," she told Candy. "I was left a small legacy which was just enough to buy the cottage and support me for a short while."

"What did you do when the money ran out?"

"Again, I had some luck," Bessie said. "My advocate helped me make some very clever investments. It's been more years than I want to count and the money hasn't run out yet."

Candy sighed. "I was never any good at saving money," she told Bessie. "I got paid what felt like a fortune to me for the two movies I starred in, but I spent every penny on living extravagantly. Why buy a car when you hire a limousine to take you everywhere? Why cook when you can eat in fancy restaurants every night? Unfortunately, after the second movie, the work dried up, but my lifestyle didn't adapt. And, to make matters worse, I don't think I learned anything from my mistakes."

"What do you mean?" Bessie asked.

Candy gave a short, humourless laugh. "Once Scott got hired to do *Market Square* the two of us went on a spending spree. We got rooms at a fancy London hotel and ate out every night." She shook her head.

"There were rumours flying that Scott was about to lose his job, as well," she confided in Bessie. "If he had, we'd have been stuck, penniless in London." She laughed again, harshly. "Of course, now I'm stuck, penniless, here."

"Which is why you were trying to get your job back with William," Bessie said.

"Exactly," Candy sighed deeply. "Everything I earned from working as Scott's agent is spent and my credit cards are at their limits. If William doesn't take me back, I'm not sure what I'll do. Eventually the insurance should give me a small boost, but that could take months to process, apparently."

Bessie didn't have any good advice to offer, but luckily Doona arrived in time to save her from admitting as much to Candy.

"There you two are," Doona said in an artificially bright voice. "Isn't a lovely afternoon to be sitting on the beach?"

Candy laughed. "No, not really," she said. "What I really want to do is get stinking drunk and complain about men. Anyone else want to join me?"

Doona exchanged glances with Bessie and then laughed. "You know, I could do with a session like that," she admitted. "I've had a rough time with men lately."

Bessie weighed up her options and then shrugged. "Why not?" she asked. "Let's go buy a couple bottles of wine and something for dinner."

Doona looked surprised and then laughed. "Why do I think this is all going to go badly wrong?" she asked.

"No doubt," Candy said seriously. "But what the he…, er, heck. Let's go for it."

Bessie grabbed her handbag and the trio climbed into Doona's car. The nearest large grocery shop was in Ramsey, so Doona headed there. Once inside, the trio split up. Doona and Candy headed for the wine section, while Bessie wandered the aisles, trying to work out what to prepare for her unexpected guests.

Candy and Doona found her standing in front of the meat counter, wearing a frown. "What sounds good?" Bessie asked the other two.

"Can you get pizza delivered to your cottage?" Candy asked. "That way no one has to fuss."

"Oh, but," Bessie began, but Doona interrupted.

"Candy's right. Let's just order pizza," she said. "No one in Laxey delivers," she told Candy. "But I can ring *La Terrazza* now and they'll have whatever we want ready when get there. It's very close to Bessie's cottage."

Bessie blinked a couple of times when she saw how many bottles of wine the other two women had selected. They'd also collected several bags of crisps and assorted crackers on their trip around the shop. Bessie and Doona insisted on paying, while Candy dug around in her handbag, seemingly unable to find her wallet.

"It's fine," Bessie assured the woman. "You can be our guest, just this once."

Candy flushed and muttered embarrassed words of thanks. While Doona loaded up the car, Bessie called in their order to *La Terraza*, ordering far more food than she expected they could eat. She'd much rather have leftovers than run out, especially with the amount of wine the other two seemed to be planning to drink. They'd need a lot of food to help soak up all that alcohol.

Doona dashed into the restaurant once they arrived back in Laxey and she was quickly back with several steaming pizza boxes.

"Oh, that smells amazing," Candy gasped as Doona set the boxes on the backseat next to her.

"Hang in there," Bessie laughed. "We're only a few minutes from home."

Back at Bessie's cottage, Doona carried in the pizza while Bessie and Candy brought in the bags from Shopfast. Bessie pulled plates and napkins out while Doona opened the first bottle of wine and poured generous helpings into glasses.

"I didn't know white wine went with pizza," Candy laughed.

"It probably doesn't," Doona told her. "But it's what sounded the best to me. You can have red if you prefer."

"It's all the same to me," Candy assured her. "Even when I had loads of money and bought the expensive stuff, it all tasted pretty much the same. At home I buy the big cardboard cartons of it, and that's pretty darn tasty when you need a drink, I can tell you."

The trio ate in relative silence for a while. Candy downed three glasses of wine with her pizza, while Bessie stuck to just the one. Doona drank faster than Bessie, but nowhere near as quickly as Candy. When the pizzas were just about finished, Doona spoke.

"Andy threw in a bonus," she told the others. "He said he's been trying new things and he was hoping we could taste-test this one and give him our thoughts." She opened the last pizza box. Inside was what looked like a huge chocolate chip cookie.

"That looks amazing," Candy groaned as she topped up her empty glass. "I wish I hadn't already eaten so much."

"It's a cookie pizza," Bessie said, staring at the surprise.

"Yep," Doona laughed. "Andy said that if people like them he might try decorating them for birthdays and special occasions. I gather it's an American thing that he's thinking might catch on over here."

"Well, it's worth trying," Bessie said, her mouth watering as she caught a whiff of warm melted chocolate, butter and vanilla.

Doona cut the cookie into slices like pizza and they each took one.

"This is wonderful," Candy sighed.

"It is really good," Bessie agreed. "I must ring Andy tomorrow and tell him I think the cookie pizza is a great idea."

Doona nodded. "I love it and it's exactly what I want for my next birthday. Unless I decide not to have birthdays anymore, that is."

Candy laughed heartily. "I say celebrate," she told Doona. "You can't stop yourself getting older, so you may as well have cake and make people buy you stuff."

Doona laughed. "That's great advice. Or maybe it just feels that way after two glasses of wine."

"Only two?" Candy shook her head. "You're falling behind already."

Doona drained her glass and then quickly refilled it. "Bessie," she said, slurring her words a bit. "I'm crashing on your couch tonight."

Bessie grinned. "You two can fight over the couch and the spare room," she told the pair. "Neither of you is going to be fit to go anywhere in another half hour."

"So how'd you end up here all alone?" Candy asked Bessie. "I mean, you never married? Why not?"

Bessie flushed and poured herself a second glass of wine. The first bottle was just about empty, but Doona was quick to jump up and open a second.

"I fell madly in love when I was sixteen," Bessie told Candy. "We were living in Ohio in those days. Then my parents decided to move back to the island, and they made me come with them and leave Matthew behind."

"That's horrible," Candy said angrily. "I wouldn't have stood for that."

"The times were very different then," Bessie told her. "Unmarried girls didn't argue with their parents. They did as they were told."

Candy laughed. "I never did what my parents told me to do," she said. "Maybe that's why I've ended up in such a mess. Although my parents weren't exactly...." she trailed off.

"Your parents weren't what?" Doona asked.

"Let's just say I didn't have a happy childhood and leave it at that, okay?" Candy asked. "There isn't enough wine on this island to get me talk about the things that I went through as a child."

Doona and Bessie both nodded. "Anyway," Bessie said, dragging the conversation back to her own unhappy story. "Matthew decided to follow me back here, but he didn't survive the crossing."

"Plane crash?" Candy asked.

Bessie smiled gently. "He was coming by boat," she told the other woman. "There weren't commercial trans-Atlantic flights in those days."

Candy gave her a strange look. "Just how old are you?" she demanded.

Doona drew a deep breath. "Maybe you don't want to ask that," she warned Candy.

Bessie laughed. "It's okay," she said to Doona. "I'm old enough to tell you to mind your own business," she told Candy.

Candy blushed. "Sorry, I wasn't really trying to be rude," she said. "Please continue with your story."

Bessie nodded. "That's pretty much it. Matthew died just before his boat docked in Liverpool. He left me the small legacy that allowed me to buy this cottage, and I've been here ever since."

"Imagine losing your one true love at seventeen," Doona sighed. "To never look at another man again. It's so romantic."

"And not true," Bessie told her.

"What do you mean it isn't true?" Doona demanded, as Candy laughed.

Bessie chuckled. "We've never talked about this part of my past, have we?" Bessie asked her friend. "In fact, I looked at quite a few men after Matthew died. Oh, I never forgot him, but I think that's true for many people with their first loves. It took me a few years to begin to feel as if I might try a relationship again, and I even went out with a few men from around Laxey, but there were never any sparks."

"I hear that," Candy said. "Nothing worse that kissing a guy and feeling nothing. So you never found a suitable replacement for Matthew?"

"I nearly did," Bessie admitted. She took a big gulp of her wine. She'd never really talked about this period in her past, and she wasn't sure she was ready to talk about it, even now.

"Go on, spill," Candy demanded, draining her own glass. "Then Doona and I will tell you all of our secrets. They're bound to be juicier than yours."

Bessie laughed heartily. "You're absolutely right about that," she said. She took a deep breath. "There was a man. His name was Peter Quayle, and he was my advocate's younger brother. It was maybe ten years after Matthew died, and the Second World War was just getting started. He was living in Australia, working in some capacity for their government or ours; I was never sure exactly which it was. Anyway, he came to visit his brother and started courting me."

"Courting you? What a lovely romantic word," Doona said with a sigh.

"What does it mean?" Candy asked.

"A woman living on her own had to be very careful," Bessie told her. "It wouldn't have done for me to be seen out and about with a young single man. I had dinner at my advocate's house regularly and was able to talk with Peter there. Occasionally we'd 'accidentally' meet up on walks around the village. That sort of thing."

"And then what happened?" Doona demanded.

"He proposed," Bessie answered, smiling to herself as Doona's jaw dropped.

"Don't tell me he died, too," Candy moaned. "That would be just too sad."

Bessie shook her head. "He went back to Australia eventually and I decided that I wanted to stay here. I loved my little cottage even then. I'd already been on my own for ten years and I wasn't sure I was ready to be a wife and mother. I decided if I loved him enough to spend forever with him, I'd have felt sure."

"Do you know what happened to him?" Candy asked.

"He married someone else eventually and they had a couple of children. He never came back to the island, not even to visit. I understand he died a few years ago."

"No regrets?" Doona asked her friend.

"You know," Bessie said, "I can honestly say that I don't have any regrets. I have such a wonderful life here."

"Where's my bag?" Candy demanded suddenly.

"What bag?" Bessie asked.

Candy shook her head. "I brought a bag with me this morning. I must have left it by your back door when I went down to the beach."

Bessie opened her back door and spotted the large bag. She wasn't sure how she'd missed it when she'd gone out earlier. Candy walked carefully over to the door and picked up the case.

"I forgot all about it," she said. "Anyway, it's makeover time."

Bessie raised her eyebrows. "Makeover time?"

"Yeah, why not?" Candy demanded. "I did my own makeup for years when I was in the movies. Let me fix you both up."

Bessie shook her head. "Thanks for the offer, but I'm not interested," she told the woman. "I rarely wear makeup and I don't really like the way it feels."

Candy nodded. "Doona, you'll let me do you, though, won't you?" she asked plaintively.

"Why not?" Doona asked, throwing back the rest of her glass of wine. "Maybe I'll learn a thing or two and that'll help me find a new man."

"If I were you, I'd be looking no further than down the hall," Candy told her.

"What do you mean?" Doona asked.

"Here, wash your face," Candy told her, handing her a tube of facial cleanser. Doona headed into the small bathroom that opened off of Bessie's kitchen. When she returned, her face was clean and shiny.

Candy, in the meantime, had spread an amazing array of tubes, bottles and other containers across Bessie's table.

"I mean that inspector of yours," Candy picked up the conversation as if Doona had never left. "John Rockwell is one fine-looking man."

Doona turned scarlet. "John's married," she said shortly.

Candy winked at her. "Happily?" she asked. She didn't wait for a reply. "Because he doesn't act like a happily married man. He acts like a man who's more or less single and not quite sure what to make of it. If I were you, I'd be working on him now. Once that marriage is officially over, the women are going to be all over him."

Doona shook her head. "I've no reason to believe that his marriage is in trouble," she said. "And besides, he isn't my type."

Candy hooted with laughter. "Okay, if you say so," she said, clearly not believing Doona. "Sit down."

Doona sat across the table from Candy and Candy began to open various bottles and tubes. "So tell me all about the loves of your life," she invited Doona, as she began to slather lotion on Doona's face.

"I've been married twice," Doona told her. "But neither of them stuck."

Candy laughed. "Sticking is the hard part," she agreed. "Go on then, which one was the love of your life?"

"Number two," Doona said with a frown. "Too bad I wasn't the love of his."

Candy laughed. "Wine break," she told Doona. "Take a quick sip before I start on the foundation."

Doona took a large drink from her glass. When she put it down, Bessie refilled it for her while Candy combined several different liquids in the palm of her hand. After a few moments, she rubbed a bit across Doona's forehead and then nodded.

"That's about right," she said. "Okay, tell me about number one first."

Doona obliged. "Matt was my childhood sweetheart," she told Candy. "We started seeing each other when I was thirteen and after school we decided it was time to get married. After about five years, though, we both were just going through the motions. We were like brother and sister, so we just agreed one day to split up."

"That happens," Candy said. "It never happened to me, but I know lots of other people that have the same sort of story."

Doona shrugged. "I never said my life was exciting," she said, sounding slightly hurt.

Candy laughed. "Now don't mind me," she said. "I'm pretty well drunk."

Doona laughed. "Anyway, we're still friends and I still have lunch with his mum at least once a month. He got remarried about a year after we split, and he and his wife have three kids, none of whom I would cheerfully spend more than ten minutes alone with."

Candy laughed until she began to cough. Bessie got her a glass of water and both women sat and watched a bit anxiously until she managed to stop.

"Sorry," she said. "I should never have smoked. It wasn't good for me. But anyway, time for husband number two, please, while I work on your eyes."

A dark look passed over Doona's face.

"You don't have to talk about this," Bessie told her friend.

Doona shrugged. "I really should," she said. "If I can't talk about him, I can't move on. I thought I was making progress, but the fact that I don't want to talk about him makes me think I'm not. Anyway, I'm among friends and at least half-drunk."

Candy grinned. "We can take another wine break," she told Doona. "Just let me get your other eye done or you'll be lopsided."

When Candy had finished whatever she was doing, Doona took a large swallow of wine. "Okay, so it was only a few years after my divorce when I met him. His name was Charles," she giggled, "well, his name is still Charles, I suppose."

"Unless he broke your heart by becoming a woman," Candy suggested.

Doona giggled again. "No, he broke my heart by being a woman-iser. And I would bet that hasn't changed a bit."

Candy frowned. "Why are men like that?" she demanded. "Go on then, tell me the whole sorry tale." Candy took a small sip of wine and then pulled out a few more makeup containers. She shifted through them, trying different colours on the back of Doona's hand until she was satisfied.

"We met at a party," Doona said with a sigh. "I didn't even want to go the stupid party, but one of my friends persuaded me that it would be fun. She was wrong. It was unbelievably dull and I was just escaping when Charles walked in. I was lost as soon as I looked at him, I really was. He was gorgeous and so much more sophisticated and worldly than I was. He totally swept me off my feet."

"Close your lips," Candy told her. Her eyes narrowed as she focussed intently on Doona's lips for a few moments, slathering them in layer after layer of gooey stuff. "Okay, you can continue," Candy said, sitting back and staring hard at Doona. "We're nearly finished with your face."

"I don't know what else to say anyway," Doona told her. "He was charming and totally different to my ex-husband. Charles was the regional manager for a big hotel chain that had just opened a new hotel on the island. He'd come over for the grand opening, and before I knew it, I was invited to the party. I met the Governor and a whole bunch of minor celebrities who had been invited to the opening weekend. By the end of that weekend, I was madly in love."

Candy shook her head. "It's hard when you fall so quickly," she said. "Take it from me, nothing good ever comes of falling in love fast."

"It's your turn next," Doona reminded her. "Anyway, Charles went back to the UK and we talked on the phone every night for weeks before he was able to come back. When he did come back, he brought an engagement ring with him."

"Oooooooohhhh no," Candy said laughing. "That should have stopped you in your tracks, girl."

Doona laughed as well. "Yeah, but I was too stupid to realise that at the time. I was flattered and amazed and I said 'yes' about a million times. We were married about two weeks later and had a glorious month-long honeymoon visiting various properties all across Europe that were in the group he worked for. No matter how bad things were later, I do have to admit that he was wonderful for that month."

"So when did it all go wrong?" Candy asked.

Bessie drew a sharp breath. "Perhaps we should find another topic of conversation," she suggested, anxious to protect her friend from the very difficult topic.

"It's okay, Bessie," Doona insisted. "It's therapeutic talking it all through. Besides, I've drunk enough to simply not care."

Candy laughed. "Good girl," she said. "So what happened after your glorious month?"

Doona sighed. "When we got back to the island, he told me that he thought it would be best if I stayed here while he travelled back and forth. He couldn't see any point in dragging me over to the UK to live since he was on the road at least five or six days a week. I was dumb enough to agree to that, of course."

"It sounds logical enough," Candy shrugged.

"Yeah, but you're saying that after a bottle of wine," Doona pointed out.

Candy began to laugh and then took another sip of wine to stop herself. "That's a great point," she told Doona. She started putting the various pots and tubs back into her bag, pausing occasionally to dab a bit more onto Doona's face.

"So he was cheating?" Candy asked.

"Not only was he cheating, but he only married me to hide the fact that he was already involved with a married woman," Doona announced.

"Don't cry," Candy told her. "I've finished and you look amazing. Don't ruin it. What do you think?" Candy asked Bessie.

Bessie looked at her friend and then blinked hard. "You look beautiful," she told Doona. Somehow, after all the layers and layers of makeup that Candy had piled on, Doona looked as if she were wearing very little makeup at all. But her cheekbones were suddenly pronounced, her eyes looked huge and sparkly, and her lips looked larger, but entirely natural. Doona looked well-rested and about ten years younger.

"Do I?" Doona demanded. She got up from the table and walked very slowly and carefully to the loo. "I look wonderful," she said in an awed tone. "Candy, you're a magician."

Candy flushed. "It's all you," she said. "I just enhanced what's already there."

"It isn't all me," Doona snorted. "I've never looked this good before."

"Let me take some pictures," Bessie said, getting up to look for her camera.

"No," Doona told her. "I'm sure a photo won't look nearly as good."

A knock on the door interrupted Bessie's reply. Bessie crossed to it and pulled it open.

"Inspector Rockwell? What brings you here?" she said to the man on the doorstep.

"I thought you were calling me John," he replied. "I just stopped by to make sure everything was okay."

"Everything's fine," Doona told him as she walked towards the door. "Candy just gave me a makeover."

John blinked at her and then nodded. "Right, well, you, um, that is, I, um."

Candy laughed. "Doesn't she look amazing?" she demanded, joining Doona, next to Bessie.

"She does indeed," John answered, looking at the ground.

"Did you want to come in for a glass of wine?" Bessie asked.

"Oh no, I can't stay," he replied. "I've got to get home to Sue and the kids. I was hoping we could all have dinner tomorrow night, though? You and me and Hugh and Doona, I mean."

"That sounds great," Bessie told him.

"I'll bring Chinese," John offered.

"And I'll bring a pudding," Doona chimed in.

"Six o'clock?" John asked the others.

"That sound fine," Bessie told him.

He nodded once, giving Doona a further quick glance, and then turned and headed back to his car. Bessie waited until he was behind the wheel before shutting the door.

"If I were a few years younger," Candy growled, "I'd be all over that man. He is seriously sexy."

Doona picked up her wine glass and emptied it. "What were we talking about?" she asked.

"Your Charles," Candy reminded her.

"Oh, as it turned out, he wasn't really ever mine," Doona sighed. "And I'm well sick of talking about him. Your turn," she told Candy.

Candy laughed. "I've only been madly crazy in love once. I ran away from home when I was fifteen and I met Hank at a bus station in a small town in the middle of nowhere. I'd just run out of money and Hank was kind enough to pay my fare to Los Angeles. I thought I was going to be a movie star, and then I fell madly in love with Hank and I didn't care what I did, as long as I was with him."

"So what went wrong?" Doona asked.

Candy laughed. "Hank became my agent and promised to make me a star. When he got me my first job in porn, I argued with him about it, but he insisted. That was when I realised he didn't really love me."

Bessie shook her head. "I'm not sure I want to hear this story," she said sadly.

Candy shrugged. "It isn't much longer really," she said. "It turns out I'm not a good enough actress for porn. I could never hide how incredibly bored I was, and after a couple of movies, Hank couldn't get me cast in anything else. He started getting both physically and verbally abusive one night and I punched him in the mouth and left. I'd already met William on a set once, when he was trying his hand at movies. I called every name in my address book that night and he was the only one that offered to help. He wired me enough money to join up with the company in New York, where they were getting ready to start their tour."

"That was kind of him," Doona said.

"William's terrific," Candy answered. "If he wasn't so obsessed with Penny, I'd have made a play for him a long time ago."

Bessie had to bite her lip before she spoke. It wouldn't do to repeat things she heard in police interviews. "And William never cheats on Penny?" she asked.

Candy laughed. "Poor William and Penny," she said. "They're both so busy trying to make the other one jealous that they never have time to enjoy being together. I'm sure Penny thinks I had an affair with William and I'm sure William thinks Penny had an affair with Scott, but in truth, it was all just pretend." She sighed "We're a pretty mixed-up group of people."

"You are, at that," Doona told her.

Candy laughed until she started coughing, and then gulped wine. "I wish I could say that we were once one big happy family, but really, we've always been one big dysfunctional family. William needs to make Penny think he's irresistible to women, so he pretends to have affairs as often as he can. Penny finally got mad about it and pretended to sleep with Scott to get back at him. Adam cheats whenever he can, but Sienna does her best to limit his opportunities. And then there's Sienna," Candy sighed dramatically. "That woman is either the best actress I've ever met or the worst. I'm just not sure which it is."

What do you mean?" Doona asked.

"She's just incredibly changeable," Candy said. "When we were travelling, I'd go from thinking she was devoted to Adam to being sure she was leaving him and then back again. She's all about the drama. If she doesn't get what she wants, she threatens to leave the troupe. William's called her on it once or twice, but usually he ends up giving in and giving her a bigger part or a nicer costume or whatever. She was the main reason I was happy to leave the group once Scott got his break."

"And you said you thought she killed Scott," Bessie remembered.

Candy shrugged. "Maybe I just don't like her," she replied.

Bessie changed the subject, and the trio spent another lively hour comparing British and American food, television and popular culture. By the time they'd run out of wine, all three women were exhausted.

"I'll sleep on the couch," Doona offered. "I don't want to climb the stairs anyway."

Candy looked like she might argue and then she shrugged. "I think I can manage a few stairs in exchange for a bed."

Bessie showed Candy to her room and got her settled in, and then she headed back down the stairs to check on Doona. Doona was standing in front of the bathroom mirror, staring at herself.

"I don't want to wash my face," she told Bessie. "I know I'll never look this good again."

"You always look beautiful to me," Bessie told her.

"Thanks," Doona said, sounding glum.

"Doesn't your face feel funny with all that goo on it?" Bessie asked.

Doona frowned. "Yeah, actually, it kind of does," she admitted.

Bessie laughed. "You should be eager to get it off, then."

"Yeah, I suppose so," Doona shrugged, but she turned the water on and splashed some on her face. "I think I'm going to need the heavy-duty cleaning cream that Candy gave me to get all of this off," she said, as she looked back at herself.

Bessie handed her the bottle that Candy had left out and then headed back upstairs, at Doona's insistence. "I'm fine. Go and get some sleep," Doona had told her.

She was unused to having more than one houseguest at a time, but Bessie didn't have any difficulty falling asleep. Her internal alarm woke her at six as normal, as well. She stretched and then got up slowly. After a quick shower, once she was dressed, Bessie peeked in on Candy, who was still fast asleep. Downstairs, Doona was stretched out on the couch, also still sleeping. Bessie sighed. They were going to miss the very best part of the day.

She left them a short note, just in case they woke up and wondered where she was, and then she headed out for her morning walk. The sun was already shining and Bessie felt good in spite of the late night and the amount of wine she'd drunk.

CHAPTER 13

*B*essie took her time, enjoying the lovely day, and when she got back to her cottage, the other two women were both up.

"Good morning, Doona and Candy," Bessie said as she swept into the cottage. "How are you both this morning?"

"A little hungover," Doona groaned. "Just a little."

Bessie laughed. "Oh dear, I'm sure I have headache tablets here somewhere."

"It's fine," Doona told her. "I've got to get home and take a shower and then get to work."

Candy was sitting at the kitchen table, holding her head in her hands. "I'll take everything you've got," she told Bessie.

Bessie tried not to laugh as she dug in a cupboard for tablets. She handed two to Candy, along with a glass of water.

"I didn't know how to use your coffee machine," Candy moaned, after she'd taken the medicine. "But I sure could use some coffee."

Bessie filled the machine and switched it on. Doona looked at her watch and sighed. "I can't wait," she said with obvious reluctance. "I need to get home and get ready for work." She gave Bessie a huge hug.

"Last night was fun," she told Bessie and Candy. "We should do it again sometime."

"Maybe with less wine," Candy said, her voice muffled by her hands, which were still holding up her head.

"Yeah, maybe," Doona agreed. Bessie let her out, and then focussed on Candy.

"Would you like some breakfast?" she asked her guest.

"Dry toast?" Candy asked.

"No problem," Bessie told her. She made the toast and by that time the coffee was ready as well. Candy cupped the mug she was given in both hands and Bessie watched a little bit of colour return to Candy's face as she sipped the hot drink. A few bites of toast later, she was practically back to normal.

"Oh, that's so much better, thank you," Candy said, as she took another sip of coffee.

"You're welcome," Bessie replied. "What are your plans for today?"

Candy shrugged. "Don't worry, I'll get out of your hair," she said. "Except I got thrown out of my hotel because my credit card hit its limit. Can you suggest a cheap place to stay? Like really, really cheap?"

Bessie sat down with her own toast, covered in a thin layer of marmalade, and a cup of coffee. She sipped her drink while she thought about Candy's request.

"I can find you a place for a few nights," she told the woman. "One of my friends has a small hotel in Peel. You can stay there, I'm sure."

"Will they have room? I tried calling lots of places, but everything was full," Candy told her. "And I can't afford very much, either," she added, looking down at her plate.

"Let me ring him and see what he says," Bessie replied. She used the kitchen phone, but ducked around the corner to talk where Candy couldn't hear her. When she came back into the room, she gave Candy a big smile.

"He only has one small room at the moment," she told Candy. "But you can use it if you want it."

"I'm not fussy," Candy replied. "As long as it has a door that locks and has been cleaned in recent memory, it'll do fine."

Bessie chuckled. "It will definitely have a door that locks, and I'm sure Jack keeps his rooms spotless. The day rate includes breakfast and dinner as well."

"How much?" Candy asked baldly.

"Let's not worry about that for now," Bessie told her. "I've told Jack to bill your room to me. Once you get your life sorted, you can repay me."

"Really?" Candy's eyes filled with tears. "You'd do that for me? Why?"

Bessie shook her head. "I'm not sure why," she told the other woman. "It just feels like the right thing to do."

"I was a porn star," Candy said. "Most women of your generation don't want anything to do with me."

Bessie nodded. "I'm not most women," she said.

"Clearly not."

"You know, when I wanted to buy this cottage, the widow who owned it didn't want to sell it to me," Bessie said. "Women didn't live on their own in the nineteen-thirties; well, nice women didn't. A lot of people have criticised me for the way I chose to live my life over the last fifty or sixty years," she told Candy. "I may not understand or agree with your choices, but that doesn't make you any less of a person. And I'm fortunate to be in a position where I can help you. Maybe some day you'll be able to help someone else in a similar situation."

Candy gave her a small smile. "You're a very special lady, and I feel lucky to have met you."

Bessie rang her car service and sent Candy on her way, this time with Dave driving.

"You do have some glamourous friends," he told Bessie, as he helped Candy into the cab.

"Take good care of her," Bessie said.

"Oh, yes, I will." Dave gave her a quick bow and then he and Candy drove away.

Bessie tidied up her kitchen and then straightened out the sitting room where Doona had rearranged things ever so slightly. She sighed.

While she was at it, she might as well clean the whole house, she decided. There were guests coming for dinner, after all. By lunchtime the house was as clean as she could be bothered to make it and Bessie was starving.

She reheated some frozen soup and cut a huge slice of crusty bread from the loaf she'd bought at Shopfast during the trip for wine the previous evening. She added a thick layer of butter to the bread and then made herself a cup of tea to wash everything down with. She didn't feel all that full when she'd finished, but she knew she'd be having a large evening meal.

After lunch she took another, shorter, stroll on the beach and then curled up with a book about the role of women in medieval society. When she heard the knock on her door, she returned to the present with a shake of her head. We're so much better off, she thought to herself as she headed towards the door.

Doona smiled at Bessie when she opened the door. "I bet you were lost in a murder mystery," she teased her friend.

"Nope," Bessie replied. "I was lost in medieval Europe."

She let her friend in, and Doona deposited a large bakery box on Bessie's counter.

"What did you bring?" Bessie asked.

"You'll have to wait and see," Doona laughed. Another knock, only a moment later, announced the arrival of Hugh and John. John was carrying a large box full of small takeaway containers, which he handed to Hugh once Bessie opened the door.

"I'll just grab the other box," he told Bessie.

"There's more?" Bessie said, shaking her head. It looked like an amazing amount of food, but she knew that Hugh would have no trouble finishing whatever John, Doona and Bessie didn't want.

Within minutes, everyone had filled a plate and settled in around Bessie's kitchen table. Hugh carried over cold drinks after taking everyone's requests.

"This is so good," Doona said between bites. "Where did it come from?"

Rockwell named the small Indian restaurant in Ramsey's town

centre. "I spent my afternoon working at the Ramsey station," he explained. "So it just made sense to bring the food from there."

"It is good," Bessie agreed.

"You seem to be spending a lot of time in Ramsey," Hugh remarked to his boss.

John shrugged. "Since I'm actually handling an investigation in Peel, it's just easier to work from Ramsey in some ways. I've actually been back and forth to Peel every day since Scott died."

"Let's not talk about that until after pudding," Doona suggested.

John looked as if he wanted to argue, but after a moment he nodded. "Did you ladies have fun last night?" he asked, smiling at Bessie.

"Candy is surprisingly nice," Bessie told him.

"And you're paying for her hotel room as well now, aren't you?" he replied. "First Penny and now Candy. I'm surprised William and Adam haven't stopped by to ask you to put them up somewhere as well."

"She needed a place to stay and she's out of money," Bessie said with a shrug. "Jack, the hotel owner, is an old friend. He won't charge me much as long as she doesn't cause any trouble."

"What makes you think she won't cause trouble?" Hugh asked with a wicked grin.

"Jack's wife," Bessie told him. "She's tough as old boots and she won't put up with any shenanigans, I promise you."

"I just hope we can get Scott's murder solved quickly and get the whole troupe off the island. I don't much like any of them," John said.

"How's Grace doing?" Bessie asked Hugh.

Hugh blushed. "She's okay," he replied. "She was pretty shook up for a few days, but she's feeling a lot better now. We had dinner together last night and talked a lot about my job and stuff. We're thinking about looking for a little house together."

"How wonderful," Bessie exclaimed. "She's perfect for you. Maybe I should buy a hat?"

Hugh turned an even brighter shade of red. "Not quite yet," he told

Bessie. "But with her in Douglas and me up here, it's hard. We thought maybe we could find a little place somewhere between the two. It's either that or maybe she could look for work up here. We aren't sure which is better at this point."

"She teaches primary school, doesn't she?" Bessie asked. "Maybe the village school will have an opening in September?"

"She's going to ask," Hugh told her. "And in Lonan as well. Then we'll work out what we want to do."

"Maybe I will start looking at hats," Bessie said thoughtfully.

Everyone had cleared their plates, except for Hugh, who had cleared his at least three times. Doona quickly collected the dirty dishes and put them in the sink.

"Pudding time," she announced, holding up the bakery box.

"What did you bring?" Hugh asked eagerly as Bessie passed around plates and forks.

"A Bakewell tart," Doona announced. She opened the box and set the large tart in the middle of the table. For a moment, everyone simply stared at it before Bessie laughed.

"I'm sure it tastes better than it looks," she said, grabbing a knife.

"I'm not so sure," John replied. "It looks pretty darn good."

It did taste at least as good at it looked, and Bessie sat back a short time later with a happy smile on her face. "That was perfect," she said, after she'd wiped her mouth.

"I suppose we can't put off the inevitable any longer," Doona said with a sigh. "We have to talk about Scott's murder and Sienna's accident, don't we?"

"Technically, no," John replied. "But I'd like to, if no one objects. Talking with you three always helps me get my thoughts in order. Before I forget, though, we've had some preliminary lab results and it doesn't look as if Scott was drugged. He was just very drunk and apparently fast asleep when he was stabbed."

"That was lucky for the killer," Doona commented. "If Scott had yelled or even moved around a bit, someone might have seen what was going on."

"It's difficult to speculate on what might have gone differently," John told her. "It was very dark and fairly noisy. We need to focus on what we know."

"Means, motive, opportunity," Hugh said. "Those are the keys, right?"

"Since we've gone over Scott's murder once already, let's start with Sienna's accident," John suggested. "Although, again, it seems like the five main suspects all had plenty of opportunity and equal access to the means."

"I can't believe no one noticed anyone tampering with the balcony," Doona said.

"Some people probably did notice," John replied. "But apparently Jack from MNH was doing work all over the place for much of the day. If someone else started doing a bit of carpentry, no one would have paid any attention."

"Motive is tricky, because we aren't sure who the intended victim was," Hugh said. "If Sienna was the target, I'd suspect Penny, but if Penny was the target, I'd suspect Sienna."

"What about Candy or the men?" Doona asked.

Hugh shrugged. "It just feels like something done hastily and in anger. No one seems to think it was another murder attempt, and I'm inclined to agree."

John nodded. "I'm inclined to agree as well," he said. "Although I'm not sure I would discount Candy or the men as suspects."

"What was Candy's motive?" Hugh asked. "And who was her target?"

"Perhaps, if Candy was the culprit, she didn't care who the victim was," Bessie said thoughtfully. "Candy's broke and she's desperate. She needs William to give her a job. Maybe she thought by sabotaging the balcony, someone would get injured and have to quit the show, creating an opening for her."

"Sounds logical to me," Doona said. "Can I make coffee?"

Bessie laughed. "Help yourself," she told her friend.

"It sounds logical to me as well," John told them. "William knew about the cast change, so if he did the damage, he did so intending to hurt Sienna. Anyone have any idea why he might have wanted to do that?"

"I can't see William doing anything to damage the troupe," Bessie replied. "Having anyone out of the cast at this point has to be damaging. I'm not sure what they're going to do for the school show tomorrow."

"It might be interesting to find out, though," John said. "I wonder if we can get tickets?"

"Grace is taking her class," Hugh said. "I can see if the school has any extra tickets."

"That's a good idea," John told him.

Hugh flushed with pleasure at the praise and then quickly pulled out his mobile and rang Grace. Doona bustled around making everyone's coffee, while they all tried hard not to eavesdrop on Hugh's conversation. After just a few minutes, he disconnected.

"We're all set," he said with a grin. "She said half the kids in the school aren't being allowed to go to the show because of all the negative things their parents have heard about it, so they have tons of tickets left over. She's going to leave four at the ticket booth with my name on them."

Bessie sipped her coffee to avoid yawning. "So where does that leave us?" she asked. "Do you think that Scott's murder and the attack on Sienna were done by the same person?"

John shrugged. "Murderers do vary their methods," he said. "So it is possible, but it really doesn't seem as if the attack on Sienna was a murder attempt, where the attack on Scott definitely was. The question is, who had a motive for both attacks?"

Bessie frowned. "Let's go through the suspects one at a time," she suggested. "Let's start with William. Everyone says he hated Scott because of Scott's success, and he might have believed that Penny had an affair with Scott, as well."

"But why would he want to hurt Sienna?" Hugh asked.

"Candy suggested that he was tired of her demands and wanted to get rid of her," Bessie said. "But he could simply have fired her or let her quit if that was the case. Sabotaging his own show seems a bit extreme."

"Okay, how about Penny?" Doona asked. "What did she have against Scott?"

"I don't think she had anything against Scott," Bessie replied. "He said he'd help her and William out. His death was bad news for her, as far as I can tell."

"What about the balcony?"

"Sienna suggested that she did it," Bessie replied. "But I can't see Penny tampering with the balcony that she thought she was going to be standing on herself."

"Didn't Sienna say she thought Penny did it to garner sympathy from William?" Hugh asked.

"It seems like quite an extreme way to get a bit of extra attention," Doona remarked.

"More extreme than pretending to have an affair?" Bessie asked.

"Potentially more dangerous," John pointed out.

"I'm not sure Penny has enough sense to realise that," Doona said.

"Ouch, that's harsh," Hugh said.

"But maybe accurate," John sighed. "Who's next?"

"Adam," Bessie said. "And he seems to me to be the best candidate if the same person did both things. He hated Scott, even he admits that, and I can see him wanting to get rid of Penny, at least for a while, so that Sienna would get a bigger role in the show and be willing to stay."

"I can't argue with that," John said. "But it just doesn't feel right for some reason."

"No, it doesn't," Bessie agreed. "I just didn't get the feeling that Adam actually cares enough about anything to take such serious action. What about Sienna?"

"She seemed to have the best motive for wanting Scott alive," Doona said. "He'd offered her a break, maybe even a big break. I can't see her being responsible for his death."

"I can see her damaging the balcony to upset Penny, though," Hugh said.

"Yeah, I can as well," Doona agreed.

"What about Candy?" John asked. "You two spent a lot of time with her last night. What did she have to say? Who does she think killed Scott?"

Doona and Bessie exchanged glances. "We didn't really talk about that," Doona said slowly. "We were just trying to keep things friendly."

"Fair enough," John nodded. "But surely you formed an impression of the woman. Did she kill Scott or sabotage the balcony?"

"No," Bessie said. "I don't think she did either thing. Scott was her only source of income. She wouldn't have done anything to hurt him. She is desperate to get her job back, but I can't see why she'd have to hurt Penny or Sienna in order to do that. They all used to work together, after all."

"There's something about her I don't like," John said with a frown.

"That doesn't make her a murderer," Bessie said firmly.

John nodded. "You're right, of course," he said. "I take it you enjoyed your evening with Ms. Sparkles."

"It was educational," Bessie told him. "She's had a tough life and she's in a difficult situation now. I think she's going to do great things once she gets back on her feet."

"I hope you're right," John said solemnly.

"Candy did say something I found quite interesting," Bessie said. "She said that William is devoted to Penny and never cheats on her, even though he wants her to think he does."

"That's just sad," Hugh said.

Bessie nodded. "It is sad, but I found it interesting. I'm not sure why."

John yawned. 'Even with coffee, I'm falling asleep," he said. "The show is at two o'clock tomorrow. I'll pick you up at one, okay?"

Bessie nodded. "I'll be ready. I'm not bringing a picnic to this one. This time I want to focus on exactly what happens on the stage."

Hugh frowned. "Not even a box of biscuits?" he asked sadly.

Bessie laughed. "Surely Grace will be bringing something for the children? I'm sure she'll be able to spare a biscuit or two for you."

Hugh's eyes lit up. "You're right. She's bound to bring them a snack, and I'm sure she'll have extra, especially if half the kids aren't going."

Doona shook her head. "The way to a man's heart," she muttered under her breath.

John laughed. "Especially a young man," he told her.

Doona insisted that Hugh take the rest of the Bakewell tart home with him. "You'll appreciate it, and I don't need the extra calories," she told him ruefully.

"The next 'aerobics for beginners' class starts next Monday," John reminded her.

"I was thinking I should save everyone the embarrassment of seeing me in exercise kit," Doona replied with a sigh.

John looked as if he wanted to say something, but he didn't. Instead, he fished his keys out of his pocket and headed towards the door. Hugh was right behind him.

"Now promise me you won't open your door to anyone after we're gone," Doona said to Bessie.

"Stop fussing," Bessie replied automatically.

"Promise," Doona insisted.

Bessie sighed deeply. "I won't open the door to anyone," she told Doona. "Now stop fussing."

Doona gave Bessie a big hug. "I worry about you," she told her friend. "I wish you didn't live on your own."

Bessie laughed. "I love living on my own," she said firmly. "Now off you go. Let me get some sleep."

Bessie sighed as she locked the door behind her friends. She did love living on her own, but Doona was making her feel quite paranoid now. She checked her back door and then checked the front one again. Everything was locked up tightly.

Upstairs, she quickly got ready for bed and climbed in. She'd left a half-read detective story on her nightstand, so she settled in and lost herself in someone else's problems. Half an hour later she was fed up.

The identity of the killer was so obvious that she'd begun talking to the book. She slammed it shut and dropped it back on the nightstand.

One day she would finish it and make sure she was correct, but for tonight she just wanted sleep. As she began to drift off, she wondered to herself whether the identity of Scott's murderer wasn't perhaps just as obvious.

CHAPTER 14

*W*ednesday was drizzly, and Bessie worried that the show might have to be cancelled, as she took a shortened stroll on the beach. She waved to the Markham sisters through their cottage window. They both frowned and looked at the sky before waving back.

Bessie found herself feeling restless as the morning dragged by. She ate a light breakfast and then spent some time going through some notes she had recently taken at the Manx Museum. After the conference the previous month, she'd been asked to submit the paper she'd given for publication.

She'd been putting off doing the necessary work of tidying it up and double-checking her references for weeks because it was incredibly dull work. That remembering the conference made her feel sad didn't exactly inspire her, either. Today, with light rain still falling and nothing better to do, she forced herself to sit down and do some of the work. By midday she felt like she'd accomplished something. She went down to make herself some lunch and wave at the sun that was doing its very best to dry up the morning's rain.

After lunch, she washed up her dishes and then checked that she had everything she needed in her handbag. The small folding umbrella that she usually carried was missing and she spent a moment hunting around for it. She'd left it to dry in the small shower in the downstairs loo, and then promptly forgotten all about it. Now she folded it down and dropped it in her bag, on top of her wallet. If the rain started back up, she'd be ready. Then she settled in to watch for John.

Doona and Hugh were already settled in the backseat of John's car when he pulled up at Bessie's cottage. He jumped out while she was locking up her door.

"I hope the weather holds," he said as a greeting.

"Me, too," Bessie said with a grin. He helped her into the car and then shut the door behind her. By the time she'd buckled her seatbelt, he was back in the driver's seat.

"Anyone have any idea what we should expect today?" Bessie asked. "I mean, can they do the show without Sienna?"

"They're doing a show," Hugh told her. "Grace checked with MNH yesterday and she was told that the show would go ahead. Apparently, instead of *Much Ado About the Shrew,* they will be performing a series of short selections from various Shakespeare plays without all the weird drama in between."

"It can't be any worse than what they were doing," Doona laughed.

"No, it really can't," John agreed.

"Apparently, they've done away with all the extras as well. It will just be the main actors doing whatever it is they're going to do," Hugh added.

"I don't think the extras really added anything anyway, did they?" Doona asked.

No one disagreed. Bessie didn't want to bring up Scott's murder on the drive. The day was getting brighter, and everyone was in such good spirits that it seemed a shame to spoil it. At the castle, the car park was about half full with several large buses. John parked and they walked carefully along the road to the castle. Another bus was just pulling in as they started their climb up the castle steps.

"It seems like they're going to have a decent turnout," Doona remarked.

"I hope so," Bessie said.

Henry greeted them with a big smile. "It's great to see you all," he said. "I have your tickets." He nodded at Hugh. "Your young lady is ever so nice," he told him.

Hugh blushed. "Thanks," he muttered.

"We aren't having a VIP section today, not with all the kids in," he told everyone. "But I've set aside a small section for you guys towards the front. I thought you'd like to be a little bit away from all the little ones."

Bessie shrugged. "We'll take whatever we can get," she told him.

Doug came over and offered to take over the ticket window so that Henry could show Bessie and her friends to their seats.

"Here we are," Henry announced as he showed them a row of folding chairs that were set up quite near the small changing room tent.

"You got us chairs?" Doona exclaimed. "I could kiss you."

Henry turned fuchsia. "I just thought that Bessie's done way too much sitting on the ground lately, that's all," he muttered, turning away.

"Thank you, Henry," Bessie said. "I can't tell you how much I appreciate your kindness."

Henry blushed even more. "It wasn't anything," he said, rushing off back towards the ticket booth before anyone else could speak.

Bessie settled into a chair and sighed. "I'm enjoying the show more already," she said happily.

The tent flap on the small tent opened suddenly, and Bessie waved at Penny, who looked over at her anxiously. For a moment, Bessie thought she was going to say something, but just as suddenly she disappeared back inside.

"Penny looked really nervous," Doona remarked, after she'd sat down on Bessie's left.

"She did," Bessie agreed.

"I wonder what that was all about?" John said from Bessie's right.

"I wish I knew," Bessie replied.

Hugh was still standing, scanning the crowd. "Ah, there's Grace. I'm just going to go and say hi," he told the others, walking quickly away.

Bessie smiled. "I'm so happy that he's found such a nice girl," she remarked.

"She does seem perfect for him," Doona said. "What do you think?" Doona asked John.

"Me? I don't know. She seems fine," John replied.

Doona rolled her eyes at Bessie. "Men," she muttered.

John looked from one woman to the other and then shrugged. "I think I'll just keep my mouth shut for now," he muttered to himself.

Bessie and Doona laughed.

A few minutes later Hugh was back. "Man, little kids are noisy," he complained. "I could barely hear what Grace was saying over all the shouting and singing."

"They are rather loud over there," Doona said, looking at all the clumps of school children spread out across the grass. "I'm not sure that William and his troupe are going to be able to get their attention for five minutes, let alone hold it for an hour or more."

A moment later William himself strode out of the tent. He headed straight for the stage and quickly climbed the steps. Then he turned to face the audience. He was wearing an elaborate costume that made him look like royalty and for a moment that was enough to capture everyone's attention.

"Ah, Shakespeare," he said, his rich baritone booming across the castle grounds. "Put up your hands if you've been forced to read something written by Shakespeare."

Just about every hand went up in the school groups.

"Keep your hand up if you thought it was endlessly boring," William continued. A round of giggles went through the crowd, and nearly all the hands stayed up.

"Put your hand down if you actually understood what you read," William said.

More giggles, but most hands stayed in the air.

William bowed to the crowd. "You may put your hands down while I tell you why I think your teachers are crazy for making you read Shakespeare."

Bessie glanced around. From what she could see, every child was fascinated by William's words.

"What did Shakespeare write?" he asked now. "Aside from a few sonnets, he wrote plays. Plays aren't meant to be read, they're meant to be experienced. They're meant to be lived. Sitting in a hot classroom surrounded by twenty-five other kids who are just as bored as you are, you have no chance of experiencing a play. Instead, you get lost in the language and bogged down by stage directions and start to forget which character is related to which other character." William laughed.

"Is it any wonder that no one wants to read Shakespeare anymore?" He bowed again to the audience. "Today, we are going to give you something a little bit different. Today we are going to show you some of the very best scenes that Shakespeare created. We like to think of it as the highlights of the plays without all the boring back-story." He laughed again.

"Before each scene, someone will take a moment to fill you in on where we are in whatever play we've taken the scene from. He or she will also give you a few things to look out for. Shakespeare was actually a very funny man, and if you spoke Elizabethan English you'd know that most of his jokes are about farting."

Hundreds of school children burst out laughing as William took a bow and then left the stage. For the two hours that followed, he and his troupe kept every single child at the castle enthralled. Each short scene was introduced, and then Candy, Penny, Adam and William, often with little more than a change of hat to mark a change in costume, made Shakespeare's words live for their audience.

Bessie was equally riveted, first awed by the madness of Candy's Lady Macbeth and then saddened by the doomed love affair that played out between William and Penny, who were somehow strangely believable as the teenaged Romeo and Juliet. Hamlet made an appearance, as did Henry VIII and Shylock.

Each introduction was cleverly written to explain the entire play in only a few sentences, and was followed by suggestions of certain words or phrases to listen out for, along with a translation of their meaning. While not everything that was highlighted was a fart joke, they managed to get enough of those into the show to keep even the most bored teenager paying attention.

When the show finished, and the actors were done taking their final bows, Bessie sat back in her seat, feeling as if she'd just experienced something incredible.

"They were so good," Doona gasped. "That was amazing."

"It really was wonderful," John agreed. "The children loved it as well."

"You can certainly see why they were so popular in the US," Bessie said. "It was like watching a completely different group of people to the ones we saw last weekend."

"What worries me is what good actors they've all just shown themselves to be," John said with a frown.

"So what was different today?" Bessie asked. "I mean aside from scrapping the *Much Ado* script. Was Sienna that big of a negative influence? Or is it down to having Candy back on board?"

"Maybe we should ask them," John suggested.

Bessie nodded. "That isn't all I want to ask them," she muttered.

John took her arm. "What else is on your mind?" he asked, with a concerned look on his face.

Bessie sighed. "I think I may know who sabotaged the stage," she said. "And I also think I know who killed Scott. After today's performance, though, I almost hate to split the company up."

"You don't really want anyone to get away with murder," John reminded her.

"No, I don't," Bessie agreed.

The pair walked over to the small tent, with Hugh and Doona following a few steps behind.

Bessie exchanged looks with John and then called out, "Hello, Penny? William?"

She could hear voices inside the tent having a whispered conversation, and then the tent flap was pulled open.

"Bessie, isn't it?" William said. "How kind of you to come and say hello. We're just getting changed, so you'll excuse me if I don't invite you in."

William was still in his king's costume and full makeup. Behind him Bessie could see Penny, now dressed in jeans and an oversized blouse. Adam and Candy weren't visible through the small opening.

"I just wanted to congratulate you on a wonderful show," Bessie told him. "I was incredibly impressed with everything you did today."

"Ah, thank you," William said, giving Bessie a small bow. "We worked very hard, as a group, to make today special."

"That was obvious," Bessie told him. "And it was impressive."

"We're splitting up," Penny announced baldly, as she joined William in at the tent flap opening.

"Splitting up? But why?" Bessie asked.

William shook his head. "That's a private matter," he said sternly. "It needn't concern you."

John leaned in and spoke. "It concerns me," he said in an official tone. "Everything this group does concerns me until Scott's murderer is behind bars."

William flushed and rolled his eyes. "Give us a few minutes to get ourselves organised," he said huffily. "Then we'll all come out and have a little chat, okay?"

"That's fine," John replied.

Bessie exchanged glances with the others as they stepped away from the tent. No one spoke as they stood and watched the groups of school children being herded back towards the car park. Grace waved and Hugh waved back enthusiastically. Bessie and Doona smiled at each other as Hugh blushed.

After several minutes, while the sound of muffled conversation came almost continually from the tent, the players emerged. Everyone was now casually dressed, although only Adam had taken the time to remove his stage makeup. The foursome filed out slowly, and then took up positions in a row in front of Bessie and Rockwell.

"You wanted to speak to us," William said grumpily.

"I did," John said. "But I think Bessie wanted to congratulate you on the performance first."

"You were all simply amazing," Bessie said, deliberately gushing. "Today was such an improvement over *Much Ado About the Shrew*, I almost didn't believe it was the same actors up there."

"We never had adequate time to prepare *Much Ado About the Shrew*," William said. "And we needed to bring in a large number of untrained amateurs in order to make the show work, which was difficult. Today was all about showcasing the very best things we've ever done together."

"Who wrote the introductory pieces?" Bessie asked. "They were absolutely perfect."

Adam bowed deeply. "They were my small contribution to today's performance, aside from the acting I did here and there, of course."

"As I said, they were very well done and they kept the children's interest all the way through," Bessie said.

"I told you we were very successful in the US," Penny said. "Today you've seen why."

"Indeed," Bessie replied. "So why on earth are you talking about splitting up?"

William and Penny exchanged looks, while Adam and Candy looked at their shoes.

"It's time," William said finally. "We've all been together for many years. It's just time to go our separate ways."

"And you all feel that way?" Bessie asked.

Adam and Candy continued to stare at the ground, while Penny twisted her hair and stared at William. The silence was starting to get awkward when Penny finally exploded.

"No, we don't all feel that way," she said loudly. She took a deep breath and continued in a quieter voice. "That is, some of us don't feel like we should be splitting up, but it's so difficult right now because there's a murderer running around. We all keep looking at each other, wondering if one of us killed Scott." She laughed harshly.

"Did you notice we did the balcony scene without a balcony

today?" she asked. "There was no way I was climbing on anything that might have been sabotaged. We all work well together, but none of us feel like we can trust anyone else in the group right now."

"Let's talk about the balcony," Bessie suggested. "Penny, when did William tell you that he was giving Sienna the Juliet part in that scene?"

"He told everyone just before the second half started," she said.

"William, when did you tell Penny that you were giving the part to Sienna?" Bessie asked William.

"Like Penny just said," William said with a sigh. "I told everyone about the switch just before the second half started."

Bessie shook her head. "I've been thinking about everything I've heard and seen over the last week or so about you folks," she said to the foursome. "I know you're all actors, so you're all very good at lying, but one thing that just about everyone agreed on was that William and Penny were devoted to each other. Oh, arguably William cheats or maybe Penny does or whatever, but the more I thought about things, the more I wondered about something."

Bessie paused for a breath, leaving everyone staring at her for a moment.

"It seemed to me that William would have warned the woman he loved if he was about to make such a big change to the play. I think he told Penny his plans earlier, maybe even much earlier. But then I thought maybe he didn't tell her, but maybe Penny knows her man well enough to have been able to see what was coming. Maybe, without saying a word, William did something that let her know that she wasn't going to be Juliet that afternoon."

William was shaking his head. "I can't see why all of this matters," he said in a bored tone. "But I definitely didn't say or do anything to let Penny know my intentions. I wasn't even sure until the last minute that I was going to change the scene. It was only after Sienna threw a last-minute tantrum, just before the show started, that I finally decided."

"How did you know?" Bessie asked Penny softly. Penny shook her head; she had tears streaming down her face.

William looked at her and then took her hand. "You don't have to answer that," he told Penny.

"It's okay," Penny said with a sigh. "I hate living with all the lies and uncertainty. It's time for me to confess."

"Confess to what?" William demanded, grabbing Penny's arm.

She turned to face him. "I pulled a bunch of nails out of the balcony rigging, hoping that it would end up really shaky and scare Sienna. I was hoping she'd quit."

"But you didn't know Sienna was going to do Juliet," William said insistently.

Penny laughed hollowly. "Sometimes you're very transparent," she told William. "When Sienna had one of her tantrums half an hour before the show started, you told her, right in front of all of us, that you'd make sure she had a bigger part in the show. I knew the only place you could make any big changes was the balcony scene, so I knew you'd be giving her my favourite role. My heart was broken," she said, as more tears spilled down her face.

William shook his head and then pulled her close. "My darling, darling, Penny," he said. "You could have killed Sienna."

Penny looked up at him. "I'd kill for you," she said with scary intensity. "I knew it wouldn't be long before she'd be forcing her way into more than just my favourite scene. I'd do anything to stop her getting you."

"She wasn't going to get me," William said soothingly. "I'm all yours."

"Except when you aren't," Penny said bitterly.

"I'm always yours," William said insistently. "No matter what."

"Ms. Jakubowski, I'm afraid I'm going to have to take you down to the station for questioning," John interrupted the pair.

Penny nodded, suddenly looking exhausted and several years older. "I really didn't mean to hurt her," she said to Bessie. "I just wanted to make the balcony feel unstable. I thought she would get up there and it would throw her off in the scene, and then William would have a reason not to use her again."

Bessie nodded. "What about Scott?" she asked the woman.

"Scott? What do you mean?" Penny sounded confused.

Bessie shrugged. "I've been trying to work out if Scott's death was tied to Sienna's accident in any way," she said. "What do you think?"

"Why would I have hurt Scott?" Penny asked, still sounding puzzled.

"Someone killed him," the inspector pointed out.

"Well, yeah, but it wasn't me," Penny replied.

"And yet, you just told William you would kill for him," Bessie pointed out.

"I meant Sienna," Penny said. "And I might have killed her if she'd stayed with the troupe and kept going after William like she was."

"But is that feeling mutual?" Bessie asked.

"I'm sure I don't know what you mean," William said. "If you're trying to suggest that I had anything to do with Scott's death, well, that simply isn't worth commenting on."

Bessie looked at him and sighed. "Sienna wanted Scott alive so that he could help her. Candy needed him alive; he was her only client and worth a fortune to her. Penny was also hoping he might help her out, and you as well. That only leaves Adam and yourself as possible murderers."

William laughed sharply. "Sorry, Adam, I think Miss Marple here is about to get you arrested."

Bessie shrugged. "I'm sure Adam hated Scott enough to want him dead, but I'm not sure he hated him enough to kill him."

"Well, if you've eliminated all of the others, it must be him, mustn't it?" William said with a shrug. "I suppose the inspector will have to arrest him as well?"

"I think you hated Scott enough to kill him," Bessie told William. "You thought he and Penny had an affair."

"A minor hiccup in my relationship with Penny," William said airily. "Sienna had an affair with him as well."

"Maybe, but as I understand it, Sienna and Adam had something of a, um, flexible relationship," Bessie said, wondering if the term was correct. It wasn't something she was used to discussing, after all.

"As do Penny and I," William said in a bored voice.

"I'm not sure that Penny would agree with that," Bessie said. "Would you?" she asked Penny.

"No," Penny said tearfully. "William's had affairs, but I've always been faithful."

"Except with Scott," William said quietly. "You had an affair with Scott."

Penny shook her head. "I didn't, actually," she told him. "It was all just pretend. I wanted to make you angry. I wanted to make you understand just how much it hurt me when you cheated. But you didn't even notice. You didn't even care."

William gave a bitter laugh. "I didn't care?" he asked. "I sat at home, alone, counting the minutes until you'd return, smelling of Scott's cologne and trying to look innocent. Do you know how difficult it was for me to pretend I didn't care?"

"No," Penny sobbed. "Because you were very, very good at it."

William shrugged. "I'm an actor. I played my part. If you'd known how devastated I was, it would have changed our relationship. I don't want anything to change what we have."

"Anyway, that was all over a long time ago," Penny told Bessie. "It can't have had anything to do with Scott's death."

"You didn't forget, though, did you, William?" Bessie said. "And you never stopped worrying that Penny and Scott might get back together."

William frowned. "I think now might be a good time to ask for my attorney," he said stiffly.

Penny gasped and grabbed his hands. She held them in hers and stared into his eyes. "Is Bessie right?" she demanded. "Did you kill Scott?"

William opened his mouth, but for a moment no sound came out. Candy began to laugh quietly.

"See what you get for pretending to cheat?" she said to Penny. "You drove the man to murder."

Penny shook her head. "I don't understand," she said quietly.

"I would kill for you," William said, echoing Penny's earlier words. "And I did. As soon as I saw Scott that night I knew why he was here. He'd been calling you, keeping in touch. I knew that he was going to take you back to London with him. You'd have been crazy not to go. He could offer you everything I couldn't."

"But I didn't love him," Penny said. "I love you."

"He would have taken you from me," William said, his eyes filling with tears.

"No, he wouldn't have," Penny insisted.

William shook his head. "I knew, a year ago, that I might lose you to him. That's when I started making plans."

"What are you saying?" Penny asked.

"I decided to kill him," William said in a monotone. "And then you stopped sneaking around with him, and I decided to let him live."

Penny shook her head. "It was all pretend," she said softly.

"But I knew it wouldn't last," William continued as if she hadn't spoken. "I knew he'd want you back one day. So I pretended that my knife was stolen. I thought that would give me an unbreakable alibi, you see. And I waited and I watched for him to try to get you back."

"Mr. Baldwin, I think maybe you should just come to the station with me and we can talk there," the inspector interrupted William's words.

William shrugged. "Penny needs to understand," he argued. "When I knew he was calling her, and then when he turned up here, I realised what was happening. He wanted her back and I couldn't allow that. He had to go." William shook his head. "It was simple really. I always kept the knife with me. It was so precious to me. That's my biggest regret, you know, using that knife."

Penny burst into tears. After a moment, Candy pulled her into her arms and began to pat her back. Rockwell took William's arm and began to lead him away. After a few steps, he stopped.

"I forgot we all came together," Rockwell said to Bessie and the others. He pulled out his phone and rang the Peel station, requesting two cars be sent to the castle. Only the sounds of Penny's sobs broke the silence while everyone waited.

As soon as the cars arrived, Rockwell handed William over to the uniformed officers from one of them. Then he turned to Penny.

"Ms. Jakubowski, I'm afraid you're going to have to come with me," he said.

Penny raised her head from Candy's shoulder. "He loves me," she said, looking at Bessie in amazement. "He loves me enough to have killed for me."

Bessie wasn't sure she had ever felt so speechless in her life. She stared back at Penny.

"All these years, I thought he didn't really care," Penny said. "If only I'd known."

"Scott would still be alive," Bessie said crisply.

"Yeah," Penny waved the thought away as insignificant. "But think how happy William and I could have been together, if only I'd known."

Bessie opened her mouth to reply, but the inspector held up a hand. "I think that's enough for now," he said sternly. "Let's get you down the station where you can make a full statement."

Penny nodded absently, clearly still thinking about William. Rockwell took her arm and began to lead her away. Behind them, Candy began to laugh.

"I don't think any of this is funny," Adam snapped at her.

Candy shrugged. "If I don't laugh, I'll cry," she told him. "Scott tried to help Penny out by agreeing to pretend to have an affair with her, and it got him killed. That's so tragic it's funny."

"You have a sick sense of humour," Adam snapped at her.

"And I hope you have some bright ideas up your sleeve," Candy retorted. "The troupe is booked for three more shows and we've just lost our two lead actors."

Adam turned pale. "Surely no one expects, that is, how can we possibly...." He shook his head. "Penny signed the contracts. This is her problem not mine."

"If we don't do the shows, we don't get paid," Candy reminded him. "I, for one, can use the money."

Adam nodded slowly. "I guess the show must go on," he muttered, spinning on his heel and heading back into the tent.

Bessie looked at Candy. "Are you okay?" Bessie asked.

"I'm fine," Candy replied, not meeting Bessie's eyes. "And as Adam said, the show must go on."

CHAPTER 15

*H*ugh drove Bessie and Doona home in Inspector Rockwell's car. The inspector could get a ride back to Ramsey after he'd finished questioning William and Penny. Hugh would simply leave the inspector's car at the Ramsey station. The atmosphere on the journey home was subdued.

"How did you work it all out?" Doona asked Bessie.

"I don't know," Bessie admitted. "It just suddenly seemed like the only answer that actually made sense. I was thinking about it all day and then, when I was watching them do Romeo and Juliet, I could just see how much in love they were, and that made me even more certain."

"They had a pretty messed up relationship," Hugh said.

"They certainly did," Bessie agreed.

The foursome met for dinner the next night. Hugh brought pizza and Doona brought a Victoria sponge.

"I wasn't sure you'd make it," Bessie told John as she let everyone in. "I assumed you'd have a lot to do with William and Penny."

John shook his head. "They both gave me full confessions, even once I brought in advocates for them," he told her. "The hardest part was getting it all down fast enough. Once they started talking, neither of them wanted to stop."

"How much trouble will Penny be in?" Doona asked, as she nibbled on a slice of pizza.

"It depends on what she ends up being charged with," John replied. "No one seems to think it was a murder attempt, so she's certainly in less trouble than William."

Doona sighed. "It's all so very sad," she said. "I just feel so sorry for Scott, who was just trying to help a friend."

"Helping a friend by pretending to sleep with them isn't really helping, though, is it?" Bessie demanded. "If he really wanted to help, he should have helped them work through their problems."

"That's a bit harsh on poor Scott," Hugh said.

Bessie nodded. "I know. I think I'm just mad at him for how bad I feel about how everything's turned out. I'm not sure that even made sense." She shook her head and then grabbed a second slice of pizza.

"Let's talk about something pleasant," John suggested, opening the second pizza box and pulling out a slice.

"How are your kids doing?" Bessie asked.

"They're terrific," he answered with a grin. "They're both really looking forward to the summer holidays, although they still have a month of school to go. Sue's taking them to Manchester for Tynwald Day weekend, though, so I'm happy to make a day of it with you guys, if the offer is still good."

"Of course it is," Bessie said. "It's just a shame your kids will miss it."

"Sue really needs to be with her mum as much as possible right now," John told her. "And the kids love seeing their old friends, too."

"Grace and I are planning on coming to Tynwald Day as well. I have the day off, after all." Hugh told Bessie.

"What are you all doing Saturday night?" Bessie asked. "Candy stopped by earlier and gave me tickets to Saturday's show. She says that we'll love it."

Hugh shook his head. "I don't think I can take any more Shakespeare," he said with a sigh.

John frowned. "I'm meant to be taking the kids to dinner and a movie," he told them.

"I'll go with you," Doona told Bessie. "I mean, after everything that's happened, how bad can it be?"

The foursome exchanged looks, but no one commented. Everyone kept the conversation away from any mention of Scott and the troupe for the rest of the evening. The three pizzas disappeared very quickly, and the Victoria sponge was equally popular.

"Be careful Saturday night," John said to Bessie as she let everyone out a few hours later.

"What could possibly go wrong?" Bessie asked.

"Maybe I should come," he replied.

"Oh, do stop fussing," Bessie said. "Doona and I will be fine."

Bessie packed a much smaller picnic on Saturday afternoon. Doona would be driving, so Bessie packed fizzy drinks instead of wine. She didn't mind the change, and this way Doona wouldn't have to watch Bessie drink wine.

Doona was a few minutes early, which suited Bessie, who was ready to go. They chatted about nothing much on the drive across the island. Bessie was feeling slightly uneasy about the evening ahead.

"It could all go spectacularly wrong, couldn't it?" Doona asked as she pulled into the car park.

"I rather expect it to," Bessie replied. "They only had a few days to work something out. I rang Henry today and he assured me that there will be a show tonight, but he couldn't tell me what show it was going to be."

Doona laughed. "Well, that isn't anything new, is it?"

The pair made their way up the steps to the castle. Doug was sitting in the ticket booth and he waved Bessie and Doona through.

"I'm sure you have tickets. Don't worry about finding them," he told Bessie.

"I do have them," Bessie assured him. They were, however, some-where in the bottom of her bag and she decided it wasn't worth putting the picnic down to try to dig them out.

"Henry has a spot picked out for you," Doug told them as they walked past him.

"No more special treatment," Bessie said insistently.

"Fight it out with Henry," Doug said, laughing.

The pair made their way into the castle grounds. They were early, so there weren't many people there yet. Henry must have spotted them right away, because he was headed towards them when Bessie saw him.

"I have your spot all set up," he told Bessie with a grin. "No objections now. This was on orders from the cast."

Bessie opened her mouth to object anyway, but Doona interrupted.

"We'll take it," she told Henry. "Lead the way."

Bessie shot her an angry look, but Doona was marching along behind Henry and didn't see it.

It was their usual spot, really, right next to the small tent in front of the stage. This time, there were a handful of folding chairs set out, with a small table in front of them.

"I knew you'd be bringing a picnic," Henry said, gesturing towards the table.

"Thank you, Henry," Doona said. "This is perfect."

Bessie added her thanks. "But it really isn't necessary," she added.

Henry just smiled and headed back towards the castle entrance.

Doona quickly slid into a seat and put her hamper on the table. "I could get used to all this special treatment," she told Bessie happily.

"It makes me uncomfortable," Bessie said, sitting down next to her.

"Well, it shouldn't," Doona told her. "You've been through a lot lately. You've earned a bit of special treatment."

Bessie added her own hamper to the table and then opened it. The pair put together plates full of cold meats and cheeses, fresh crusty bread and butter, a bit of fruit and a few more biscuits than were strictly good for them.

A few minutes into their feast, the tent flap opened and Candy poked her head out. She waved, and then turned and said something to someone in the tent before walking the short distance between the tent and Bessie and Doona.

"Hello, ladies, thank you so much for coming," Candy said with a beaming smile. "I hope you enjoy the show tonight. We've put a lot of effort into it."

"I'm sure it will be wonderful," Bessie said, politely untruthful.

"I'm really looking forward to it," Doona said.

"I have to get ready now, but stick around after the show," Candy told them. "We have some exciting news to share with you."

She was gone before Bessie could ask any questions. "Well, that's intriguing," Bessie said to Doona.

"They deserve some good news, after everything that's gone on," Doona replied.

A few minutes later, just minutes before the show was due to start, Sienna and Adam emerged from the tent. They were both dressed in elaborate Elizabethan dress. Sienna was on crutches and she made her way slowly towards the stage with Adam hovering by her side. Adam helped her up the handful of steps on to the stage and then Sienna crossed to a small stool that had been placed near the front of the platform. She settled in, adjusting her long skirt until her cast was no longer visible. Adam took the crutches away and Sienna waved at the audience, some of whom cheered.

Adam carried the crutches off stage and then returned to the centre of the platform to address the audience. His introduction was broadly similar to the one William had given to the schoolchildren, except tonight, apparently, the emphasis was going to be more on the hidden "adult" humour in the scenes.

Bessie frowned. She hadn't come to see "adult" humour, but an hour later, when they broke for a short interval, she had to admit that they'd done a wonderful job of making the show funny and a little racy, without being crude or offensive.

"They are really good," Doona said. "Sienna's better than I expected."

Adam had apologised for her inability to move quickly during his introduction, suggesting that the scene changes would take a little bit longer than ideal, but it didn't seem to disrupt the flow of the performance.

"I'm amazed that they managed to incorporate some of the local performers into so many of the scenes and get them up to speed so quickly," Bessie said.

"I suppose they didn't have much choice," Doona replied. "They couldn't do every scene with just the same three people, no matter how talented they are."

The interval was only a quick ten-minute one, and Bessie and Doona simply continued making their way through the contents of Bessie's hamper. The second half of the show was as entertaining as the first, even if Juliet had to sit on a stool rather than stand on a balcony. When it was all over, Bessie and Doona joined the rest of the crowd in a rousing standing ovation.

As everyone around them began to gather up their picnics and pack up, Bessie and Doona settled back in to wait for the cast.

"I think I enjoyed that even more than Wednesday's show," Doona said.

"I definitely did, because I wasn't having to think about who killed Scott throughout the whole thing," Bessie replied.

Doona nodded. "There is that," she said. "But I think Adam and Sienna and Candy work really well together. They seemed less tense without William watching their every move."

"We certainly were," Candy said. "William was, well, difficult is the best word. He was difficult to work with." She had emerged from the tent in jeans and a T-shirt with "Manx National Heritage" printed across it. Adam wasn't far behind, and he was helping Sienna across the uneven grass. They too were now casually dressed.

"He was difficult and he was a murderer," Sienna said in a soft voice. She shuddered and leaned into Adam, who slipped an arm around her. "I can't believe that he killed Scott. I just can't get my head around it."

"Well, whatever the reason, you were all wonderful tonight," Bessie said, smiling at them. "I can't tell you how much I enjoyed your show."

"Thanks," Candy said. "I guess we were pretty good last night, too."

"Did you get a standing ovation last night as well?" Doona asked.

"Yeah, and something a bit better." Adam smiled, giving Sienna a squeeze.

"Come on, then, don't keep us in suspense," Bessie said.

"One of my friends from London came over to see the show last night," Candy told her. "I didn't even know he was here, but he saw the show and after it was over he, well, he made us an offer we can't refuse."

"How wonderful," Bessie said. "To do the show elsewhere or something else?"

Candy laughed. "Oh, something else, for sure," she replied. "After tomorrow's matinee, I don't think any of us will ever do Shakespeare again."

Sienna laughed. "I just hope I stop dreaming in iambic pentameter."

"So what will you all be doing?" Doona asked.

"I'm going to be managing these two," Candy said with a grin. "That will be a full-time job, for sure."

"And Sienna and I have been offered roles on *Market Square*," Adam said excitedly. "They've decided to have Scott's character go missing. I'm going to play his brother who flies in the from the US to try to find him."

"And I'm Adam's girlfriend, who comes along with him," Sienna added.

"What a wonderful opportunity for you all," Bessie said.

"We're all over the moon," Candy replied. "We have tomorrow's show to do and then the production company is flying us back to London on Monday. Our new adventure starts with rehearsals on Monday afternoon."

"And you're not acting?" Bessie asked.

"Not for now anyway," Candy said with a shrug. "Maybe something will turn up, but I'm happy managing these two anyway. There's no doubt in my mind that they're going to be huge stars."

"In that case," Bessie said with a smile, "I insist on getting your autographs now, while you're still willing to talk to me."

Everyone laughed, and the trio happily signed sheets of paper in the small notebook Bessie habitually carried. After that, there was an awkward pause before Candy spoke.

"The thing is," she said, looking at the ground, "well, we're all just so very grateful to you for figuring out what happened to Scott and everything." She sighed. "We really can't thank you enough for helping us all out. I've paid your friend for my room, by the way, out of my share of what the troupe is getting for the shows here. I, um, paid for Penny's room as well. It didn't seem fair that you get stuck with the bill, but I couldn't see her paying from prison."

"Thank you," Bessie said. "You didn't have to do that, but thank you."

Candy flushed. "As I said, we're all so grateful. It was the not knowing, you know? I kept looking at them all, wondering who killed Scott and why. I couldn't sleep at night, and I'm sure Adam and Sienna were the same."

"It was awful," Sienna said. "I was so afraid that Adam had done it that I could barely function."

"Gee, thanks," Adam said, dropping his arm from around Sienna. She grinned at him.

"I didn't really think you'd done it," she told him. "But I couldn't imagine anyone doing it, not really. It all sort of feels like a bad dream, even now."

Adam nodded. "It doesn't feel real," he agreed with Sienna. "But at the same time, I feel immensely grateful to you," he told Bessie.

Bessie just laughed. "Promise me you'll remember me when you're rich and famous," she teased.

"We will," the three told her solemnly.

"And have fabulous lives," Bessie added with a smile.

The group hug that followed felt like a suitable goodbye.

GLOSSARY OF TERMS

MANX TO ENGLISH

- **fastyr mie** — good afternoon
- **Kys t'ou** — How are you?
- **moghrey mie** — good morning
- **skeet** — gossip
- **ta mee braew** — I'm fine
- **Thie yn Traie** — Beach House
- **Treoghe Bwaane** — Widow's Cottage (Bessie's home)

ENGLISH TO AMERICAN TERMS

- **advocate** — Manx title for a lawyer (solicitor)
- **aye** — yes
- **bill** — paper money
- **biscuits** — cookies
- **booking** — reservation
- **boot** — trunk (of a car)

- **car park** — parking lot
- **chippy** — fish and chips take-out restaurant
- **crisps** — potato chips
- **cuppa** — cup of tea (informally)
- **diary** — calendar
- **exercise kit** — exercise clothes
- **fairy cakes** — cupcakes
- **fizzy drinks** — soda (pop)
- **flat** — apartment
- **fortnight** — two weeks
- **fringe** — bangs (in hair)
- **glove box** — glove compartment
- **headlamps** — headlights (on a car)
- **holiday** — vacation
- **interval** — intermission
- **midday** — noon
- **mobile** — cell phone
- **pavement** — sidewalk
- **petrol** — gasoline
- **plaits** — braids (in hair)
- **pudding** — dessert
- **tannoy** — public address system
- **telly** — television
- **tin** — can
- **torch** — flashlight
- **thick** — stupid
- **trainers** — sneakers
- **uni** — university (informal)

OTHER NOTES

CID is the Criminal Investigation Department of the Isle of Man Constabulary (Police Force).

The emergency number in the UK and the Isle of Man is 999, not 911 as it is in the US.

"Noble's" is Noble's Hospital, the main hospital on the Isle of Man. It is located in Douglas, the island's capital.

When talking about time, the English say, for example, "half seven" to mean "seven-thirty."

When island residents talk about someone being from "across," they mean that the person is from somewhere in the United Kingdom (across the water).

The TT (or Tourist Trophy) is a motorcycle road-racing event held on the island every May/June. It is held in a time trial format over approximately thirty-seven miles of closed public roads. The course takes in the mountains as well as travelling through several small towns and villages.

A "ceilidh" is a social event with folk dancing.

Tynwald Day (5th of July) is the Island's National Day where their independence is celebrated and their parliament meets outdoors on Tynwald Hill, the approximate geographic centre of the island. All laws enacted during the previous year are read out in both English and Manx and any Island resident can present a petition to the government for consideration.

Someone who tries to "chat up" someone is flirting.

A hen night is the female equivalent of a bachelor party, where the bride-to-be and her friends go out and celebrate the upcoming nuptials, sometimes with a great deal of drinking.

Bonfire Night (5th of November) commemorates Guy Fawkes' attempt to blow up the Houses of Parliament in 1605. It is usually celebrated with a bonfire and fireworks. Children sometimes make an effigy of Guy Fawkes and "beg," saying "penny for the guy," although this tradition is dying out.

When Bessie asks if she needs to "buy a hat," she is asking if Hugh is planning to propose soon. British women, especially in the recent past, used to buy new hats to go with new outfits to attend weddings, and the phrase has remained in common usage, even if very few people still wear hats to weddings.

A-Levels are exams taken after the UK equivalent of an American high school and their results determine whether you are accepted into the university you are hoping to attend, or influence your job prospects.

Self-catering is staying somewhere on holiday (vacation) with at least limited kitchen facilities within your accommodation, so that you can prepare meals for yourself rather than having to eat in restaurants for every meal.

The road between Castletown and Douglas takes travellers across the "Fairy Bridge," and everyone knows that if you don't "wave to the little people" some misfortune will befall you.

The following quotations from Shakespeare are used in chapter two:

"To be or not to be," is from *Hamlet, Prince of Denmark*, Act III, Scene i.

"Oh, Romeo, Romeo, wherefore art thou Romeo?" is from *Romeo and Juliet*, Act II, Scene ii.

"Out, damned spot! Out, I say!" is from *Macbeth*, Act V, Scene i.

"To sleep, perchance to dream," is from *Hamlet,* Act III, Scene i.

In chapter five:

"Heaven has no rage like love to hatred turned, Nor hell a fury like a woman scorned." This comes from William Congreve's *The Mourning Bride,* Act III, scene viii.

In chapter six:

"Every cloud has a silver lining," is a paraphrase from John Milton's *Comus: A Mask Presented at Ludlow Castle.* In part it reads:

Was I deceived, or did a sable cloud

Turn forth her silver lining on the night?

ACKNOWLEDGMENTS

As ever, thanks to my fabulous editor, Denise, who hardly ever complains that I make the same grammar mistakes in every single book!

Thanks to my favorite beta reader, who is also my favorite mom, Barb.

Once again, thank you to Kevin for the beautiful cover photo.

Thanks to hubby and the kids for letting me work without too many complaints and for believing in me, even when I don't.

Adam, Penny and William (Bill) get my special thanks for letting me use their names in this story. They are nothing like the characters here, being instead incredibly talented thespians that I am privileged to know. Thanks guys, I hope you enjoy the adventures of your fictional namesakes.

And an extra special thank you to my beta reading team (in reverse alphabetical order), Ruth, Margaret, Janice, and Charlene, who do so many things to make Bessie better!

Aunt Bessie's adventures continue in:
Aunt Bessie Enjoys
An Isle of Man Cozy Mystery
Diana Xarissa

Aunt Bessie enjoys planning for a pleasurable Tynwald Day celebration with her friends.

Elizabeth Cubbon is called "Aunt Bessie" by nearly everyone in the small village of Laxey that she calls home. A number of murders have thrown her normally quiet life into turmoil and at her age (just don't ask her exactly what age that is), she feels like she's had enough.

Aunt Bessie enjoys getting through the whole day without anyone stumbling over a dead body.

It's her friend John Rockwell's first Tynwald Day and Bessie is delighted when she, Doona, Hugh and Grace get to share the spectacle and festivities of the Manx National Day with him, without anything going wrong.

Aunt Bessie enjoys a quiet breakfast at home, until the police come pounding on her door.

It seems someone at Tynwald Day had murder on his or her mind after all, and suddenly Bessie finds herself caught up in the most complicated murder investigation she's ever had the misfortune to experience. This time Rockwell is doing his best to keep her as far away from the investigation as he can and Doona seems to be trying to keep Bessie under constant surveillance. If there's one thing Bessie definitely doesn't enjoy, it's someone getting away with murder.

ALSO BY DIANA XARISSA

The Isle of Man Cozy Mystery Series

Aunt Bessie Assumes

Aunt Bessie Believes

Aunt Bessie Considers

Aunt Bessie Decides

Aunt Bessie Enjoys

Aunt Bessie Finds

Aunt Bessie Goes

Aunt Bessie's Holiday

Aunt Bessie Invites

Aunt Bessie Joins

Aunt Bessie Knows

Aunt Bessie Likes

Aunt Bessie Meets

Aunt Bessie Needs

The Isle of Man Ghostly Cozy Mysteries

Arrivals and Arrests

Boats and Bad Guys

Cars and Cold Cases

Dogs and Danger

The Markham Sisters Cozy Mystery Novellas

The Appleton Case

The Bennett Case

The Chalmers Case

The Donaldson Case

The Ellsworth Case

The Fenton Case

The Green Case

The Hampton Case

The Irwin Case

The Isle of Man Romance Series

Island Escape

Island Inheritance

Island Heritage

Island Christmas

ABOUT THE AUTHOR

Diana Xarissa lived on the glorious Isle of Man for more than ten years before returning to the United States with her family. Now living near Buffalo, New York, she enjoys having the opportunity to write about the island that she loves so much. It truly is an amazing and magical place.

Diana also writes mystery/thrillers set in the not-too-distant future under the pen name "Diana X. Dunn" and fantasy/adventure books for middle grade readers under the pen name "D.X. Dunn."

She would be delighted to know what you think of her work and can be contacted through Facebook, Goodreads or on her website at www.dianaxarissa.com.

Find Diana at:
www.dianaxarissa.com
diana@dianaxarissa.com

CPSIA information can be obtained
at www.ICGtesting.com
Printed in the USA
LVHW011117170319
610949LV00053B/3233/P

9 781502 737885